PRAISE FOR PERCIVAL EVERETT

"Percival Everett is a genius. He's a brilliant writer and so damn smart I envy him."—Terry McMillan

"If Percival Everett isn't already a household name, it's because people are more interested in politics than truth."—Madison Smartt Bell

"The audacious, uncategorizable Everett. . . . [He] mixes genre and tone with absolute abandon, . . . never does the same song twice. . . . Brilliant."
—*The Boston Globe*

"Percival Everett has made a career out of flouting expectations . . . [forging] a nervy, caustic body of work that defies easy categorization."
—*Los Angeles Times*

"Everett is a fearlessly experimental author."—*Esquire*

"It's hard to pigeonhole Percival Everett. Working between the traditions of the academy and the African American tall tale, he writes with a sharp satirical voice."—*Playboy*

"A spare, yet powerful writer."—*The Seattle Times*

"Everett's books are unfailingly intelligent and funny, formally bold and intellectually ambitious."—*LA Weekly*

"Everett bends language like Superman bends steel. . . . [He] swoops, swerves, zigs and zags."—*San Francisco Gate*

"[Everett] is a first-rate plotter, an incessantly readable stylist, a modernist with his play with form and structure, and an intellectual whose novels and short stories are often mini textbooks on whatever has captured his interest. He is also a superb satirist and humorist."—*Bookmarks Magazine*

I AM NOT SIDNEY POITIER

A Novel

Percival Everett

Graywolf Press

SAINT PAUL, MINNESOTA

Publication of this volume is made possible in part by a grant provided by the Minnesota State Arts Board, through an appropriation by the Minnesota State Legislature; a grant from the Wells Fargo Foundation Minnesota; and a grant from the National Endowment for the Arts, which believes that a great nation deserves great art. Significant support has also been provided by the Bush Foundation; Target; the McKnight Foundation; and other generous contributions from foundations, corporations, and individuals. To these organizations and individuals we offer our heartfelt thanks.

Published by Graywolf Press
2402 University Avenue, Suite 203
Saint Paul, Minnesota 55114
All rights reserved.

www.graywolfpress.org

Published in the United States of America

ISBN 978-1-55597-527-2

2 4 6 8 9 7 5 3 1
First Graywolf Printing, 2009

Library of Congress Control Number: 2008941967

Cover design: Kapo Ng@A-Men Project

For Henry and Miles

I AM NOT SIDNEY POITIER

CHAPTER 1

I am the ill-starred fruit of a hysterical pregnancy, and surprisingly, odd though I might be, I am not hysterical myself. I'm rather calm, in fact; some might say waveless. I am tall and dark and look for the world like Mr. Sidney Poitier, something my poor disturbed and now deceased mother could not have known when I was born, when she named me Not Sidney Poitier. I was born after two years of hysterical gestation, and who knows what happens in a mind when expectant, anticipative for so long. Two years. At least this was the story told to me.

To make a long and sad story abbreviated and sad, this is how I have put it together: My mother, famously eager to have a child and likewise famously odd, offbeat, curious to all who met her and famously very much without a partner, one day told her neighbors, near and not so near, that she was pregnant. Everyone nodded in appropriate and understandably sympathetic, if not outright patronizingly though benignant ways, but then much to their surprise, horror to some, befuddlement to nearly all, my mother's belly began to inflate. Her belly grew quite large from all reports, but after the customary nine or so months there was no baby. This full and soon to be overfull, too-full term had been preceded by two hysterical miscarriages, both matters of public knowledge and joking, and so there was already plenty of room for doubt. And then after ten, eleven, twelve months there was still only brown belly-skin stretched drum-taut over what many believed to be a volleyball, and so everyone understood that my crazy mother, volleyball theory notwithstanding, was suffering, or perhaps perpetrating, yet another hysterical or, more likely or precisely, insane

3

pregnancy. Then after twenty-four months I was in fact born and not terribly quietly, mind you, as my mother woke many people with this emergency, at first by knocking, then by howling like a coyote, and so my entry was well attended and well documented by a shocked few who told a shocked, though mainly uncaring, many.

It was also, as one might suspect, a bit of a hysterical delivery. My mother's wailing caught the attention of a nearby woman who called another neighbor woman and soon there were three of them huddled like conspirators around the spread-eagled legs of my mother, staring at her privates and believing that nothing would be forthcoming. One of them had a notion to summon the doctor from down the street, and so she did. The short, waddling doctor, bleary eyed and out of sorts, arrived and asked a reasonable enough question: "What week are you in?"

"One hundred and four." This came from the first woman.

The claim was backed by all present, including my mother, though her exact words were, "Far too many!" She then wailed, "Stand back, girls! Two years he's been forming and now he's coming!"

The doctor thought in his Thunderbird-booze haze that all of them were crazy while the huddle of neighbors believed only my mother was crazy. Then the doctor pulled out his stethoscope and gave the belly a long listen. Standing back, he said, "This woman is going to have a baby."

Another wail from my mother.

"I'd say imminently."

"Would you like me to boil water?" one of the women asked.

"If you'd like," the doctor said. "Tea would be nice."

But my coming was not as imminent as my mother might have liked as the labor proceeded to last some forty hours, a forty hours that saw a parade of curious well-wishers, voyeurs, file through the house: some drinking coffee, some eating popcorn, and all commenting on the very strange gestation period and even stranger actual existence of a baby. The doctor was quite sad he'd been called because even though he had taken the Hippocratic oath, he thought that there were better things he could have been doing, not the least of which was finishing the bottle he'd abandoned, though the neighborhood women finally used the kitchen to prepare much food that he found to his liking. As it happened, I finally burst out, though perhaps *burst* is not the right word as I came along feet first and oversized head last, all ten pounds of me, nearly tearing my mother apart, all of this very slowly. Her screams filled the streets like screams.

The birth astonished everyone in the community, perhaps no one more so than my mother, who viewed me as nothing less than an immaculate conception. Even news crews from as far away as San Diego and a couple of university sociologists and biologists came around to sneak a peek. The best I can figure is that my mother was in fact hysterically pregnant and that in month fourteen or so of that pregnancy she somehow managed to find and utilize the sexual organs of my father (a term I of course use in the strictest zoological sense), who may or may not have been Sidney Poitier, and she actually did become pregnant, and so here I am. Twenty-four months in the womb was the local legend, and so as a tyke I was seldom called by my odd name Not Sidney, but instead I was tagged *Elephant Boy* and on occasion *Late Nate* and once *Ready Freddy* by a boy who had moved to Los Angeles from Ohio. That one never did make sense to me.

As described, my birth was a difficult one, to say the least, sheer hell to say the most, a scary thing certainly, a near-death experience for my mother, a near-life one for me. She became obsessed with the belief that her pregnancy need not have ended so painfully, and that belief led to a campaign that she took very seriously, a campaign against all vaginal births. Our house was perpetually cluttered with T-shirts and posters with the same image and slogan: a vagina in a circle with a line through it and *MISCS* which stood for *Mothers In Support of Caesarian Sections.*

Though my mother, her name was Portia Poitier, was absolutely, unquestionably, certifiably crazy, she was not without resources. Perhaps she simply was lucky, I will never know, and therefore neither will you. When I was two, in 1970, she invested every dime she had in a little-known company called the Turner Communications Group that would later become Turner Broadcasting System. Every dime she had came to about thirty thousand dollars, most of a settlement from an elevator accident at her job with the phone company—a lot of money at that time, and for someone in our neighborhood it was a fortune. It turned out to be enough to make her filthy, obscenely, uncomfortably rich. Not as *filthy* rich as she would have been had she lived a little longer. Instead, I became *filthy* and insanely rich. In fact, so much stock did she have that Ted Turner actually paid her a visit shortly before her death. I was seven and remember the manic white man exploding into our house like a pale, mustachioed, talking tornado.

"Hello there, young fella," he said to me with that fast southern accent, engaging and alarming at once. "You seem like a nice young man."

I was standing on the porch of our house when he arrived, and a couple of the guys had just ridden by on their bikes calling out, "Hey! Where's your trunk, Elephant Boy!?" My mother, who had spoken to Turner numerous times on the telephone, called him Teddy.

The neighbors stared at us from their yards and through their windows. My mother, not out of any distrust but out of disposition, had kept her wealth guarded, not spending more than would seem ordinary. What she did spend her money on was hardly perceptible to those outside our home: books, music, and language lessons for me, and really good, sensible, and therefore ugly, shoes. She would spend hundreds of dollars on a pair of shoes that no one suspected cost more than thirty. My white and blue Oxford shirts came from London's Savile Row, she told me, though I had no idea why that mattered. All I knew was that I hated the shirts that no one else wore, longing every day for a T-shirt or a jersey of some kind.

Turner clicked his tongue against his impossibly white teeth and surveyed the neighborhood. He seemed comfortable in his skin and that made me comfortable with him. "Your mama's quite a businesswoman, yessireebobby, quite a business mind." I kicked a couple of toys away from the center of the floor. "Is that Lego you're playing with? I love Lego. Didn't have Lego when I was a boy, had an erector set. You've probably never seen one. Used to cut my poor fingers to kingdom come, blood all over the little screws and bolts. Always loved building things. Are those brownies I smell? Don't tell me your mama can bake brownies too? Don't you love them when they're just out of the oven, all warm and gooey and smelling to high heaven? Chocolate all over those screws and bolts. Yep, some businesswoman, your mother." That was what he was like and I have to say I liked him, and he genuinely liked my mother and loved the fact that she had had such faith in his business. And she liked him, called him Teddy, as I said. When he asked her why the kids had called me *Elephant Boy,* she told him that they were just jealous. He chewed his brownie and stared at me; her answer seemed to satisfy him.

"Tell me, Portia, just what kind of name is Not?" he asked.

"It's Not Sidney," my mother corrected him.

Turner was puzzled momentarily, then nodded his big head and laughed. "Oh, I get it."

Then it was my mother's turn to look puzzled. I never knew the story of my name. One might have thought that my mother imagined that our last name, rare as it was, was enough to cause confusion with Sidney Poitier, the actor, and so I was to be *Not* Sidney Poitier. But her puzzled expression led me to believe that my name had nothing to do with the actor at all, that *Not Sidney* was simply a name she had created, with no consideration of the outside world. She liked it, and that was enough.

My mother died shortly after that visit from Ted Turner. An illness came over her. That was how it was put to me. *An illness has come over your mother.* Within weeks death came over her as well. She passed away in her sleep, and I was told that was a good thing—no suffering, no pain. Even then I wondered why that was a good thing. We had no family, and certainly no one in the neighborhood would take in the abject spawn of the crazy lady, the product of such a strange and probably demonic, prolonged gestation. Had they known I was worth millions of dollars *Elephant Boy* might have been slightly more attractive, but they didn't know and they wouldn't have believed it if I or anyone else, even Ted Turner, had told them, even if they had known who Ted Turner was.

Enter Ted Turner once again. Turner saw my mother's substantial investment in his dream as a kind of symbol and charm for his success. My mother was the kind of grass-roots, if not proletarian, person he wanted to imagine his media world touching, however tangentially, on his way to great and obscene wealth. Anyway, Turner showed up and, to the drop-jawed bewilderment of the neighborhood and city, took me away to live with him in Atlanta. To say that I lived with or was raised by Turner is misleading and simply or complexly untrue. I lived at one of his houses and was left pretty much to my own unformed devices. The staff of my part of the household, mostly black women, prepared my meals and took care of my needs, and my teachers, mostly black women, came to the house to educate me. I hardly ever saw Turner or his family, though for a while, during puberty, I found a place to secretly watch his leotarded wife, Jane Fonda, perform her disco exercises by the pool. Her ribs jutted from beneath the spandex, and I felt more than a little lust, though I held no crush.

To Turner's credit even he was not comfortable with the scenario of the rich do-gooding white man taking in the poor little black child. Television was polluted with that model, and it didn't take a genius to understand that something was wrong with it. My situation was somewhat different as I was in fact extremely wealthy as a result of my mother's business acumen.

I was supposedly free to make decisions concerning my own life. The house staff was run by a statuesque woman from St. Lucia.

Claudia, with her massive afro and keen stare, made it clear to me, on more than one occasion, since she had decided: that, though sweet, I was a bit of a numbskull; that it had been made very clear to her that I was paying the bills out of my own pocket and not Ted Turner's; that she worked for me and not for Ted Turner; that her job was to please me, not Ted Turner. She liked the truth of that; I could tell by a certain tilt to her afro. And so did the two women who took care of my part of the house along with her. My teachers were a string of girls from Spelman College who thought I was either simply adorable or a stinking pariah, a pathetic social abomination better left unhandled, if not unconsidered. One, however, Betty, was a raving socialist who liked me, liked teaching me, and liked especially the fact that I had money to burn, *real money* she called it, and I trusted her because she spoke of it openly. She imagined that one day I might use my wealth for good. Still, she had some difficulty accommodating the reality of my residing in Ted Turner's house. I was eleven when I told her that I actually paid rent to live there and so really wasn't being cared for by Turner at all. Technically I was paying rent, but the money was being funneled back to me through some kind of manipulation of stock options. I understood the concept if not the machinations. I was slightly precocious, and Betty liked that about me. Betty was my first crush, though I never imagined her working out to disco music the way I did with Jane Fonda. Betty called herself "big boned," and she was even in my eyes a little plump, but I thought she was beautiful.

She taught me about Marx and Lenin and Castro and the ills of American democracy and the fall of the Roman empire and about how the British lost their empire because they were likely as not to stand around in sheer amazement upon recognizing that they were not loved by their colonized peoples. She taught me that America preached freedom yet would not allow anyone to be different. She usually told me all of this while stuffing her face with big greasy sandwiches from Hardee's and greasier chicken from Popeyes. Wiping her mouth the while and sighing, she was likely to say, "This is why I'm big boned," and then she would let out her rather endearing snorting and loud laugh.

"Multinational and defense corporations, those greedy bastards, they are the real powers of this country," she said. "The mass media and the oil, they're the movers, the facilitators. Politicians are just tools used to make us think we have some choice and a little power."

I was rubbing my shoulder under the coarse white fabric of my karate dogi. A bigger boy had roughed me up the day before, and I was awaiting the as-usual, one-day-too-late visit from my martial arts instructor.

"Ted is in the media," I said.

"My point exactly." She looked around the room as if to be sure no one was listening. "He's precisely the kind of pestilential, poisonous, pernicious parasite I'm talking about." She often gave in to some inexplicable and strange, but I thought quaint, alliterative urge.

"I like him."

"You're a child."

"He likes you," I said.

This threw her off. "Why do you say that?"

"He said so."

"When?"

"I don't know."

"What exactly did he say?"

"He said, 'You know, Nu'ott, I like that big-boned teacher of yours.'" I affected my best, but not very good southern accent. I was confused by how much Betty enjoyed hearing this. "Do you like him, too?" I asked.

"Of course not, Not. That man is the devil. You be careful around that white man. And around whitey in general."

"Why do you say he's the devil?" I asked.

"Young brother, young brother, you have no idea. Money be green, we be black, and the devil be white. That's all we know and all we need to know. Trust me, your big-boned sister."

"I just don't see why him being white makes him the devil. My mother liked him. My mother was smarter than you. I like him. And he likes you."

"Stop saying that." She reached into her bag for some hard candy and unwrapped it. She stared at me while she put it in her mouth. "Why do you insist on repeating that he likes me."

"I said it only twice," I said.

"That, Not, is called repetition. I'm amazed. Really, you would think that after all I have tried so untiringly, diligently and untiringly to teach you, you would know that."

"You said 'untiringly' twice."

"I did not."

"Are you saying that 'you did not' or that 'you did, Not'?" I asked.

"I did not say untiringly twice, Not."

I didn't press the matter, but felt mightily puzzled by her behavior.

"Besides," she said, "you must have misheard him." She re-arranged her big bones in her seat. "What expressly, explicitly, exactly did he say?"

"He said, hating to repeat myself, 'Nu'ott, you know, I like that big-boned teacher of yours.'"

She bit into her candy. I think it was butterscotch. "And why does he say your name like that?"

"I don't really know," I said. And I didn't. I imagined that he considered Not to be an actual name and couldn't believe it would be simply the single syllable it was. So, it came out *Nu'ott*, the same way god became *ga'awd* for the evangelist on the street in downtown Decatur.

One sunny day Turner and I were sitting in the garden between our parts of the mansion and he was rattling off figures and theories about television, not caring whether I understood or not. I in fact enjoyed our one-sided chats and viewed them as important and essential to my education.

"Now, it's true that we don't have significant market share at the moment," he said, "but good old country persistence will win out. It does every time. This is a simple war of attrition, and if we resolutely stick the course we'll gain a foothold and, well, that will be that. But you can't show the news and *The Three Stooges* all the time." He looked at me. "And aw hell, son, who can afford to make brand-new crappy shows, and who wants to? Especially with so many crappy shows just sitting in cans waiting to be aired again? I'll let the networks waste their money on making the new trash. I'll take their stale old crappy shows and air them again and again until they sit in people's heads like jingles."

"Jingles?"

"I need a new pair of Weejuns. And I want to apologize again about this abstruse arrangement. Boy that's a lot of *a*'s in one sentence. I know it must seem strange to you. Hell, it's strange to me, this situation of ours, I mean."

"I'm okay."

"You ever see that kidney-sick little boy who can't grow on that *Diff'rent Strokes* show? Well, I think that's just obscene, Not. Not him, but that picture, that model of the black child being raised by some great white father. I'm not that arrogant. You think I'm arrogant like that, Nu'ott?"

I just looked at him.

"Maybe I am, a little bit. Arrogant, I mean. Lord, I can't help it. I'm an American."

"So am I," I said.

"Well said, son. Society, some like to call it the culture these days, shouldn't be subjected to that kind of pernicious and deleterious rubbish, the Arnold and Webster model. That's why I'm going to take over television and air that trash every day several times a day instead of only once a week. That way we'll all become desensitized to its harmful and consumptive effects by sheer overexposure.

That's what I mean by jingles. They'll become meaningless and innocuous little ditties." He popped a stick of gum in his mouth and offered one to me. "It's cinnamon. Have you ever been sailing, Nu'ott? Of course you haven't. I love sailing, the bright sun on your face, the sea smell, that breeze running through your hair." He looked at me. "My hair anyway. Yep, I'm going to take you sailing. It's a shame about that sick dwarfish boy with bum kidneys, never growing and all that."

I asked if Jane would be coming along with us on the sailing trip. I had an image of her deck-lounging in a bikini stuck deck-lounging in my brain.

"I don't know," he said. "She's mad at me a lot these days. I think I talk too much for her. I'm not the silent cowboy type like her daddy. Don't you just hate raisins? They're too sweet, if you ask me. And they look like flies, don't you think? Flies without wings. And they're too sweet."

Weekly I would be driven into town by Claudia as her big hair filled the space behind the wheel of the Volvo station wagon that had been purchased with my money. In town, I was allowed to ride my bicycle while she did the shopping. I was always receiving beatings from boys with whom I sought to play. It would always start the same way.

"What's your name?" a kid would ask.

"Not Sidney," I would say.

"Okay, then what is it?"

"I told you. It's Not Sidney."

"Ain't nobody called you Sidney."

"No, it's Not Sidney."

The boy would make a face, then look at his friends and say, "What's wrong with him?"

And I would say, I always thought in a polite and nonthreatening way, "Nothing's wrong with me. My name is Not Sidney."

This would be about the time the first punch found the side of my head. They were understandably and justifiably frustrated and angry with me. They thought that I was being, if not petulant, then wearisome, but I saw myself as merely answering the question honestly.

As I mentioned, I had a martial arts instructor. Claudia hired him after my third thrashing. He was a stocky Korean man named Raymond, a name I found disappointing, and he came by the mansion every Thursday. This was unfortunate because my trips to town were on Wednesdays. Though he was able to observe the damage, debrief me on the tactics used against me, all of his instruction was lost into the air during the following six days, so that by the next Wednesday I was facing either a brand-new attacker or an old one with new tricks.

"Okay, Not Sidney, show me what that bully did." Raymond said to me. We were standing on the lawn near the pool in our bright white dogis, he with his black belt and I with my white. "How did he come at you?"

"He was bigger than me," I told him, "and he grabbed me around my neck and punched me on the top of my head with what felt like iron knuckles and then, while I was holding my head and trying to find balance, he punched me viciously twice on the shoulder. I think I have nerve damage."

"That's simple to fix," he said, reassuringly. I thought at first he was referring to the aforementioned nerve damage, but I remembered that he always said that, and after he said it, I was to be either hurt and/or humiliated. "Grab me just the way he grabbed you." Raymond leaned over and allowed me to place him in a headlock. I didn't like that position, A, because of the anticipation of whatever demonstration of defensive measure was coming and B, because his hair stank of cigarettes, some kind of coconut-perfumed substance, possibly shampoo but unlikely, and god-knew-what-else. "So, what you do is you reach over his head and put your index and middle fingers into his nostrils like so and yank the bastard's head back thusly!" He did so, thusly, which was synonymous with roughly or violently, as he always did, thusly, and threw me to the mat with a hollow and sick and sadly familiar thud. I of course landed on my already-bruised and nerve-damaged shoulder. "Simple, right? Do you get it?"

"Simple."

"Now you try it," he said.

Raymond put me in a snug, and what I found to be meaningful, headlock and said, "Go!"

But I could not reach over his shoulder and certainly not around his misshapened, oversized, and smelly head to come even close to his red and bulbous nose with nostrils ample enough to accommodate a few fingers each had they been able to get there. "I can't reach," I said.

"Keep trying," he said and gave my head a squeeze and a little twist that incidentally must have affected my spine because my shoulder pain lessened. "Close your eyes and visualize your actions, your movements. Picture everything. Imagine you are me."

I shuddered at the very thought. Still, I couldn't reach his nose, and now I was finding it extremely difficult to breathe. I tried to say as much, though I'm sure it sounded like mere gurgling to him, and then he let me go by tossing me to the mat. Rather thusly.

"We'll have to come up with another stop, another strategy altogether." He paced. "This is the thing, you can't let him get you in the headlock in the first place. Yeah, that's the thing." He studied me for a long scary second, as if to figure out what part of me might make the most noise upon breaking. "Okay, okay, come at me as if you want to put me in a headlock."

I did, but it must have looked incredibly silly since he was at least a foot and a half taller than me. As instructed, I went at him like the complete fool I was. He stomped my left instep with one of his turned-in monkey-looking feet, hooked that same foot behind my right ankle, and popped me in the chest with the meaty heel of his hand, sending me sprawling onto the mat.

I lay there and he stood over me. He put his fist in his palm and bowed. "Our time is up today, Not Sidney. I will see you next week."

"Thank you, Raymond."

One of my favorite places, no doubt for its relative safety, was the small public library in Decatur. The librarian became accustomed to my face, and when she finally asked me my name and I told her, she simply said, "What an interesting name." So, I liked her. She let me go into the old part of the stacks where the books were dusty and damp, and many were falling apart. I loved the smell of the books there, with their staleness and floating dust. I studied and studied, devouring all sorts of books, confused much of the time. I could hear my mother's voice. "Read. Always read. No one can take that from you. The evil picture box [her name for the television] won't make you smarter, but books will. Read. Read. Read." And then she would lock me in my room with the *Britannica*. It was in the stacks of the library that I found a book by an Austrian psychiatrist named Anton Franz Fesmer. The slim volume was titled *Passive Carriage Manipulation*. The manipulation described was very much like hypnosis and perhaps more like the thoroughly debunked mesmerism; the similarity of the names was no doubt in great part responsible for Fesmer's notable lack of recognition. Fesmerism was a method of gaining control of a subject without the subject's awareness. The idea was a beautiful one, and it of course appeared to me as the perfect form of self-defense. The program had, however, one, rather huge, procedural hurdle. It required that the practitioner stare for some time, minutes, at the subject. The claim was that once one got better at it, the time of eye contact would become shorter. Fesmer also claimed that, unlike hypnosis, the subject's actions would not exclude those that he or she would find offensive or unacceptable when not under the influence. I read the book twice and on a Wednesday went to the playground and got my ass kicked.

"Why are you staring at me?" Those were the last poorly formed words I recall hearing.

But I persisted, and I practiced on Claudia, Betty, and Ted and finally had my first success with Raymond.

"What's wrong?" he asked.

I stared at him.

"Not Sidney, why are you looking at me like that?" Then his eyes glazed over, and he said nothing.

I had him stand open, defenses down, exposed, and he received my punch to his midsection. He crumpled and became immediately un-Fesmerized. And so I stared at him again, and he slipped under. I beat him up fairly well that day, and he went home sore without any inkling why.

I still couldn't Fesmerize Claudia, but I thought I might have gained just a bit of influence over Betty when I had her toss away the remaining portion of her Arby's roast beef sandwich, something she had never done before.

Wednesday came, and I found myself at the playground. The biggest of the bullies was there alone, and without the others to show off for he showed little interest in me, except to say, "Hey, little motherfucker, you wait till later."

I stared at him. I was about twenty yards away, no doubt trembling though I really don't recall, and I launched my gaze at him, complete with one eyebrow raised, as clearly described in Fesmer's procedural guide. The bully, his name was Clyde, asked me at what I was staring, his precise words being, "What you starin' at, li'l motherfucker," the "li'l motherfucker" saving him from ending a sentence with a preposition. However, I kept to my immediate business of raised-brow staring. Irritated, and no doubt bubbling with sadistic urges, he started toward me, grinding his fist into his palm the way he always did before pounding me. I felt my stomach tighten and tremble, but I stayed with it, and by the time he'd dragged his knuckles the twenty yards to me, his dull bovine eyes were glazed over like Raymond's. I issued post-Fesmer instructions to him to not only protect me, but to allow me to strike him in the face whenever I pleased. When I said, "Oh, dumbshit," he was to lean over and put out his chin. I practiced once, and then just had to do it again. I was somewhat impressed by the punching skills that Raymond had somehow taught me.

It all worked beautifully that day, and I found myself equipped with a tool that I knew would serve me for the rest of my life, a kind of psychological Swiss Army knife. The problem with the method was and would be the fact that not all people can be Fesmerized, and when they are impervious to it, they are not, sadly, oblivious to the person who is staring at them like some kind of maniac. So, if it doesn't work, one comes across like an insane and possibly dangerous person. Unfortunately, I was never able to come up with a reliable profile for susceptible subjects. At first, I thought it was dumb people who made good subjects. I thought this until I was one day beaten to within an inch of my life by a remarkably stupid boy named, simply, Sidney, who had the obvious problem with my name. My staring bounced harmlessly off his pit-bull head like so many marshmallows. "What you be starin' at?" he shouted. "You, yeah, I talkin' to you!" I have to admit that I was distracted by his diction, and so perhaps my stare was somewhat weakened. By the same token, Betty, one of the smartest people I knew, turned out to be highly susceptible to the old Fesmer eye. The weapon was revealed to me as flawed and unpredictable and unreliable, and so I resigned to use it sparingly.

Betty was teaching me about the evils of supply-side economics when Ted came into the room. Betty was just finishing a sentence, ". . . and though Keynesian economics is no kind thing to common people, Say's Law is truly the work of the white, European, devil mind."

"I'd have to agree," Ted said.

This startled Betty. She had not seen him enter.

"I believe that the market is driven by demand," Ted said. "Otherwise, people get screwed up the hind end. The only thing that ever trickles down to poor people is rain, and that ain't much more than God's piss."

Betty didn't want to agree with Ted, but she nodded.

"How's our student doing?" Ted asked.

"Very well," Betty said. "Not Sidney is quite smart."

"He's got his mother's brains. Have you ever had one of those itches in your ear that you have to scratch with your tongue inside your mouth? In fact that's the only way to get to it."

Though I had a boy's crush on Betty, I knew that I was but eleven and that all the brains and money in the world wouldn't make her kiss me. I in fact had a kind of crush on Ted as well, and so I found that what I really wanted was for the two of them to kiss. So, I tried to Fesmerize them. I couldn't stare them into submission at the same time and decided to begin with Ted, as I remembered that I might have had earlier success with Betty during the sandwich incident and so chose to save her for last. I raised my left brow and sharpened, then leveled my penetrating gaze at Ted. He stared back at me for a while with an expression that could only be called *quizzical,* and I thought that I might have been making some headway until he said,

"Nu'ott, what's wrong with your eye?"

"He does that sometimes," Betty said. "I think it's gas."

"That doesn't look good."

A less persistent person, or a saner one, might have stopped at that point, but I gave it another push.

"Looks like the boy's gonna pop. Nu'ott, you all right?"

I gave up. "Yeah, I'm fine."

"Funny little episode you had there."

"Just thinking," I said.

"Okay, well, I'm going to talk to a man about a German shepherd dog. They're great dogs. I especially like the way they walk, all slung low like that. You're in charge, Betty." He said that, then leaned over and gave Betty a kiss on the cheek before exiting the room.

Betty was taken by surprise, but hardly offended.

I was more confused than ever. Had my Fesmered suggestion been received and, more importantly, processed? Was I in fact responsible for that unexpected, unseemly, and glaringly inappropriate action? I was left not knowing if I had succeeded or failed, a state worse than failure itself.

"He kissed you," I said to Betty.

"Oh, that wasn't a kiss. That was what we call a peck."

"Why do you think he kissed you?"

"It was a peck, Not Sidney."

I let the matter rest, though I was no wiser or more percipient for my experiment or for having witnessed the event that I might or might not have caused. The only thing that was clear was that Ted and Betty now believed there was something wrong with me. I suppose I could have likened my new tool to a sort of psychological Swiss Army knife, as I said before, but to continue the metaphor, I could never know whether I was opening the scissors, saw blade, corkscrew, or leather awl, or whether it would open at all.

No one was more surprised than I when Ted invited Betty to join Jane, himself, and me on a sailing day-trip, except perhaps Betty, who surprised herself into a silk sundress and equally inappropriate wedge-soled sandals and onto a bus to St. Simons Island. Jane was glamorous and aloof, attributes that I imagined fed each other. From behind her oversized dark sunglasses she addressed me politely and warmly, pronouncing my name as she had learned it from Ted, *Nu'ott*. She received Betty politely yet somewhat less warmly, as she was baffled by the presence of the chubby tutor in the silk wraparound. Joining us also was a niece of Jane's, daughter of her brother, a freckled girl about my age named Wanda Fonda who took an immediate, intense, and indefatigable shine to me.

It was sunny, but there were some clouds drifting around, and it was almost cool. It was cool enough that big goose bumps formed on Betty's hefty thighs that were continually in view because of the attack of wind at her dress, despite her hands busily clutching fabric. Betty looked sorely out of place as she stepped aboard the *Channel Seventeen,* and I'm certain she felt that way as well, more so after Jane peeled off her raw linen trousers and white linen shirt, revealing her yellow bikini and cartoonishly narrow waist. There were no goose or duck or sparrow bumps on her as she lay out on the deck and appeared to have the sun's rays zero in on her like a spotlight.

While Ted motored the sloop out of the slip and toward open water, Wanda Fonda had attached herself to my side. "What kind of name is Nu'ott?"

"My name is Not Sidney."

"Okay, Not Sidney," she rather nicely said. "Just what kind of name is Not Sidney?"

"One my crazy mother dreamed up."

"I think it's a nice name. I find it much better than my name. I hate that my name rhymes."

"It's not so bad. At least it doesn't get you beaten up all the time."

Wanda Fonda put her surprisingly strong grip on my forearm and sighed. "Do they beat you up?"

I was saved by Ted calling me over to him at the tiller. I moved to him, Wanda Fonda tethered fast.

"Nu'ott," he said, "what we're sailing today is a sloop. A sloop has one mast and two sails — mainsail and foresail. This fractional rig sloop was made by some Frenchies named Beneteau, was made in their factory in South Carolina. They grow great peaches up there. I love to suck on the pit, but then I never know what to do with it. The wind is the most important part of sailing. Without wind, there is no sailing. Today you'll learn about the wind. Next time, knots. Yep, today you just sit back and watch and I'll teach you about the wind and the beat and the close reach and the reach and the broad reach and the run, about luff and what it means to be in irons, about coming about and jibbing and about sails. You ever see what the sun can do to a convertible top over time? I had a little MG when I was in college, and the sun turned the top into a shag carpet."

"Nu'ott, I'm going below for some lemonade," this from Wanda Fonda. "Can I bring you some?"

"You can bring me a tall glass, Wanda Fonda," Ted said. The girl was always called by both names. "Bring some for Betty, too. You want some lemonade, Betty? Maybe you want some iced tea instead?"

"Lemonade sounds nice," Betty said. She was sitting not far from the tiller.

"You want some lemonade, Jane?" Ted called forward.

Jane waved her hand in the air in a way that could have meant yes or no or my nails are perfect.

"What about you, Nu'ott?" Wanda Fonda asked me, again.

"No, thank you," I said.

With that Wanda Fonda disappeared down the companionway.

We passed under the sweeping suspension bridge, and Ted turned to me and said, "This is the Not Sidney Lanier Bridge." He chuckled. "Just joking. I think Sidney Lanier was a poet or something."

I looked at the bridge, looking both east and west along its length, but could not see where or if either end ever found land.

Once past the bridge Ted switched off his motor and raised the mainsail. The feeling of moving under the power of the wind was thrilling even though we weren't making great speed. The motion of the sloop was hypnotic, at least to me. To Betty, it was nauseating. She swayed against the boat's rhythm and took on a greenish cast.

Wanda Fonda came back with a tray of glasses of lemonade.

The sweating glasses made me instantly wish that I had said I wanted some.

"You look like you're going to upchuck, Betty," Ted said. "Do me a favor and lean over the side when you do."

Betty looked at the glass of lemonade being held out to her by the freckled Wanda Fonda, then turned to release her last meal into the Atlantic.

"Attagirl," Ted said.

"Uncle Ted?"

"Yes, Wanda Fonda?"

"I'm glad you brought Nu'ott with us."

Ted smiled warmly at me. "Of course I brought him out here. He's a sailor at heart. A lover of the sea. An admirer of the wind. A free spirit. A mighty Viking! Or perhaps a Moor."

My eleven-year-old ears liked the sound of that.

"Go up there and raise the foresail, Wanda Fonda."

I watched as she did. The girl pulled a line and the sheet of canvas slid up the front side of the mast and I thought it was just beautiful. The sun found Wanda Fonda's face and I thought she was beautiful as well.

We sailed on, tacking once to make a forty-five-degree turn. Betty tried to put on a strong front. Ted tried to talk to her over the roar of the wind, and she politely pretended to listen, but she was not faring well. Wanda Fonda had found again her station next to me and had even managed to inch her arm close enough to mine that we ever so slightly touched.

"I'd say we make a run!" Ted shouted. "Ready to come about, Wanda Fonda?"

Wanda Fonda's lithe body sprang into action as she made her way forward and grabbed a crank and some line, I didn't know what, and clearly listened for Ted's next words.

Which were, "Hard-a-lee!," if hard-a-lee is three words and not one. Ted let loose the line behind him, then pushed me down into the cockpit and let the boom swing quickly over me. The sail luffed, making a sound I immediately loved, then caught the wind as the boom swung out well to the starboard side of the boat.

Wanda Fonda dropped the foresail, then cranked as fast as she could, and the blue and white spinnaker went up and ballooned out.

"That Wanda Fonda is a heckuva sailor," Ted said.

Now, with the full strength of the wind, we were really moving. The spray, the sun, the breeze, Jane's thighs, it was all intoxicating. I closed my eyes and enjoyed the movement, the smells, the wet luxury of it all. The sky was the bluest I had ever seen, and the ocean seemed a part of it.

Betty was lying on the long cushion now, her face turned to the sky, as green as I had ever seen a person and growing paler. Jane was unimpressed by the coming about and lay still and magnificent under the sun; her skin seemed to bronze in front of me. She grew darker as Betty grew lighter.

Betty looked from stem to stern and then to Ted and asked, "How much did this boat cost?"

"A lot," Ted said.

"Does it bother you to have so much?" she asked.

Ted paused, perhaps considering the question, perhaps considering lunch, and said, "Not yet."

"Well, it bothers me," Betty said.

"Then I won't share it with you." Ted laughed. "Did you know that horses can't throw up? That's all a cow does, back and forth, stomach to stomach, but a horse can't. Strange."

"Do you have a girlfriend?" Wanda Fonda asked me.

"No, and I don't want one," I said.

"I go to a private school. All girls."

"Girls beat me up, too." I turned to hear Ted telling Betty about how to make perfect pickles every time. "Where the bathroom?" I asked.

"The head," he said.

"What?"

"It's called the head. The bathroom is called the head."

"Where's the head?"

"Below," Ted said. He turned to Betty. "Now, Nu'ott's mother, she had a head on her shoulders. Brilliant woman. I wish I'd hired her, but, you know, I never thought to do that. Perhaps because I'm a privileged white male."

"Come on," Wanda Fonda said, taking my hand. "I'll show you."

I peed into the toilet, mostly into the toilet as the rocking of the boat made the project a challenge. When I came out, Wanda Fonda had pulled her pants to her ankles, revealing loud pink, high-waisted panties.

"Would you like to see my tattoo? We've all got them."

I had never seen a tattoo, and I was, honestly speaking, interested, but I said, "You should pull up your pants."

"Are you scared?"

"I think so," I said.

"Of me?" she asked.

I nodded. "What's the tattoo a picture of?"

She pulled down the front rim of her underwear and revealed a red circle with a stem, obviously a fruit, and I said, "An apple?"

"No, stupid, it's a cherry."

"I don't get it."

"It has to do with sex."

Oddly, it was when she called me stupid that I first took a liking to Wanda Fonda. Enough of a liking that I decided to try my cyclopean eye at Fesmerizing her. I leaned into my stare. Before she could complain or clock me one across the head, she relaxed into that cow-eyed state that I so welcomed. I looked about the cabin and wondered what I might have her do, and I came up with nothing. I did have her pull up her pants. Then I remembered that I was eleven, almost twelve, and though sexual activity or exploration with Wanda Fonda was clearly out of the question, I did very much enjoy the idea of seeing actual tits. I instructed Wanda Fonda to go up on deck, make her way to Jane, and toss Jane's bikini top overboard. I knew that it was already undone; the ties were lying teasingly alongside her as she lay facedown on her towel. I gave a post-Fesmer suggestion that she would remember none of my instructions and spend the rest of the trip fawning over Betty.

I followed back up the companionway topside. Wanda Fonda went directly to Jane and stood over her, blocking the sun.

Jane lifted her head and looked back at Wanda Fonda. "What is it, Wanda Fonda?"

The girl said nothing, but as Jane raised herself while lifting her shades to get a better look at the face over her, Wanda Fonda snatched the bikini top from the towel and tossed it into the air. The wind played with the abbreviated garment top for many seconds before letting it fly away from the boat and high into the air. Jane sat up and watched the article's flight.

I looked at her breasts, and though I was sort of thrilled to be seeing them, I thought finally that her chest looked a lot like mine, only puffier.

"Why did you do that, Wanda Fonda?" Jane asked.

"Do what?"

Jane didn't become even slightly upset, she just lay back down and said, "Never mind."

It was all terribly disappointing, the breasts and the reaction. The sight of Jane's breasts was made the more uninteresting by the fact that she simply didn't care that I was seeing them. She paraded her boobies out and about for the rest of the time on the boat. Her eyes, hidden behind the dark glasses, became of far more interest to me. It was her eyes, the ones I couldn't see, that seemed to work on my under-construction libido. I wanted, needed to see Jane Fonda's eyes. I therefore set to the business of casting my cyclopean stare her way.

"What's wrong with you, Nu'ott?"

I was terrified once again that I would be thought insane, but I persisted, raised my left brow another millimeter.

"Excuse me, but would someone, Ted, please ask this child what's wrong with him?" Jane said.

I wondered as I worked on her, if her sunglasses would diminish the effectiveness of my gaze. I could not see behind them to detect any shift toward the desired cow-eyed state, so I pushed my suggestion that she toss her glasses overboard. It turned out that the dark lenses must have actually amplified my power because she whipped them from her face and tossed them out into the ocean without the slightest pause. Jane's eyes were sad-making, not weak, not really sullen, but cheerless, tenebrific. I pushed the suggestion that I was sorry and that she should not associate me with the action, but I knew that I needed to back off. My ability, two successes in a row, scared me greatly. I remained quiet for the rest of the trip. Betty was entertained mercilessly by the cherry-tattooed Wanda Fonda and Jane sat around with eyes and tits unabashedly uncovered and Ted railed on about the first television—"It was nothing but static, but what moving static it was"—and how baseballs were made—"In Haiti, by women who bend all the way down and stand all the way up with every stitch"—and whether inflammable and flammable were really the same word—"I mean, invariably and variably don't mean the same thing." Except for the wind-driven ride itself, I had pretty much controlled the action on the boat.

I never saw Wanda Fonda again, and Jane barely acknowledged me when I would greet her by the pool. I continued to sail with Ted, and time went by. Tutors came and went. My wealth grew, or so I was told by Ted's accountant, an Indian man named Podgy Patel.

"You have vast money," he said in his singsong accent. "Vaster this week than last."

"How much money do I have?" We were sitting in the living room of my quarters.

"How old are you?"

"Thirteen."

"Let me just say 'vast.' The actual figure might frighten you."

"Tell me."

"I cannot." He smiled the smile he always smiled, a smile I imagined he would wear whether he was being tickled, being praised, or being fired. "I can only say that your wealth is . . ."

"Vast," we said together.

"Very good," he said.

"What if I want some money?" I asked.

"Just ask."

"What if I want fifty thousand dollars?"

"Just ask."

"What if I don't want to ask?"

"Write it down."

"Can't I just go to the bank?"

"You are thirteen. They will not give you fifty thousand dollars."

"But you will," I said.

"Of course, it is your money."

"And I can do anything I want with it? I can throw it off a building downtown if I want to?"

"That sounds foolish, but yes."

"Okay, I want fifty thousand dollars," I said.

"Do you really? Or are you just saying that?"

"No, I want it."

"I'll bring it by this afternoon."

I felt for some reason defeated, even though this smiling Podgy Patel man was telling me that I was insanely wealthy. "Never mind," I said. "I guess I don't want the money."

"I knew it."

Like most people I am smarter than some, dumber than others, skinnier than most, and fatter than a few, but none was ever more confused than I was. I flew with confusion always parallel to me, and a whole internal chase at my rear. The one matter that was not confusing to me, but seemed to escape all others, was the fact that the only thing that was certain to become obsolete, would necessarily become wearied and worn, was the truth. I knew this in spite of the *truth* that I had had little truck with the *truth* in my life. It was not that I considered myself a resident in a den of lies, but rather that my history was shrouded and diced and soaking wet with hysteria and contradiction. Contradictions or no, my trajectory through life, though different from most, was, nonetheless, a trajectory. The move from my bizarre early childhood in Los Angeles to my strange latter childhood in Atlanta was abrupt, yet somehow seemingly seamless, the sudden death of my mother and my induction into the world of a media icon notwithstanding.

A few years disappeared into wherever time goes and with them my childhood, Claudia, the cook, and my karate instructor. Betty graduated from college and married a Morehouse man from Ohio whom I never met. For a couple of years I received the occasional, uninformative postcard from Akron, usually depicting something called the Soap Box Derby. I lived in my part of the house pretty much alone as the Russian woman who cooked for me spoke no English and the woman who cleaned refused to speak to me. I saw Ted often.

By the time I was in high school, it was common knowledge, or at least it was no secret, that I lived at Ted Turner's house. To my teachers my name was odd, but to my classmates I was Sidney or Not Sidney or something other than Sidney. My *real* name became a mystery to be solved for many. Still, I was beaten often, but now in an attempt to have me give up that bit of prized information, namely my name. There was some upside, as some of the looser girls would offer to kiss me if I told them my name. I would gladly agree to the arrangement. I would receive the kiss and then say, "My name is Not Sidney." Unfortunately, the *looser* girls often would and could be more violent and fierce than the boys, and so they would offer up an entrée of whup-ass with sides of hair pulling and scratching.

A steady diet of humiliation leads to a kind of immunity or desensitization to abasement and discomfiture and so I found myself caring less and less, and the less I cared the less anyone seemed interested in beating me up. Lack of interest or not, the beatings continued, perhaps because they had become a habit or ritual for a few. Sadly, that journey to pointless and profitless immunity often is completed with a degree of permanent injury, usually to the brain and/or nervous system, but I luckily made it through without any perceptible lasting marks—physical, physiological, or neurological. Psychic damage, however, is far more difficult to assess, though I think I was saved from even that by my sense of irony.

My mother's insistence on my reading as much as possible made me bored in school. I never imagined that I was terribly bright, but I turned out to be extremely well educated. I made friends with a squat, square-headed, bespectacled white boy named Eddie Eliazar in my American history class. He had an overdeveloped fondness for World War Two–era airplanes and suffered all the ridicule and only a fraction of the beatings I endured. I imagined that his diminutive stature saved him the physical abuse. We shared a crush on and competed for the attention of our history teacher, Miss Hancock, a narrow-shouldered blond woman with pale blue eyes and long legs who was not so much beautiful as perhaps honest looking. Eddie attempted to wow her with plastic models of Messerschmitts, Zeros, and Corsairs while I became obsessed with the concealment of FDR's disability from the American public, my real interest being the definitions of *disability* and *public*. About this interest, Miss Hancock would say, "How fascinating," a response that I loved then, but would later come to recognize as code for any number of things. There were clearly codes in her employ that fell short of my understanding, but it soon became evident that my emerging resemblance to Sidney Poitier was not lost on her and that an inappropriate and, I must say, welcomed relationship began to surface. The girls of my school were too accustomed to teasing, ignoring, or beating me to observe any maturation or change in my appearance or bearing, but Miss Hancock, unfortunate name and all, did notice and with much zeal, eagerness, and a surprising and confusing amount of enterprise.

The relationship took flight, not unlike one of Eddie's Messer-schmitts, when after school one day Miss Hancock asked me if I would accompany her home and move some bags of topsoil and manure from the trunk of her car to her garden shed. I should have read her signals, as she told me all this while crossing and uncrossing and recrossing her smooth, miniskirted legs and applying dark red lipstick. But I was naïve, dumb, inexperienced, fifteen and, most importantly, stupid. So, I rode with her in her powder blue Mustang convertible, top and tinted windows up, to her modest house at the edge of Decatur. I got out of the car and walked to the back, waiting for her to open the trunk, which she did and all I saw was a spare tire, a jack, and jar of petroleum jelly. I looked at her, I imagine, rather blankly.

She responded by saying, "Do you know what fellatio is?"

I told her I did not, but the subtext was becoming clear. I had heard other guys talking about encounters, desired encounters of this kind, but I felt this was all being wasted on me. I was a sexual imbecile. More than that, I was an innocent, a stowaway. I had come to her country with no visa, passport, and with no destinations in mind. I had come to move topsoil from the trunk of a blue Mustang to some garden shed in the backyard.

In her house, and I'm not certain how she got me in there, the teacher put her mouth on my penis and sucked on it. My eyes rolled back into my head, and I recalled the long, drawn-out, luxurious days of my youth. I was lying in the backyard, staring up at the forever cloudless blue California sky, except that it was brown. I could hear my mother in her study by the open window, dictating into her recorder her ideas about politics and the culture. I was alone, as I was always alone. No one would play with me, the freak. But somehow I loved the moments in the backyard, my mother's ranting a kind of white noise from the house and the sounds of boys playing elsewhere a comfort because that meant they had no interest in torturing me. I lay there and identified the birds, my trusty Peterson guide beside me. I was enjoying the memory of a Rufous-sided Towhee when sharp pain brought me back.

I did have some idea what fellatio was, but I hadn't known the extent to which teeth were involved. I was contemplating this while sitting in the garden at home. Ted joined me.

"When I was a boy I always wanted to collect me a jar full of fireflies, but I never did," Ted said.

"Have you ever been seduced?" I asked.

"Once or twice," he chuckled. "When I was younger. What about you? And why are you sitting like that?"

"Do you know what fellatio is?"

"Why, yes, Nu'ott, I do. It's when one person wraps his or her lips around the penis of another and either sucks it or rubs it with the tongue, sometimes causing ejaculation. It's also referred to as giving head, a hummer, or a blow job, though blow seems antithetical to the actual action employed. Why do you ask?"

"Someone did it to me," I said.

"Who?"

"My history teacher."

"A woman?"

"Yes, a woman," I said.

"An attractive woman?"

"I guess."

"Well, you know, that doesn't sound too bad on the face of it, but it seems a little inappropriate." Ted folded a stick of gum into his mouth. "Gum? It's Juicy Fruit." When I shook my head, he looked back at my part of the house. "Do you get lonely living here all by yourself?"

"Not really."

"These are Italian shoes. I've often wondered why those Italians should be so good at making shoes. They don't walk more than other people. When I was a boy I read this story about a man who lost his arm in an accident. Scared me so much I taught myself to tie my shoes with one hand."

"But wait. Ted, how do you get to choose which arm you'll lose in an accident?" I asked.

Ted stopped working his gum for a second. "That's a very good question, Nu'ott. I hadn't thought of that. I guess it had better be my left. So, are you going to turn this teacher in?"

"Do what?"

"Report your teacher for making improper advances to you, a minor. Did you like it?" he asked.

"Not terribly," I said. "It did feel kind of good before the biting."

"It's up to you, but I say report her. She's contributing to the delinquency of a minor. And apparently giving defective blow jobs."

"I don't think I'll tell on her," I said. "She seems kind of sad."

"Everybody is always maligning the granny knot, but I think it's every bit as good as a square knot. Left over right and right over left. Who the hell cares? What do you think?"

"What are you talking about?"

"You know, I miss that Betty." Ted looked down at the peonies near where we sat. "She was a smart young woman."

"She's in Ohio with some minister dude with dreadlocks. She sends me postcards."

"Minister dude? God save us. Are you going back to the history teacher's house?" Ted asked.

"I don't know. I don't think so."

"I wouldn't recommend it," he said.

"Is that fatherly advice?" I didn't mean what I said in any snide way, but I could imagine him hearing it like that. But he didn't.

"No, this is just advice from a fellow penis owner," he said. "These things don't come with a manual. As far as I can see, nothing of any importance comes with a manual."

"And so that's why we have television," I said.

Ted looked at me blankly for a second, then said, "I guess so, Nu'ott. I guess that's right. Everybody should have a headstone. You know what I want written on my headstone when I die? I want it to read, *I have nothing more to say.*"

I nodded. "What does my mother's headstone say?"

"I don't know, son. I never actually saw her grave. I learned of her death because she had named me executor of her will. I suppose her stone gives the dates of her birth and death and maybe says something like *Loving Mother.* I think that's kind of standard."

I didn't say it to Ted, but I wanted to see my mother's grave. I wanted also to come up with something fitting for her headstone.

"I remember your mother's cookies. Damn, they were good."

I thought about the cookies and didn't remember them being so tasty, however, they were remarkably uniform in size and color.

"This teacher, does she have full lips? Does she wear makeup? How short are her skirts? Just trying to get a picture of the whole thing."

Hormones and a weak spine conspired to put me again at the split-level ranch home of Miss Hancock. I hadn't during my previous visit been able to take in the décor, but a quick glance around made me appreciate in what a confused state I'd been and to conclude that Miss Hancock was not like most people. Three of the walls of the living room were tiled with patterned mirrors, allowing broken reflections of everything and nothing in particular, and on every surface—the mantel of the fireplace, the coffee table, the top of the television—were little dinner bells, the size of a shot glass and smaller, from the fifty states, from amusement parks, from funeral homes, from hotels and motels and hostels, county and state fairs. I walked around the front two rooms while she went into the kitchen for iced tea.

"Why all the bells?" I asked.

She handed me an already sweating glass of tea. "I like bells," she said. "You can ring any one you like. All, if you want to. I want you to ring my bell." She laughed at that.

I sipped the too-sweet tea. I searched for something to say to her, anything. "Which one is your favorite?"

"That's easy." She walked across the room. I watched her legs beneath her short, pleated skirt. She wore knee socks. She picked up a little blue porcelain bell from the top of the television. "This bell is from a motel in Sparta, Mississippi, the Tibbs Inn. In the restaurant they had barbecue, Tibbs Ribs."

"Why was that so special?" I asked.

"It wasn't really, but the bell is blue. It's periwinkle. It's the only periwinkle one I have. Take off your pants."

"I don't know about this, Miss Hancock." I took a step back. If I had only added a "gee" in front of my statement, I could have been completely the cliché I felt like—Beaver Cleaver getting a hummer.

"Call me Beatrice when we're here."

Her name caught me off guard and I had a notion to laugh, but I suppressed the deeply buried tickle.

"I really don't know about this," I said.

"Of course you know, Not Sidney. Didn't it feel good last time? I was sure you liked it."

"Well, sort of."

"Okay, take off those pants and we'll try it again. We do it until we get it right. How does that sound?"

I backed into a large-wheeled tea cart and set a rack of tiny bells swinging and dinging.

"See, you've upset the bells. The little bells are crying out. Now, stop backing away from me."

"I'd better go home," I said.

"If you leave, then I will fail you and you'll never graduate from high school and you'll never get into college and you'll waste away on the street until you turn to drugs and die hopeless, helpless, and alone."

"All of that from turning down a blow job?"

"You'd better believe it."

"You can't do that," I said, not so much worried about the picture she had painted, but offended on principle.

"Can and will."

"I'll report you," I told her.

"Go ahead, report me. Who will they believe? Me, teacher of the year, or you, a kid without a proper name, angry because he couldn't live out his fantasy with the hot teacher?"

"It's 'whom.'"

"What?"

"It's 'whom will they believe.'"

"Shut up and take off those pants. Be a good boy and I'll pretend none of this silly stuff ever happened."

I unfastened my belt, understanding at that moment how what was happening had nothing to do with sex, only and simply power, watching as she approached me like the predator she was. She reached out and grabbed the waistband of my khakis, pushed them down past my thighs. My penis hung there unimpressive and unimpressed. Beatrice dropped to her knees and took me into her mouth. Hormones got the better of me and I began to swell, at least my penis did, but before I could get completely hard she'd start in with her teeth and my organ would retreat. It went like that for a bit, back and forth, pleasure and pain, arousal and repulsion, erection and deflation. She sucked away like a maniacal vacuum and I stared down at her, hating her for threatening to fail me, while not caring actually if she did fail me, fearing her for her clumsy teeth and my compromised position.

I had nothing to do but watch and so I leaned into my Fesmer gaze. She seemed turned on by my staring, reading it as intensity, and so she sucked harder. The sight of her working away like that was somewhat comical. What came with her increased excitement was, sadly, more employment of teeth, but I focused and stayed with it, and my suggestion was mainly the cessation of biting. The gnashing and gnawing did subside, and I believed I had put her under, so to speak, and so I *encouraged* her rather strongly to give up the idea of failing me in history.

Without the chewing and chomping, the fellatio became pleasurable in that animal way that any kind of genital manipulation is pleasurable to a teenage boy, in spite of her name being Beatrice, in spite of the audience of dinner bells, in spite of my being a victim.

The biting stopped, but I was bitten nonetheless. Beatrice Hancock flunked me and I sat there, dumbfounded, feeling more or less exactly like someone who might actually flunk history. I didn't like the feeling, though I was momentarily fascinated by it. She gave me a look when I glanced up from my report card, as if she'd been aware of my attempt to manipulate her mind. I wondered if sexual arousal or distraction had served to diminish my Fesmeric thrust. Perhaps with my penis already in her head there was no more room for any more of me, including my unspoken and poorly formed mental suggestions. The failing mark was certainly an attack, perhaps even an insult, and still it meant little to me. However, it was now a matter of principle, a matter of fair play, decent behavior, and so I found myself marching down the corridor to the principal's office.

The principal was a squat, bell-shaped man named Clapper. Mr. Clapper had been made hard and tough by years of dealing with abuses to his name. He or the custodian or both were ever vigilant in erasing the Clapper-driven graffiti from the walls of the crapper.

He did not stand when I walked in. He looked at me with his good eye. "Why are you in here, Not Sidney Poitier?" He called everyone by his or her full name to show off his memory.

"I have a complaint," I said.

"You know you're looking more and more like that Sidney Poitier every day." He tilted his head as if to get a better view. "Yes, very much like him. Tall and dark like him. Thick red lips like his."

"Mr. Clapper."

"What kind of complaint?"

I looked at the open door.

"Don't worry about that," he said.

"It's about Miss Hancock."

"Have a seat." When I was seated, he said, "Go on. What did Miss Hancock do?"

"She failed me."

"That's her job," he said.

"I did A-grade work."

"That's not for you to say." He leaned forward and interlaced his fingers on his desk, staring at me. Had I not known better, I might have guessed he was trying to Fesmerize *me*.

"She took me out to her house, supposedly to move bags of top-soil and manure, and then she—" I found myself unsure about how to proceed with my accusation. I could not say *blow job* to the prin-cipal and neither could I say to him that Beatrice Hancock had *given me head* or *fellated* me, so I landed, like a blind roofer, on *rape*. "She raped me," I said, regretting it before I had uttered the final word.

I never heard such laughter. Mr. Clapper turned beet red, his tongue rolled into a tube and pushed out of the O of his mouth as he coughed, and tears trickled down his corpulent face while he pointed at me. I think he said, *that's rich,* or maybe, *you wish,* or *that bitch,* which made no sense. But it was clear, clearer than clear, that he did not believe me.

I got up and walked from his office into the outer chamber and looked at all the wide-eyed potato faces of the staff who had evi-dently overheard the exchange. They didn't laugh out loud, but they found me plenty amusing.

As much as I didn't want to care, I was unable to let the matter rest. The whole thing gnawed at me, much in the manner of Miss Hancock. Things were of course made worse by the story buzzing through the entire school. I was used to the pointing and laughing, the insults and beatings, but somehow, in that strange universe of high school, my universe of high school, that abuse made sense. But now what lay at the core of my ridicule was a lie. Even Eddie Eliazar turned against me; I had either lied about his beloved Beatrice Hancock or, worse, been with his beloved Beatrice Hancock. He was obliged to hate me either way. One thing surfaced through this, a kind of bodily discovery. I realized that I was not small. At just over six feet and looking much like Sidney Poitier, I was becoming a man. One of the usual bullies approached me in the cafeteria.

"You gonna eat that cupcake?" he asked.

I was sitting alone, in my usual place, wherever there was an empty seat alone. "Why, do you want it?"

"Yeah, I want it."

I looked at the yellow-and-white-topped cupcake. I never had any intention of putting the heavily buttercream-iced sawdust in my mouth, but I said, "I think I'll keep it." I looked up at him, surprising myself that I had not even thought to attempt Fesmerization. And then I stood. As it turned out I was a good three or four inches taller than the bully.

I saw retreat in his eyes, but he was pushed forward by the pressure of his friends and everyone else in the cafeteria, for that matter.

"I think I'll eat it." I took a bite of the awful thing.

"I'm gonna fuck you up," he said.

"Okay," I said. "Fuck me up."

Now even his friends were nervous. The bully turned to his backup singers and said, "Let's go." And they went.

What should have been a moment of triumph for me, standing up for myself and even settling the matter without blows, turned oddly sour as I realized that the kids around me were now afraid of me. By so daringly stepping away from my role as victim, I was to be feared, or at least made to feel like a shit for abandoning the rules.

I hated everything about everything. The rules that had been broken, the trust that had been broken, were all broken by that slutty history teacher, that orally fixated predator who didn't know that *normalcy* was coined by a dumb president.

At home, I ate alone and in the dark. I paced the grounds. I was walking back and forth the length of the pool on Saturday morning when Ted came out in his trunks for a swim.

"Hey, Nu'ott," he said, then dove into the deep end. He came up and looked at the sky. "I've never been struck by lightning. You?"

Had it been anyone but Ted I would have thought he was speaking metaphorically. But he was talking about lightning. "No," I said.

"I bet it hurts like hell."

"Well, my teacher failed me," I told him.

"Wow."

"I went back to her house, I don't know why, and she did it again and I asked her not to and she said she'd fail me if I didn't let her and so I let her and then she failed me anyway."

"Wow."

"I went to the principal, but he laughed." I sat on the edge of a pool chair. "You know, I really don't care, but I care. Know what I mean?"

"Absolutely." He went under and came back up.

"What should I do?"

"I can't tell you that, Nu'ott. You can climb the ladder of command if you want, but I can't say that's what you should do. You have to decide what you need out of this, what's important to you. I wonder if you know the lightning's coming. A fellow told me that when he got struck he felt like he had glass in his shoes. Welded his zipper shut. If I were you I might go to the school superintendent." Then he was submerged again, swimming to the far side.

The following Monday I skipped school and went to the office of the superintendent of the school system. The downtown building that housed that office was glass and steel and looked like it was probably outdated and obsolete before it had been completed. Everyone there seemed shocked to see an actual student on the premises and stared at me like I was an experiment of some kind. I believe I got in to see the superintendent only because they were all so confused by my presence.

I stepped into the plush, tastelessly decorated office to discover that Dr. Gunther was a gray-haired woman with square glasses. From looking at her I felt confident that if she had ever seen a penis she certainly had not put the thing in her mouth. I had the immediate thought that I might fare better with her than I had with Mr. Clapper. She asked me to sit and if I'd like some water. I sat in the low, hard chair and said no to the water.

"What may I do for you, young man?" She pulled a pad of paper in front of her. "First, what is your name?"

"My name is Not Sidney Poitier."

"I can well imagine." She studied my features. "You do look a little like him. Now, what is *your* name?"

"Not Sidney Poitier. My name is Not Sidney Poitier."

She appeared suddenly nervous, perhaps afraid, casting sidelong glances at her door and phone. "And you're here because?"

"I'd like to report the inappropriate behavior of a teacher," I said.

"Sexually inappropriate?"

"Yes. Of the oral variety." I said this and looked away from her at one of the two big-eyed clown paintings on the wall behind her.

She appeared to be genuinely concerned. "Just where are you in school?"

"Decatur Normal."

"And your principal is—"

"Mr. Clapper."

"Yes, of course," she said.

"And the teacher in question?"

"My history teacher, Beatrice Hancock." I took pleasure in saying her name, so I said it again. "Beatrice Hancock."

"And what did she do?"

I decided to not beat around the bush, but dove straight into it, to offer the shock of it. "She drove me to her tacky house, got on her knee-socked knees, and gave me what I have since learned is called a blow job."

"She did, did she?"

"And, to tell the truth, she wasn't very good at it. I don't think it's supposed to hurt."

She cleared her throat. "Well, never mind that. This happened once?" Dr. Gunther asked.

"No, twice."

"I thought you said it hurt."

"It did, both times," I said.

"Why did you let it happen a second time?"

"She forced me."

Dr. Gunther stared at me for a few seconds. "Did you tell Mr. Clapper that Miss Hancock did this to you?"

"I did. He laughed."

"You don't mind if I call him, do you?"

I shrugged. As she asked her secretary to get Clapper on the phone I realized what a bad idea it was for me to be there. This woman didn't believe me and wasn't going to believe me. I thought she might call security at any second and that I would then be just one twitch away from getting shot by a product of this very school system. She smiled, rather insincerely, at me while she waited, receiver pressed to her small gray head.

"Mr. Clapper? Yes, this is Superintendent Mrs. Dr. Gunther Junior down here in the central office. Oh, I'm fine. And how are you? And how is your wife? And how are your children? I'm sitting here in my office with a tall young black man. Do you have a student named Poitier? Really. So, that actually is his name." Her sounds became absurd and muted, and then she was nothing but a working mouth in front of me, like a crab eating. I wanted to dash out of there, down the glass-and-steel corridors and into the street, but I didn't. Then the sound of her voice came back and now it was laughter, cackling, witch-cackling laughter, which at once frightened me, irritated me, and justified all of my not-so-kind preconceptions. She hung up the phone, looked at me, and laughed harder.

As I walked out of the building and into the light spring air, I realized that I truly did not care, not even about the principle. I had no desire to see Miss Hancock punished and no notion to give her a piece of my mind. It of course helped me in not caring to remember that I was filthy rich. Grades and diplomas, perhaps sadly, simply didn't matter to me. And as far as blond Beatrice Hancock was concerned, at least she had learned to suck a penis without drawing blood, and so I had performed a sort of public service, offering a measure of protection to the next in her line of victims. I was fairly clear in my desire to become a high school dropout. I decided right then to light out for the territory, as it were, to leave my childhood, to abandon what had become my home, my safety, and to discover myself. Most importantly I wanted to find my mother's grave and put something fitting, perhaps beautiful, on her headstone. What? I'd yet to figure that out. The warm and humid spring air filled me with clean inspiration and a sense of independence.

And so, this became a prophetically, apocalyptically instructive, even sibylline, moment. I was, in life, to be a gambler, a risk taker, a swashbuckler, a knight. I accepted, then and there, my place in this world. I was a fighter of windmills. I was a chaser of whales. I was Not Sidney Poitier.

CHAPTER 2

I was my own person, so I was told, so I believed, and so I was treated by Ted, and so I therefore had no reason to sneak away from my so-called home, to leave covertly in the night without a word. Instead, I found Ted sitting on his veranda, surrounded by flowers he once told me he never liked, reading the *Atlanta Journal-Constitution*'s sports page while having breakfast.

"I don't know why this is a continental breakfast," he said, pushing a croissant with a finger.

"I'm leaving," I said.

"Well, the day had to come." He bit into a cheese Danish and looked up at the sky as he chewed.

"I'm going to drive back to Los Angeles."

"That seems like a likely destination. However, you don't have a driver's license," he pointed out.

"I bought a fake one."

"You don't have a car."

"It pays to have money," I said.

He nodded and put down the Danish. "I've often wondered how the soldiers in the Civil War could do it," he said. "Imagine, charging across a pasture with men getting blown to smithereens to the left and right of you and you keep going. What is a smithereen?"

"I bought a used Toyota. At least I think it's a Toyota. At any rate, most of it is blue."

"It must be, then, a Toyota. Well, you've got all my numbers and Podgy's number and I assume some cash. Call Podgy and he'll get you whatever you need, wherever you are. Call me if you need

help." He went back to reading his newspaper. "I don't know why
I bought that basketball team."

"Good-bye, Ted."

"Come back soon."

I left Atlanta, the mansion, my so-called home, and Ted, recalling
Ted's words as I drove west on Interstate 20, then exited off the free-
way and took US 278, looking for a road that was less road, possibly
a more scenic route, "Once you leave Atlanta, you're in Georgia."
And as I recalled his words, they came true. The troubling truth
took the form of a flashing blue bubble atop a black-and-white
county sheriff's patrol car. I watched as the nine-foot-tall, large-
headed, large-hatted, mirror-sunglassed manlike thing unfolded
from his car, closed his door, and walked toward me—one hairy-
knuckled suitcase of a hand resting on his insanely large and nasty-
looking pistol, the knuckles of the other hand dragging along the
ground. I had a thought to be terrified, and so I was.

He said to me through the completely rolled-down window of
my yellow and mostly blue Toyota Corolla, "Hey, boy." Those were
his exact words, though I cannot capture adequately his inflection.
It was not a greeting as much as a threat, somehow a question,
certainly an attack. His dented badge said Officer George, and I
found that funny.

"Officer," I said as a greeting and as a question.

He took my greeting as a smart-ass remark, which it might have
been, I don't know. But I could tell from his depthless eyes that
he didn't like it. I imagined his eyes as blue lifeless marbles even
though I couldn't see them, hidden as they were behind his mirror
lenses, but I assumed they matched the rest of his features. He said
again, "Hey, boy." More threatening this time.

"Sir?" I said.

"Okay, boy, first thangs first. Why don't you let me see your
license and registration?" But it was not a question.

I leaned over to reach into the glove compartment for my registration, which was as bogus as my license, and at that point I was
startled by shouting, though I could not make out clearly what was
being said. It sounded like, "That thar be far nuff, nigger! Sitch on
back straight and git out the veehickle!" This was punctuated by
the brandishing of his huge pistol. That I heard clearly.

"I was just reaching for . . ." I tried to say.

"Y'all done heard me na, boy! Move na! Move yo black ass.
Na, git out chere, raght na!"

My first thought was this man sounds like Jesse Jackson. My
second thought was not to mention my first. I got out of the car,
and he turned me around roughly and used his forearm to press
me against the rear window. He slid me down the length of the
car and leaned me over the short trunk, patted down my sides
and the insides of my legs. He jerked my left arm behind my back,
slapped on a cuff, then pulled back the right. "Don't move, nigger!"
he said.

"Okay," I said.

"Shut up! I don't want to hear another word outta yo mouth,
you understand me?"

I said nothing.

"I said, do you understand me?!"

"Yes, sir."

"Shut up!"

His voice faded a bit as I imagined him backing toward his patrol car. I heard him on his radio. He said, "I need backup out here
on 278 near the mill. Had a little trouble with an uppity nigger."

Before I could whistle "Dixie" or any other tune there were
three more black-and-white patrol cars and similarly brown-shirt-
clad miscreants swinging their long arms around me. There was a
lot of whooping and chattering and hoo-hahing and head scratching about whether my license was phony, about whether my car
was stolen, it was just too clean, and about whether I was or was
not that "actor feller." A short very round one offered up the expert

knowledge that "them thar movie cameras make you look older and fatter." To this another said, "Then how many cameras on you, Cletus?" They had a big laugh. I didn't laugh, leaning as I was still with my face against the trunk of the car.

Officer George brought his face close to mine. "Well, Poitier, I'm afraid you're under arrest."

"For what?" I asked.

"You hear that?" he asked his cohorts. "Did you hear that?" Then he got even closer to me, his breath smelling like something dead. "Well, fer one thang, sassin' an officer of the law, which around here is the same as resistin' arrest. Now, there's speedin' and failure to stop immediately when I turned on my light. And then there's bein' a nigger."

"That's not a crime," I said, then realized just what I was saying. "I'm not a nigger."

They laughed.

"This chere is Peckerwood County, boy," George said. "And chere, you's a nigger. And it's a crime if'n I say it is."

I was, to say the very least, terrified. To say the very most, in my mind, I was bending over as far as I could to kiss my ass good-bye. I was taken to the town of Peckerwood, the county seat of the county of the same name. I was denied my cliché one phone call, my car and belongings were taken to who knows where, and I was being called Sidney Poitier by the deputies and the jailer. They were encouraged to do so, pleased to do so, because of my insistence that my name was Not Sidney Poitier. Dressed in actual prison stripes that made me feel a little like Buster Keaton, I was arraigned by a judge who also had the surname George and shared all physical features with Officer George, save his size. The little snaggletoothed jurist pounded his gavel and said, "A year at the work farm!"

"Don't I get a lawyer?" I asked.

"Two years!"

Evolution might have been glacial where they were concerned, but not with me. I kept my mouth shut after that. I considered attempting a bit of Fesmerization, but I was terribly afraid of the effects of ineffective staring.

The upside was that I was getting out of the town of Peckerwood, Georgia, though my impression of it was formed without a proper tour. The downside, and I mean down, was that I was getting out on a blue-and-white county bus bound for the Peckerwood County Correctional Prison Farm. The bus was at least thirty years old, smelled of urine and, oddly, carrots, and had caging on the inside of the windows. I was shackled to a slight white man, maybe twenty years old, with grease-slicked-back dishwater-blond hair, and from the way he stared at me I knew he liked neither me nor the fact that I was black nor the fact that we were chained together. If only I could have gotten to a phone I could have called Podgy, gotten some money, and probably bought my way out of this mess. Then it would have been back to Atlanta to hire a lawyer, and I would have wound up owning Peckerwood County. It occurred to me even then: Who would want to own Peckerwood County? The reason it was what it was was because there was absolutely nothing and no one there of any value. It was a terrestrial black hole, rather white hole, a kind of giant Caucasian anus that only sucked, yet smelled like a fart. We rolled through pine trees across spider-webbed and cracked asphalt deeper into the county's colon. We stopped finally at the farm. Shacks and more shacks, rows of dusty nothing, with many trees that managed to provide no shade at all. We filed out of the bus, twenty black and three white souls.

"What do they grow here?" I asked no one in particular, but for some stupid reason said it out loud.

"This here is a dirt farm, boy," a mirrored-lens-covered set of eyes shouted at me. "Our dirt crop ain't what it used to be and it never was!" That's what I finally figured out he said. It sounded like, "Dis chere a dir farm, boi. Aw dir crop ain't wha eah yoost to be, but den tit neber wa." This would be how all the guards sounded all the time, and so I had no idea what they were telling me to do or not do.

They gave me a moth-eaten army-surplus blanket and a bar of soap and a tin cup and a quilt-thin mattress to put on the metal slab that was my bunk. The toilet was a hole in the middle of the aisle in the center of the shack. In other words, we were sleeping in a big outhouse. All of the men in my shack were black, as lost looking as I was, but finally not so much different from the rest of the inhabitants of Peckerwood County. The older men pushed me and insulted me, called me nigger, and forced me to the bunk nearest the toilet hole.

That first night I was awakened by a big white potato face looming over me. I of course had no idea what he was saying, at the top of his lungs, but it was clear that he wanted me to come with him. He took me out into the yard and handed me a shovel, opened his mouth, and let out, "Way dunt ye digs me a hole ri chere, boi?" But it wasn't a question.

Since there was a shovel in my hands and ground beneath my feet, I assumed he wanted me to dig my own grave, so I started. The ground was rock hard, and the shovel didn't make a dent.

"Put yer bac inter it!" he said.

I did, leaning onto the implement and scratching out a little stubborn earth at a time. I worked away; the tobacco-chewing Nazi stood over me while I became soaked with sweat and grief.

"Keep awn deegin'."

It was so dark and still so hot. I was about two feet down into a sizeable ditch when another peckerwood joined us. He looked at me and said, "Why'n ye takin tha dir outta my hole, boi?"

"Because I was told to," I said.

"Ja hear tha?" the second said to the first.

"Sho nuff."

"You'n a uppty nig, aintcha?" the first said. "We's awl gyine put y'all in da cain."

"Ya, in da cain," the second said, laughing a kind of panting-dog laugh. "We see haw he see thangs in the mornin'."

I had no idea what they said, but I knew it couldn't be good. They dragged me some yards away and stuck me all folded up into a four-by-four-foot corrugated-tin cube in the middle of the camp. I felt hot and sick in the dark and thought that I was about ready to die. I recalled all the prison movies I had seen, not many, and wondered if some good-hearted trustee or brave fellow prisoner would appear with a much-needed drink of water or a biscuit or a leathery scrap of dried meat. None did. However I was sure that the cliché shower scene was certainly on the program. I had the thought that things could not get any worse, and then I heard the thunder. It rained much of the night. With the heat and the humidity, the rain and the confinement, I felt hot and cold and parched and soaked.

The next morning I was dragged out of the *can,* not the *box* as I might have called it (it being a box), and was nearly blinded by the intense sun. I was distracted from the stinging light by the stinging blows to my midsection and the side of my head. I stumbled into the mess line and received a platter of gruel and a tin cup of warm pond water. We were then lined up chained to a partner, in my case the same fellow as the day before, and marched toward a bus, the top of which was laden with shovels and hoes and slings.

The bus was an oven. I felt my stomach turn as soon as I boarded. It stank of the sweat of men, the piss of men, and the shit of men. And though we prisoners were soaked and sickened, somehow neither the smell nor the heat seemed to affect the guards whose jackets remained on and buttoned, the brims of their Stetsons remained pulled low, and the ammo belts were worn snuggly around their corpulent middles. I sat near the back of the bus, my face pressed against the diamond-patterned cage, my right wrist shackled to the white man's left. The foul-smelling behemoth belched and roared to life, and we bounced out to the highway. The sad guts of Peckerwood County rolled by in a blur, and the sight of it did not lift my spirits. A red pickup with a couple of teenagers riding in the bed pulled even with the bus and then started horn blowing and shouting. I could not make out what they were saying, their being from Peckerwood County, but the quality and substance of their noise were clear. I heard "nigga" a lot and "darkie" and "slave." Then, as the pickup sped up to avoid oncoming traffic, it began to fishtail. Then the bus began to fishtail, and I could see that this was not a good thing. I gripped my fingers tight around the plastic molded seat, pulling against my shackle mate's attempt to pull his hands to his face, which by the time I looked was wide open in a Munchian scream. My grip failed as the bus began to capsize. We tumbled across to the far side, then across the ceiling as the bus somersaulted down the embankment. The air was filled with screams and choking sounds and dust and crying and dust and swearing and dust. It came to rest upside down.

I don't believe I was knocked completely unconscious, but it did take me some time to gather myself and evaluate my predicament. My first assessment led me to the ridiculously obvious conclusion that I was deep in what my mother would have called dung pudding. I was lying facedown on my faceup shackle partner. He was out cold, an immediate plus that soon became a minus as I detected the odor of gasoline. Fearing the bus would explode into flames at any second, I yelled at his dead face.

"Hey!" I looked around. Then, "Peckerwood!" I closed my eyes and listened to the moaning and weeping all around me. I did not believe myself to be injured, though I considered the possibility that shock and adrenaline might be covering any pain. The gas fumes found my nostrils again. "Peckerwood!" I shouted. I crawled over his body and dragged him across the ceiling to the emergency door at the rear of the bus. At some point it had been welded shut, but the accident had torn the doors off. My shackle mate began to come around as I pulled both of us through mud and away from the wreckage. I sat up and leaned against a thin tree and watched. The guards were dead or unconscious. Many of the prisoners were not moving either. Others were locked into place by their incapacitated cuff buddies. My partner sat up and looked at the mess with me. He looked at me.

"I thought the bus was going to blow up, so I dragged you over here," I said. "I was wrong."

"Let's go," he said.

"What?"

"Let's get outta here. You stupid or somethin'? We gotta run."

Of course he was right. The Peckerwood justice system had proven to be anything but, and if I remained I faced perhaps another year tacked onto my sentence for surviving the crash.

"Come on, boy!" the cracker shouted, getting up to pull me into moving with him. "Run!"

And so we ran. Without looking back. Without looking at each other. We roughly yanked each other this way and that, not thinking about destination or even direction, moving only to put distance between the wreckage, the guards, the cops, and ourselves.

We ran through a hollow and got scratched thoroughly by a stand of some kind of thorny bush. Finally we stopped running, panting like dogs. Peckerwood tugged the chain and I pulled back and suddenly we were wrestling with it. He tried to yank me past him, but he lost his balance and I fell on top of him. He must have injured his back in the bus crash because he screamed out in pain that I had not inflicted. I stood up and over him, my hands on my knees, trying to catch my breath.

"My back be fucked up," he said.

I fell to sitting on my butt.

"What your name, boy?" Peckerwood asked.

"Poitier."

"What? That sound like some kinda girl's name."

"What's your name?" I asked.

"Patrice," he said. He spat on the ground between his feet.
I said nothing.

He started to get up, pulling me by the chain. "Let's go."

"Where?" I asked.

"South," he said.

"Atlanta," I said.

"I gots people southa here."

"That's what I'm afraid of."

"I sayd we'se going south, boy," Patrice said. He struggled to his
feet and gave me his best cockeyed dangerous look, but when he
pulled on the chain he grimaced in pain.

"Atlanta," I said again, observing how my yank at the chain caused
him such discomfort. "I've got people and money in Atlanta."

"You ain't got shit, nigger."

I tugged the chain again, this time with a bit more authority.
"Well, I don't have an injured back, you stupid moron." I pulled
once more and watched him wince. "Atlanta." As I said it I realized
I didn't know how I planned to get us there. I knew only that we
needed to head east.

Due east we ran, or as close to east as I could guess, as hard and
as fast as we could go, which wasn't very because of Patrice's injured back and our inability to move with any coordination whatsoever. We fell over each other like a couple of Keystone Kops, pulled
ourselves up over each other, scrambled up steep hills and tumbled
down muddy yet rocky embankments. We listened the while for
the barking and howling of dogs, but heard nothing. I wouldn't
have thought to be concerned about dogs at all, but Patrice said,
"Them dawgs is fast and if'n dey catch yo ass, yo ass is last week's
poke chops."

We paused for another necessary breather, this time sitting side
by side on a fallen log. I looked at him and realized just how ugly he
was. His face was somehow much too big for his head; his crude
features sprawled everywhere to no good effect. "Why do you

think they chained us together?" I asked for no reason other than to make conversation.

"I guess that thar warden guy has got hisself one of dem senses of humor," Patrice said.

"No doubt."

Patrice looked at me and then at the sky. "Atlanta," he said. "That don't sound so bad. Dem's some purty gals in Atlanta."

"What did you do?" I asked. "Why did they put you in prison?"

"I stole me a fuckin' car. Twere the finest midnight blue Buick deuce and a quarter with cream yeller insides you ever laid yo sad darkie eyes on, boy. And then I drove the thang into my girlfriend's living room, the lyin' cheatin' bitch. What about you?"

"Apparently it's illegal to be black in Peckerwood County."

"If it ain't, it oughta be." He focused his eyes on the sky again. "Atlanta. If'n I had me some money I could be Charlie Potatoes in Atlanta." He winced at a pain in his back.

A dog barked in the distance. We got up and ran. We climbed a short hill and found on the other side what could only be called a raging river. The water was churning, violent, wearing steadily away at boulders of all sizes. It was about fifty yards across, but it looked like a mile. The river's noise was deafening. The din served to cover any sounds dogs might make, but also made them seem closer and more real. I could not hear what Patrice was yelling at me, but I understood that we had to cross. I took the first step into the, if not icy then cold as hell, water. The water pushed first at my ankles. I was surprised by the strength of the current even in the shallow water. Then it pushed at my knees, my thighs, until I was chest-deep, and it was all I could do to move my feet at all. I tried to drag my feet through each step, feeling the water wanting to lift me. I clung to slippery, slimy rocks. I picked up a foot to step over a stone and felt the force of the river seeking to push, pull, twist, and suck me into its flow. I glanced back at Patrice. He was tracing my path, gripping the chain that connected us in the fist

of his cuffed hand. Suddenly I was weightless, completely without purchase, and I was gone, sucked under and popped back up
like a cork. I felt a momentary snag as Patrice tried to hold onto
a boulder, but then he was with me, bobbing and thrashing and
crashing into each other and every rock we could find. I was pulled
completely under, and I could see my mother's face. I was in our
old kitchen and she was baking cookies, talking about investments
and the changing face of media. "News will be the new entertainment," she said. "Trust me, Not Sidney. It won't be enough to report it, news will have to be made. It's going to be a bad thing, but
it's going to be." She slid the first batch into the oven and closed the
door. "That's where we've gone. Everything in this country is entertainment. That's what you need for stupid people. That's what
children want. Drink your milk." Then my head was out again, and
I was sucking in much-needed air. Though Patrice was tethered to
me, he seemed very far away. I saw that we were passing a calmer
section of water and I tried to kick toward it, but I had no control.
Patrice was able to swing around into the friendlier water where
he grabbed an overhanging branch. He screamed as he pulled me
to him. We pulled ourselves into the safety of some driftwood and
panted like dogs.

"Thank you," I said.

"For what, nigger?"

"For pulling me out."

"She-it, I ain't pulled you out." He hacked and spat. "I kept yo
ass from pullin' me in."

We dragged ourselves onto the bank, up and away from the
river. It started raining, pouring. I was surprised at how bad the rain
felt even though I was already soaking wet.

"Well, at least them dawgs gonna lose our scent trail for a
while," Patrice said, coughing up and spitting out more river.

I caught a whiff of him and wondered if that was true about the
dogs losing our scent. I looked back and imagined the redneck track-
ers and the bloodhounds coming to the river's edge. It wouldn't take

much more than a below-average intellect to conclude that we had crossed over, so to speak. We climbed and then came down a hill into an open scar of land. A rusting and idle backhoe was standing near a pit. The rain fell harder, and thunder rattled in the distance. The place seemed to be a construction site, but nothing was being built, and so I thought it was a fitting metaphor for Peckerwood County. The ground was sloppy with mud, and we sank to our ankles with each step. Then we heard the sound of a car or truck, and we jumped into the pit. We splashed and fought with the mud and standing water in the bottom until we were plastered against the red clay wall. The engine noise faded, and we looked around to find that the hole was about ten feet square and as high.

For minutes we tried to climb the clay walls, but not only could we find no purchase on the slimy face, we defeated our efforts by our retarded, out-of-sync motions. It was a miracle, if you're receptive to such language, that one of us didn't end up strangled by the chain.

"This isn't working," I said.

Patrice looked at me with his eyes. I thought I could see panic seeping into his face.

"You stand on my shoulders," I said.

"Why?"

"So you can reach the top and then pull me out."

"Why you gonna be on da bottom?"

"Your back is hurt," I said.

He shook his head. "Naw, I ain't fallin' fer it. I don't trust you. You want me to do all the work pullin' your lazy nigger ass up."

"Okay, I'll stand on your shoulders, and then I'll pull you out. Does that sound better?"

"Right. You think I'm stupid? You'll get up there and next thing I know you're runnin' to Atlanta and I'm still in di hole."

I looked at him, then held my cuffed wrist in front of his face. "Patrice, we're chained together. I can't leave you."

"Oh, yeah."

I tried to climb up on his shoulders, but his back just wouldn't allow it. I leaned over and helped him step onto my shoulders, then I stood as tall as I could with my right arm raised as high as I could reach. Patrice reached up with his right hand, the chain pulling at his left. Mud fell down into my face. He grunted, a sound not so different from his talking, and swore, and finally said, "I got me sumpin'." The sumpin' turned out to be a root, and he managed to get his body out and clear. He grunted even louder, even screamed once as he pulled me up.

"We'd better get out of this road," I said.

The rain let up, and the heat of Peckerwood County found its full form. Now, without the rain, I was as wet with perspiration. We staggered a mile or so away from the muddy pit and collapsed on our backs in high grass.

Patrice looked over at me and said, without provocation, "You know, I don't like you. Nigger."

"I can well imagine."

"I don't even like yer name. Potay."

"That's fine by me."

"You makin' fun of me, boy?" he asked.

"Nature beat me to that," I said.

He hopped to his feet, and of course I did as well. We stood there staring at each other. I wish I could say I felt nothing, but I found a bit of hatred in myself for this redneck fool. I could see that he was not only ready to throw a punch, but that punch was forthcoming. I had seen the behavior so often in my life as a constant bully victim. I decided it was a good time to attempt to Fesmerize him. Up went one brow, and I leaned into my gaze.

"What you starin' at, boy?"

I said nothing.

Then he punched me, a left to the face, that hurt much less than I imagined it would. We yanked at the chain back and forth, trading a couple of punches. Even while we rolled around in pathetic mortal combat I considered that the presence of at least a meager intellect was necessary for Fesmerian success.

Though I'd had much truck with being beaten up, I was not an experienced fighter. I was, however, more fit and slightly larger than my opponent, and it turned out that Raymond's sadistic karate instruction had stayed with me more than it was reasonable to expect. I was able to block most of Patrice's punches and keep him more or less off balance. However, what he lacked in skill and size he compensated for in stupidity, a stupidity that made his movements highly unpredictable. For example, a couple of times he tried to run away from me, forgetting that we were linked together, only to get yanked back like a dog on a long leash. He would then come flying back at me with the wildest roundhouse punch. I realized during the scuffle that my instinct to throw a blow was simply absent, and I realized as well that if I did hit him and managed to knock him silly or out, then I would be tethered to deadweight, a dumbbell, if you will. Finally, I was on top, straddling his torso with my knees pinning his shoulders to the ground.

That's when the business end of a rifle was shoved in my face.

At the other end of the weapon was a singularly ugly redheaded boy of perhaps twelve years. I had never thought a child could be ugly, but his mouth was too small for his pie face, and yet his teeth were those of a larger person. All this set below a nose out of something by Erskine Caldwell. And all that on a head far too large for his scrawny body. Even with the gun pointed at me I wondered immediately how I could take in so many features so quickly and wondered further if he could close those lips over his bathroom-tile teeth.

"Y'all be careful wit dat peashooter naw, boy," Patrice said.

I moved away from Patrice, and we slowly found our feet.

"Why you two chained up like dat?" The boy looked at Patrice, but kept the rifle pointed at me. "You takin' him to jail?"

"Yeah, sumpin' like that," Patrice said. "You live round chere?"

"I lives over dat ridge, through the holla, up a hill, and past the branch." He pointed. "Not far."

"Who you live wit, boy?"

"My ma and my sister."

"What 'bout yer pa?"

"Ain't got no pa."

"What 'bout neighbors? You got neighbors?"

"Ain't got no neighbors."

"What 'bout kin? Cousins? You got cousins?"

"Ain't got no cousins."

I watched and listened to those two idiots.

"What yo name?" Patrice asked.

"They call me Bobo."

"Well, Bobo, you gots a spider on yer gun." When the boy looked down, Patrice knocked the rifle away. He also managed to knock the boy to the ground. "Dumbass," Patrice said.

I grabbed the rifle and realized that the boy was not moving. I put my hand behind his head and felt a rock there. "He hit his head," I said.

"So what? Let's go."

"He might be hurt." I touched the boy's wide face and said his name a couple of times.

His eyes opened and he leaped up and away from me to hide behind the legs of Patrice.

"You got food at your house, boy?" Patrice asked.

"We got some."

"Take us there."

I kept the rifle.

It was no short walk to the boy's house. As if the heat and humidity were not enough, it was dusk when we came to the *branch,* and mosquitoes were swarming. The house turned out to be a shack right out of every hillbilly's origin fantasy. Had it been constructed of logs it might have had a rustic charm, but being made

of clapboard and tin it had no charm at all. On a line hung from
a post to a stunted tree hung clothes at wild and odd angles. Just
in front of the porch was an open well surrounded by loose and
broken bricks.

"Sis!" the boy called out.

A young woman stepped out onto the rickety porch. A look at
her face left no doubt that she and the boy were related. The way
she tilted her head to locate our sounds told me she was blind.
"Bobo, who you got out dere wit y'all?"

"We don't want no trouble, ma'am," Patrice said, sounding
almost human. "We just want some water and sumpin' ta eat."

"Dey's chained together, Sis."

"Do you have any tools?" I asked the boy, but he only looked
at me and ignored my question. I glanced at Patrice.

"You got any tools?" Patrice asked.

"Yeah, we got some tools."

"Go fetch us'all a chisel and a big hammer."

"We gonna come in naw," Patrice said to the woman. "You be
a good girl and fix us up some food."

The woman knocked over a chair on her way to the stove. "I
gots some beans a-cookin'," she said.

The place was a mess. Piles of clothes were everywhere. Clean
or dirty, I couldn't say. There was no fire burning in the place. The
stones of the fireplace were thick with soot, and the timbers that
held up the tin roof had been darkened by smoke as well.

The woman dropped a couple of bowls and spoons onto the
table. We ate. The beans were awful, and they were cold. I looked
and saw that there was no fire in the cookstove. But I knew I needed
the energy if I was going to keep running, so I chewed and swallowed and tried to kill the taste with some very stale bread.

Patrice talked with his mouth full. "What yer name?"

"Sis," she said.

"What that short fer?"

"Ain't short fer nothin'."

"Huh. Sis," he said to himself. "That's a purty name. Got any coffee?"

"I'll git it."

I looked up from my bowl at Patrice. "What does this taste like to you?"

"Taste like food, that how it taste."

Sis came back with the coffee just as Bobo arrived with the mallet and chisel. Patrice and I jumped up for the tools and went and sat at the hearth. I put the chisel to his cuff and pounded it.

Bobo said, "One of 'em's a nigga."

"Which one, Bobo?" Sis asked.

"Da black one."

"Which one dat be?"

The cuff fell away from Patrice's wrist, and he set to work on mine. He said, "I the white one."

"Which one is you?"

"This one."

My cuff came off, and I stood and walked across the room, grabbing the rifle from the table as I did. "I'm the black one, and I'm over here," I said. "That should clear things up."

Patrice tried to stand up, but let out a yell and fell backward. "What's wrong?" Sis asked.

"It's his back," I said. "I think he's hurt pretty bad. Here, help me get him to a bed."

We put him on a cot surrounded by piled clothes. I looked down at him, helpless there, and I resolved to leave him in the morning. Somehow he read that intention in my face and said, "If'n you does, I'll sho nuff tell where you headed." With that, exhaustion took him, and he fell asleep.

"Is you really black?" Sis asked me.

"He sho am," Bobo said.

"My great-grandpappy used to have him some slaves," the blind woman said. "They say he owned a plantation."

"How nice for him," I said. I felt myself growing sleepy. "Listen, I'm just going to sit over here and close my eyes for a bit." I held the rifle cradled against my chest and drifted.

My dream spiraled like all things spiral: life, reflection, desire toward some truth, but never aimed directly at it. The year was 1861. Somehow I knew that and somehow I knew that I was in New Orleans, though I had never been there and certainly hadn't been there in the nineteenth century. Though it was only March, the air was wet and hot, wetter than air should be, hotter than air should be. My clothes, my clothes were magnificent. I was dressed in a canary yellow frock suit, fitted at my trim waist and just a little snug across my chest. My shirt was white and crisp in spite of the humidity, and I realized that for some reason I was not perspiring like those around me. People watched me, I believed, with some admiration and some respect and perhaps fear. The yellow of my suit made my dark brown skin seem smooth in the bright sun. Other slaves wore tattered work clothes as they labored loading and unloading cargo. The ship's captain, with whom I was dealing, was wrapped in drab attire, as was the white dock foreman, a short, fat man in a vest. They all called me Raz-ru, and I heard a black man refer to me behind my back as *the claw*.

"That does it, Raz-ru," the captain said, handing me a copy of the shipping bill. "Tell me, will we ever see Mr. Bond down here again? Or are you taking over everything?"

"Maybe," I said, intentionally leaving it unclear about which question I was answering. "Maybe."

As I walked away from the docks a black man named Jason joined me. I greeted him by name. He was taller than I, very slender, and his voice was unusually high pitched.

"They says the war is comin', Raz-ru. They says we gonna be free men," Jason said.

"Who is they?" I asked.

"Everybody."

I stopped and looked him in the eyes. "I hope it's true. I believe it is true. Are you ready for it?"

"I'm ready."

"Good man. Stay ready."

Then I was wandering with less ease, but more than I would have expected, through a crowd of white men, ugly faces, some with tobacco-stained chins, some dressed in finery. I was in an auction hall, and the merchandise was slaves. The item on the block was a man about my size, built very much like me, square jawed like me. The auctioneer barked out his attributes, said he was as strong as an ox, could lift and run all day and didn't mind the heat or the humidity. He then gestured, and the man ran back and forth through the aisle, the muscles of his back rippling, his head down. The first bids were called out, and I heard fifty, then seventy-five, but I didn't hear what price he finally fetched.

A sudden hush fell upon the room as what looked very much like a white woman was pushed onto the block. But she couldn't have been white because she was on the block. In New Orleans there were hundreds like her, but this woman wore the clothes of a so-called lady, and by that I mean that she was dressed from the waist up as well as below, given a respect that any other slave could never have expected. She stood with her back straight, her chin out, defiant. All the slaves behind the block came together as if a choir and then, as a choir, sang "Swing Low, Sweet Chariot," their voices soft, mellow, round, their gaze a collective one, dumb and lost.

"I have here a high-, high-yellow bitch of good lines," the auctioneer called. "Her good white blood is evident, but I can guarantee her hot and steamy nigger disposition. From her hips you can see she's probably not much for breedin', but she's great for rehearsin'. Her skin might be white, but she bleeds black. A fine luxury purchase for the discriminating gentleman."

Before the bidding began, a familiar voice rang out, offering five thousand dollars. It was the voice of the man who owned me.

Hamish Bond stepped forward, dashing and comfortable in his camel dress coat, his tightly cinched green cravat, his camel top hat, his oiled hair graying at the temples just below the brim. Bond was not nearly as tall as me, but he carried himself entirely erect, as if he had been constructed anew for the day.

"I have a bid of five thousand dollars from Mister Hamish Bond," the auctioneer sang. "Five thousand dollars. Do I hear any other bids? Five thousand once. Twice. Sold to Hamish Bond."

The woman looked liked every other mulatto in New Orleans, but Bond paid for her and took her back to his place in the Quarter. I arrived a couple of hours later to find myself standing in the kitchen, hearing about the new acquisition from the last high-yellow object of affection, Michelle.

She moved around the kitchen in a long dress, a scarf around her head. Her dark eyes blazed. She moved with some grace, but not much. "Raz-ru," she said, pointing at the ceiling. "She's up there right now, in that room that used to be mine. And I have to wait on her, treat her with respect and deference."

The cook, another young mulatto woman, said, "The way we used to have to treat you."

"Shut up, Dolly," Michelle said. "No one asked you."

"I have to treat her like she's more than nothing while he tiptoes around her like she's made of glass or some such, like she's white like he is. Why did I fall from favor, Raz-ru? He used to treat me like that. Why no more? Did he drill deep enough to strike black, and now he needs a new well?"

"And he'll need a new well again," I said.

Dolly came over, a big wooden spoon in her hand, talking like the voodun princess she was, "Might be the last well he get." She stirred the air with her spoon. "It's comin'. Change be comin'. It's in the air. Soon, Master Hamish won't be having his yellow cookies."

"Dolly, go about your business!" Michelle said. "Take the tea up to that . . . that new one."

Michelle watched Dolly leave. "Samantha Moon, that's her name.

She was living high and mighty up in Virginia, thinking she was white, and then the truth came back to roost. She got to live free for a long spell and she ought to be happy about that, but she doesn't believe she is what she is. I would also feel sorry for her except that she had those free years that I didn't have. I'm beginning to think the only difference between being black and being white is that if you're white you just don't know about your blood, you're dumb to your blood, ignorant about that one drop. White people fear that one drop like we fear the rope."

"Yes," I said. "Yes, but they also love that one drop. Like the way Bond loved you and will love her. Fleetingly." I studied her face. "Tell me, do you really love that man?"

"He is so kind." Her face did a dreamlike thing, it became long, then fat and I had to think to fix it and I was not sure it was ever the same.

"The devil is often kind. He controls with his kindness. His darkies collect and sing him praises for his kindness. They huddle together and parade like a single creature behind that wagon he calls kindness. He kills with his kindness."

"You ask me why I love him," Michelle said, her dead-doll eyes locked on mine. "Why do you hate him so?"

"You don't need to ask that." I realized I was still holding my hat in my hands. I was nervous because I had no place to go. "So, this woman upstairs, who has been dragged from her home, sold on the block, she cannot accept her blood?"

"Cannot and will not, Raz-ru."

"She may soon wish that her blood will accept her."

"She will not," she said.

"Then she is more than a fool. She is stupid."

And in the dream, the words felt strange in my mouth, the faces seemed in soft focus, no hard edges, no sharp contrasts, except that rage burned inside me, my not so much feeling it as knowing it. The slaves irritated me with their love of singing. Michelle irritated me with her love of Bond. I irritated myself with my artificial dignity, my station as *boss Negro,* a meaningless designation. The chorus of slaves appeared in the kitchen. *Swing low, sweet chariot, coming fo' to carry me home.* With the awful music as background I wondered about the pale woman upstairs and wondered why her blood mattered to any of us, except of course that she, like us, was property, and somehow it was an offense that she did not care or that she was incapable of holding that fact in her head. The choir of slaves kept singing, and I turned to shout at them, "Would you niggers please shut the fuck up!"

They looked shocked, taken aback.

"Just shut the fuck up," I repeated.

Grumbling, they disbanded, and the scene broke away into pieces, and I found myself being asked by Bond to sing a song for him and his sea captain visitor. Though I did not want to, I could not stop the song from finding my throat. My mouth opened and out it poured while I tasted bile. "Blow the man down," I sang, and as I did, my voice deeper than usual, I sought to punctuate it with irony that of course fell on deaf ears. "Give me some time to blow the man down," I sang the last line and then walked away from them as a storm approached.

Finding myself in the room of the new mulatto princess I was at once confused, outraged, and saddened. I could find no words to share with her, and it soon became clear to me that she was not only unaware of my presence, but unable to see me. The wind blew the French doors open wide, and the curtains danced like loose sails. Samantha Moon tried to push against the wind to close the doors, but she was beaten back. Then Bond dashed in from the veranda and, as if fighting a wind that possessed agency, he closed the doors and locked them. He went to Samantha Moon and helped her to her feet. They stared deeply into each other's eyes, as deep as they could stare, and kissed. I wanted to puke over and over while they wrestled through brief and uninteresting sex, not knowing why I was made so sick, not knowing why they were having sex. All this while a slave who looked just like Barry White stood at the foot of the bed singing, "Can't get enough of your love, babe."

Spiraling around and around I found myself standing on the

deck of a riverboat. As it docked dozens of black people gathered on the hill beyond the dock and began to sing, sing in that mellow and sweet-sad and sickening way of gospel music, sing praises to the master arriving home. I followed Bond and Samantha Moon off the boat and across the dock. There he placed her on the seat of a buckboard that had been decorated with magnolia blossoms and red and white ribbons, and he stood in the bed of it. The wagon carried him and his mistress to the plantation, the singing Negroes dancing behind, singing, cakewalking, grinning, grinning, grinning. One short, spry, bald black man high-stepped the whole way beside the wagon. I lagged behind, wondering at once what I was doing there as Raz-ru and what I was doing in this dream that certainly could not be my own.

Samantha Moon was standing on the veranda wearing a veranda-standing dress, her light skin catching the moonlight. She was asking me why I hated Bond and why I hated her. I told her that I did not hate, but that I was sad for her, for her inability to accept herself, for her refusal to acknowledge her real self. She glided across the room and went on about Bond.

"He has raised you like a son, even broken the law to teach you to read. He never beats any of you," she said.

"You?" I repeated.

She look upon me, puzzled.

"You mean *us*."

She stepped more fully into the moonlight, I imagined to appear whiter.

"Oh, yes, he's a good master. Good ol' massa Hamish. He sho nuff good. He don beat us or nothin'." I stared at her. "How would you describe a relationship where one of the good things to say was 'he doesn't beat me'? Do you know about his past?" I asked.

"He told me all about it. How he was a slave trader, and he was known as Captain Strike Down and about the Rio Ponga. He told about the burning village that haunts his dreams. He also told me that it was not only white men doing evil, but blacks as well. He told me about Geezo, the black king whose men were burning the village. He told how they would split open heads and run their fingers through the brains of still-living people. He told me all of it, Raz-ru."

"And you believed him. I suppose you would want to. Poor rich Hamish Bond, living with the guilt of ruining so many lives. I don't see him sharing his wealth with the ruined. No, he stays rich and we stay slaves because there were black men as evil as him. So says he. It is his burden to care for us."

Then stuff happened, as stuff happens in dreams, things that I either cannot remember or in fact didn't happen, though it seems like those things, forgettable as they apparently are, must have happened. But there I was, knowing that Bond had left the plantation only to test Samantha's love by leaving her alone to the advances of Charles DeMarion, evil neighbor slave owner, beater of slaves, raper of slaves. Knowing also, as I stood outside the closed doors of the drawing room that Samantha Moon was in there with Charles DeMarion and that I would be running in to save her from his inevitable attempt at rape.

And so I did respond to her cry for help and why, I'm not certain. Would I have run in to save a dark slave from his raping hands? Was it her carriage? The way she believed herself to be white? Was I defending her honor? Defending white womanhood? Or was it, sicker still, my attempt to protect the property of the master I so hated? I hated myself as I ran across that room. I pulled him away from her, and he began to beat me with the crop he always carried. I stood tall and punched him. All this while a choir of black voices floated over us, singing, "I Shot the Sheriff."

Michelle came running into the room, looked at the unconscious DeMarion and then to me. "Run, Raz-ru! Run before he calls the sheriff!"

I ran. I ran for all I was worth, which was a pretty penny I was told, through the acres of tall cotton, through the towering stands of sycamores, over the eroding levee and into the stagnant and

stinking swamp where I knew my white pursuers would not follow — not into the swamp, into the deepest of black backwater, full
of poisonous snakes and angry gators and long nights with light
from only wild eyes. I was happy to be there. A wet hell, but a quiet
heaven. All the singing was hushed.

Tornado. Rain. Bird calls. Spiraling. The blue uniform of the
Union Army fit tight across my chest and loose in the trousers.
The war was pretty much over. Growers like Bond and DeMarion
were wanted for having burned their crops and had fled into hiding. The city of New Orleans was awash with blue uniforms like
mine. The former town palace of Hamish Bond was empty, and I
sat there in it, candles burning on the dining-room table, dusk turning to night outside. Samantha Moon walked into the room from
the courtyard and was startled by my presence.

"Come in," I said. "How does freedom taste? Oh, that's right,
you've already tasted freedom. Does it taste the same? Is it sweeter?
More bitter? Does it go down easily? Like your master's sperm?"

"You're disgusting," she hissed.

"I thought you might find me so."

"What are you doing here?"

"I'm here to light the candles." I stood and walked toward her at
the other end of the table. I picked up the six-candle holder. Only
five burned. Narrow candles with tall flames. I held the light close
to her face. "Are you able to see yourself more clearly now? I think
that I can see you more clearly. Now that you're free. And now that
I'm free."

"Where is Hamish?"

"Hamish," I said. "I don't know where he is, but I will find him
and I will kill him." I pushed the candles closer to her face. "Can
you feel the hot? The heat? The heat they say we darkies burn with?
Can you feel my heat?" I moved my face closer to hers and spoke to
her left ear, the ear on the side of her heart. "You do feel the heat,
Samantha Moon. You've always felt the heat between us. It's starting deep down, isn't it, like a tickle someplace. You feel it because

here I am, waiting to reconnect you to your blood, ready to infuse you with your history, sad and ugly though it may be." My breath touched her face, and it seemed to me she found it sweet smelling, the way her eyelids fluttered. I whispered to her, "You long to be filled with the juice of lost fruit, don't you? You need your denied tale, the one I hold between my legs. You feel the blood, don't you, Samantha Moon?" Her breath was fractured, catching snags as it left her. "The heat, Samantha Moon, the heat."

Her lips trembled as she leaned toward me, aching for my kiss.

"Sadly, I don't feel the heat," I said.

She began to weep.

Then Hamish Bond was in the room. He held a long sword and leaned on it like a cane, like a swashbuckler. "You've made the lady cry," he said.

"I'm glad you're here," I said. "It saves me the trouble of finding you."

"You would kill me. After all I've done for you? I remember the village so vividly, so vividly. It was on the Rio Ponga in Africa. You think we white men are bad, but you should have seen those black pagans. I saw more than one whack off the top of a head and run his hand through some poor nigger's warm brain while he could still feel it. I was sickened by them, sickened, I say. And there, under the body of a woman was a two-month-old tar baby. I put myself between one of Geezo's men and caught a spear through my leg. I saved that little monkey and brought him home, treated him like a son, taught him to read, to move through the white man's world." He stared at me while moving closer to Samantha Moon. As he did, Samantha Moon's skin grew darker. With each step her skin became more like mine. "I should have saved myself the wound and let the spear strike that little bastard dead." He looked over at Samantha Moon and was startled.

I pulled out my service revolver and shot him in the chest.

The room became filled with hovering sullen, perhaps angry, perhaps relieved, black faces, and none of them sang.

Then I was in a brothel, plush red pillows soft and comfortable behind my naked back. My arm was slung over the back of a velvet davenport, my reddened and sore knuckles grazed the flocked wallpaper. A long-legged white woman with strawberry blond hair, pale blue and vacant eyes, crawled sensuously, yet awkwardly, toward me. I watched her over the distance, coming across the worn oriental rug, her deep red-painted nails like bloody claws. She came to me and kissed her way up my leg to my soft penis, then she took me into her mouth.

My penis was wet. I could feel that. I swam in the darkness of sleep, slowly remembering my pursuers, where I was. I opened my eyes to see the boy asleep across the room. I looked to my left and saw Patrice asleep on the cot. I looked down to find the top of the blind woman's head in my lap. I scooted away and fastened up my trousers.

"Which one are you?" she asked.

"I'm the black one," I said.

She spat. "I had me a notion."

We sat in silence for a while, and then I asked, "Is it just you and your little brother?"

"Yeah," she said. "He thinks Mama just went out to de stow. But she ain't comin' back."

"How long has she been gone?"

"Over a year now. She run off with the scrap-metal man."

"How long have you been blind?" I asked.

"How you know I ain't been born thisaway?"

"I don't. That's why I asked."

"I was ten year old when Mama threw a pail of lye in my face. You can see I'se all uglied up with burn scars."

"Hardly noticeable," I said. In fact it was difficult to see the scarring, though it was there, and it made me sad to see it.

"Mama said she couldn't keep no man on account dey liked me, and one day she got mad and threw the lye onto me."

"I'm sorry."

"Den she had Bobo and blamt everthin' on him." She seemed to look off into space, but of course she wasn't. "How old you be?"

"I'm eighteen."

"You young," she said.

"I look older."

"You sho sound older. I like the way you talk. You sound fancy."

"I don't know about that."

"Well, you don't sound like nobody from round chere."

"I can well imagine."

"What dey arrest you fer?"

"Being black," I said.

"Hmmm. I heard tell that was illegal."

"It is in Peckerwood County, anyway," I added. "I just want to get to Atlanta so I can forget about this place."

"I always wanted to go to Atlanta," Sis said. "Doan know why. Cain't see nothin', that fer sho."

"Did you go to school?" I asked.

"For a while. Den Mama threw that lye into my face and I never went back. She said I was ugly and the other chilluns would laugh at me. And I couldn't see no board or books no way. I heard one of Mama's beaus say she dint send me 'cause she was afraid she get charged wit buse."

"Abuse," I corrected her.

"Abuse."

"You don't have to be able to see a book to read it," I said. "You could go to school. You still could."

"Dat's crazy talk."

Those words hung in the air awhile. Patrice snorted, gagged a bit, then settled back into his snoring.

"Is yer friend a good-lookin' feller?"

"First, he's not my friend. I don't know. Somebody might think he looks okay. He's looks a little like that old move star, Tony Curtis."

"I ain't never seen no movie," she said.

"You haven't missed much."

"You got family in Atlanta?" she asked.

I shook my head and then realized the uselessness of that. "No. Sort of. No, I don't. I used to live there."

We sat quietly for a while, listening to Bobo and Patrice snoring in the darkness. I could see a bit of the moon through the far window.

"You think we'll make it to Atlanta?" I asked.

"I don't see how," she said. For once she didn't sound stupid or out of it. "Not on foot anyway."

"Well, on foot is all we got," I said, feeling rather colloquial.

"But if'n you was to jump the freight."

I tilted my head. "What?"

"The freight train. It goes to Atlanta. And it be going real slow up the ridge. Kinda steep. I jumped on it when I was little. We rode it fer fun. We always jumped off befo' it topped the hill."

"Where is the train?"

"The train ain't always there. It come by once a day going one way and at night goin' tother."

"Where are the tracks?"

"Across the branch, through the holler, over the hill, and round the bend. At least that where it used to be. I ain't been there since Mama burnt out my eyes."

"Which train goes to Atlanta? Day or night?" I felt terribly sorry for Sis, but she was making my head hurt.

"Day, I think."

"And how far away are the tracks?"

"It's a fir piece," she said.

"How fir?"

"Fir nuff."

"Is it two miles or twenty?" I asked.

"Yep."

"Well, which?"

"Depends on what way you go," she said. "Any fool know that. Bobo could show you the way, I think."

I looked over at the sleeping child. "I'm pretty sure he could. Do you think he would?"

She didn't answer. She leaned back, her face in shadow now, and she might have gone to sleep. I looked at Patrice's sleeping face, then over at the boy. These were sad people, and for the world I wanted to think of them as decent. Perhaps they were decent enough, but the place that made them was so offensive to me that all who lived there became *there*. I wondered how a little education might benefit them, but I came to the same conclusion. Well, sort of a conclusion, as I hadn't reasoned toward it at all. I believed they were all ego, but hardly conscious. As insipid as that model of mind seemed to me, it proved useful in my surface understanding of them. And I could see that any sort of hypnosis was unlikely to work as there was no sub- or unconscious to tap into.

"You two luv birds through yapping?" Patrice said.

"I thought you were asleep."

"I was tryin'."

"How is your back?"

I didn't know why I was asking. I certainly didn't care. Now that we were no longer chained together, there was no reason for us to remain together, except that Bobo probably would not take me to the train tracks, but he would lead the way for Patrice. I needed Bobo and therefore I needed Patrice, that was my conclusion, with a *therefore* and everything.

"I'm in treemundus pain. So, what was you and Sis talkin' 'bout?"

"I thought you were awake," I said.

"You was keepin' me awake. There's a difference. And I heard y'all, but I tweren't listenin'."

"Another interesting distinction."

"So, what she say?"

"She said there's a freight train to Atlanta that runs near here."

"Where?"

"That's the problem. We need Bobo to show us how to get there."

"And I ain't goin' do it, less'n y'all take us to Atlanta wit y'all," said Sis, sitting up and bringing her face back into the moonlight through the window.

"Ain't happenin', Sis," Patrice said.

"Then y'all on yo own." She crossed her arms on her chest and stuck out her chin in defiance.

"Well, naw, Sis, there ain't no reason to be all like dat," Patrice said. He reached over and put his hand on her knee. "I bet a purty gal like you got so many beaus round chere that you really don't want to leave."

"Ain't no beaus and you can stop yer sweet talkin'. We's going to Atlanta wit y'all or nobody goes."

"I don't want to argue," I said, "and I don't much care who hops the train with me. I just want to get on and get out of this hellhole. Bobo, what time does the eastbound train go by?"

"About dusk. If we leave at dawn we'll jus' make it."

I leaned back and closed my eyes again. "We'll need our rest," I said. "I'll need mine anyway."

I slept a dreamless sleep this time, but I awoke to the nightmare of Patrice and Sis having sex in the cot. Across the room Bobo was eating cold beans out of the pot on the stove. I covered my ears to block out the grunting and moaning. Luckily the noise was short lived, and soon they were both snoring. I tried to repress my humanitarian thoughts of helping the poor blind girl find a school so she could learn to read.

At first light I was standing out in the yard, happy for the sun to be coming up, happy to be out of the beans-, sweat-, and sex-stinking confines of the cabin. Then Patrice walked out with Sis dressed in a fresh tattered calico dress. Their faces appeared even more vacant than before.

"Ain't it a beautiful mornin', Potay?" he said.

"I cain't even see and I know it beautiful," Sis said.

"What's going on?" I asked.

"We's in luv," Patrice said.

I shook my head. "And?" But I knew what was coming and then it came.

"Sis and Bobo is comin' wit me to Atlanta," Patrice said.

Bobo stepped out of the house and stood by them. He pulled at his sister's sleeve.

"That's great. Congratulations." And it kept coming.

"Since you know folks there, we was thinking maybe you'd let us stay wit you fer a little while, til I get on my feet, ya know?"

"Are you crazy?" As I asked the question, to which I of course knew the answer, I remembered that I needed the boy to lead me to the tracks.

The hounds howled in the distance. The sound was chilling.

"If them is Jubal Jeter's dawgs, they gone be on y'all real fast," Bobo said. "Dem dawgs is mean, too."

"I'll do what I can to help," I said.

"See, Bobo," Sis said. "I told you, Potay be a good nigger."

I looked at the three of them, standing there against the backdrop of that cabin like an Andy Warhol parody of *American Gothic*, residents of a cul-de-sac at the end of Tobacco Road.

It was just sunrise, and the air was already hot and sticky. As parched as I was I refused to drink any water from the well. I could only guess how many rodents had fallen into it to drown and decompose. Neither was I hungry enough to consume just one more bean or rock-hard piece of bread. The hounds called and they sounded closer.

"Let's get out of here," I said.

Before we could leave, Sis and Bobo grabbed a few things, and Patrice had an idea to throw the dogs off our trail. He covered the

ground with black pepper and every other seasoning he could find
in the house.

"It'll take 'em awhile to sneeze dat out," he said. He giggled. "I
wish I could be here to see when dey do."

Finally, we set off, Bobo leading the way, struggling with his
oversized rucksack and a brown paper bag. Sis and Patrice followed
after, each carrying a worn leather valise as she held his hand for
guidance. A bad situation no matter how one looked at it, unless
of course you were blind and in fact they all were, and perhaps I
as well. I noticed the sad detail that Sis's shoes did not match. Both
boots were black and worn, but the heel of one was at least a half-
inch higher than the other and so she limped. I brought up the rear.
I carried the boy's twenty-two rifle, mainly so no one else would,
but a bit of thinking made me realize how quickly the presence of
that weapon in my hands could get me killed, so I tossed it into the
brush just after we crossed the creek.

The sun cooked us as we dragged ourselves up and down hills.
Patrice helped Sis over fallen logs and over puddles, and I imagined
I saw some tenderness there. Perhaps I did. Then we came to the
tracks. Bobo assured us that we had made it with a couple of hours
to spare, so we found some shade and rested.

"Will you help me find one of dem schools?" Sis asked me.

"Sho he will," Patrice said.

"And I kin go to school, too?" Bobo asked.

"You sho kin," Patrice said. He leaned his head back and looked
up at the clouds. "What I wouldn't give fer a drank."

"I got a bottle in my suitcase," Sis said. "Thought it might come
in handy." She opened the leather bag and pulled out a mason jar
with a lid. It was filled with a clear liquid.

"Well, dang it to mercy, I knowed I loved you all along," Patrice
said. He took the jar, unscrewed the lid, and took a whiff. "Lawdy,
that smells fine, finer than frog's hair." He took a swig and coughed.
"Here, honey, have a bite."

Sis took a long drink and wiped her mouth with her sleeve. She handed the jar to Bobo and he did the same. Bobo gave the jar back to Patrice. I was thoroughly and absolutely disgusted, yet somehow not surprised at all.

Patrice pushed the jar toward me, but I waved it off. I watched them drink themselves unconscious, and I realized that it didn't matter where they were, they would never be going anywhere.

The train's whistle blew. It was coming and I was the only one awake. I did not wake them. The locomotive passed, and I walked to the tracks. Just as Sis had said, the train was moving very slowly up the grade. I found an empty boxcar and easily climbed into it. Alone. I left them sleeping there where they belonged, with one another.

CHAPTER 3

I didn't want to believe, nor could I imagine, that Ted was manipu-
lating the crosshairs of the planchette to make the Ouija Board
answer my questions in a particular way, but it was the only viable
explanation. To my sad question "Will I be stuck in Atlanta forever?" the board said, "Could be." To my panicked "Am I crazy,"
it was similarly noncommittal, saying, "Perhaps." And finally to
my offhanded question, "Was I really in utero for twenty-four
months?" it was irritatingly and aggravatingly more definite, giving the response "Without a doubt."

Ted and I were sitting on the edges of lounge chairs by the pool.
Jane was steadily swimming laps, her large feet and long legs pro-
pelling her slinky red-bikinied body.

"You know where the name of the Ouija Board comes from,
Nu'ott?" Ted asked. "It's from the French and German words for
yes. Could just have easily been called the *non-nein*. Of course
that's just one theory. There are probably many. I find it simply
strange that the skin they pack sausages in is edible. Edgar Cayce
thought they were dangerous."

"Sausages?"

"No, Ouija Boards. Why would Edgar Cayce care about sausages? Maybe he did. He was a weird dude. And sausages are everywhere." Ted looked at his bare feet at the end of his chinos. "Let me
ask it a question. Why can't the Democrats come up with decent
slogans?"

"I think that might be a long answer," I said.

"My point exactly. Republicans run around chanting 'America,
love it or leave it' and 'Freedom isn't free.'"

"The board can't handle that," I said.

"We ought to market a better one. Pigs are really smart, you know."

I hadn't said it, but I'm certain Ted knew it. I felt like a failure. I had set out on my own and had come back with my pathetic tail between my legs. Actually, I was more than a little bit lucky to have come back with a tail at all, much less one unbothered by my unseemly Peckerwood County–work-farm brethren. Failure might have been too strong a term only because I hadn't had any real goals when I set out. That finally was my awakening, my revelation from that brief and both eye-opening and eye-closing experience, that I, sadly, had no direction in life, and my new mission became to discover some mission.

"You could go to college," Ted said.

I shrugged. "I'm a high school dropout."

"With scads of money, my friend, with scads of money."

That was true, and I knew just what he meant, which in itself might have been evidence enough that I didn't need a university. However, at last, I was large enough in stature to not be pushed around physically, and suddenly I wanted, for whatever reasons, to be near people my own age, most especially women. Even as I thought it I knew I was being naïve. People had never treated me well, and I had no reason to expect they would change just because I was bigger.

"Definitely," Ted said. "College would be great for you. A time for searching and growth, for exposure to new and uninteresting subjects. I think that they should be called tax cells instead of brackets."

My first letter to the so-called development office of Morehouse College offering them a bit of a portion of a scad of my wealth yielded no response. The second letter was actually mailed back to me with my name and signature circled and *ha ha* written in red ink beside it. I hated using Ted's pull, but he insisted, and so he wrote to them, introduced me, and slightly more than suggested that I could be talked into being loose with my dough. I got a call from a woman named Gladys Feet, and she wanted very much to buy me lunch. I agreed to meet her at a restaurant downtown.

I arrived at the restaurant first and sat at the table to wait, with my doubts. I had had to go around the barn, as my mother would have said, just to try to offer these folks money. I watched as the hostess pointed me out and saw the reaction on Gladys Feet's face. Gladys Feet was an average-looking woman in all respects, dressed in an average navy blue business suit with a white blouse, but she wore extremely high stiletto heels. The heels made her look like an actor in a corporate porn film. She smiled as she approached and I stood. "Mr. Poitier," she greeted me.

"Hello, Ms. Feet," I said with a remarkably straight face.

She sat. She was a bit flustered. "I can't get over how much you look like Sidney Poitier. A young Sidney Poitier."

"More every day, it seems," I said.

"So, let me first say how pleased we are to discover your interest in Morehouse. It's so rewarding to me personally to meet interesting people wanting to contribute to the education of talented black men."

Her speech put me off a bit, and as she slickly spouted the words I realized that my scads of money gave me a considerable amount of power. A seemingly simple notion, but one that I had either been too stupid to acknowledge or too stubborn to accept. I cut right to the heart of the matter. "Ms. Feet, I am a high school dropout. I want to go to college, and I'm willing to buy my way in."

"I see. Well . . ."

I interrupted her. "Three hundred thousand toward anything you need, no questions, no strings. If I flunk out, the money is still yours. If I quit, the money is still yours. If I receive the stellar education you advertise, well, just remember that I have a lot more money."

"I don't know what to say," Gladys Feet said.

"Say I'll be admitted in the fall." I was speaking with a confidence that I didn't quite recognize and certainly didn't feel was justified. I was somewhat saddened by the knowledge that the confidence derived from my wealth or, more precisely, the awareness of my wealth.

"I don't have the power to . . ."

"Three hundred and twenty-five thousand."

"I'll be right back."

Gladys Feet left the table, and I ordered another cola. And as promised she was back quickly, a smile on her face, smoothing her skirt before she sat.

"Welcome to Morehouse," she said.

"Just like that?"

"Done. Tell me, is your name really Not?"

"Not Sidney," I corrected her.

"Not Sidney."

"That's what my mother named me."

"It's quite an interesting name."

"If you say so."

"May I ask, is your father Sidney Poitier?"

"No." I answered quite definitely, but the fact of the matter is I was not quite definite; I did not know. I had no reason to suspect that Sidney Poitier was my father, but I also had no idea who my father was. I knew nothing about the man, whether he was a man or a basting syringe. Nothing. I'd asked my mother a couple of times during my short years with her about him, but her answers were either so vague and confusing as to be useless or no answer at all. Once after dinner, as we sat in front of the television watching an *Adventures of Superman* rerun, I asked, "Was my father handsome?"

She replied, "Some might say yes."

"Was he smart?" I asked.

She stared at the television. "Why is it that after all the bullets have bounced off Superman's chest, he then ducks when the villain throws the empty gun at him?"

I looked at the television and wondered, knowing also that my quest for some detail about my history had been again thwarted, albeit with a very good question. I never pressed terribly hard, thinking that someday the story would surface, but then she died.

I looked up to see Gladys Feet staring at my face.

"The resemblance is remarkable, uncanny," she said. I believe she caught on that she was making me decidedly uncomfortable. She changed the subject. "So, what is it you plan to study?"

"I haven't decided," I said. "Psychology maybe or philosophy. I don't know. I want an education, that's pretty much it." I sounded so much like a student. I liked it. "I don't even know how I can decide what to study until I have that."

"That's a very clearheaded way to approach it," she said.

"Don't be patronizing," I said. "I'm giving you money and that's what matters to Morehouse. Perhaps I'll get an education, perhaps not. That's up to me. But don't be patronizing."

"I apologize."

"You needn't be sorry. It's your job to be that way."

"How old are you?" she asked in a way that suggested she was making a comment rather than looking for an answer.

"I'm eighteen years old. Nineteen, if you choose to count my extra year in the womb."

"Excuse me?"

"I'm eighteen," I said.

She shook her head. "You seem wise beyond your years."

She was being patronizing again, but I let it go. It was obvious she couldn't help herself. I wondered if there was a name for her condition. She wasn't exactly kissing my ass and she wasn't exactly flirting with me, but with a little shove she'd have shit on her nose and I'd have a date. Perhaps she was not precisely doing anything. Perhaps each and every one of her moves and gestures was approximate.

Perhaps she was smarter than I thought, smarter than me. After all, she was collecting three hundred and twenty-five thousand dollars from me.

"May I ask you a question?"

I wanted to inform her that she just had, but I nodded instead.

"How much money *do* you have?"

"I don't know. It changes daily. Hourly, I'm told."

"I see." She tugged at her collar as if a little hot.

"One other thing," I said.

"What's that?"

"I don't want anyone to know about my gift to the school."

"Okay. That's a simple matter."

Autumn approached with more heat than most of the summer had served up — nasty, humid, searing heat that made it impossible for one to remain dry. At least I couldn't seem to remain anything but soaked with perspiration. It was September and I was a college student, a sweat-drenched college student, a fact that didn't seem to matter as the first thing I learned was that I was as much of an outcast at the university as I had been in high school, only that here instead of beating and teasing me, they simply ignored me. I could have made my first day a little easier had I just once beforehand visited the campus. Then I might have at least had an inkling where one or two buildings might be, but no, I stayed away, reading and thinking. The latter activity, I was certain, would finally be my downfall. Downfall sounds a bit melodramatic or even vain, certainly romantic, as if I believed I occupied or expected to achieve some station, but the fact was I believed thinking or overthinking finally would not serve me well, if at all. Perhaps it's not even thinking I'm talking about, but pondering or wondering or stewing or whatever the hell I'm doing right here.

I managed to register for all my classes, just as all the other freshmen so managed and, I assumed, without much less surprise than I. It was a complicated matter that might or might not have had a computer involved. My classes were what one would expect, predictable survey courses, composition, and a rudimentary introduction to calculus. I decided to try to get into an upper-division English course titled the Philosophy of Nonsense taught by some guy named Percival Everett. I needed his signature to add the course, and so I went to his office. I found his door open and before I tapped on the jamb to announce myself I saw that the room was lousy with sports equipment, basketballs, inflated and not, tennis and squash rackets, a hockey stick, a baseball bat, a baseball glove on his desk, and a pair of boxing gloves hanging on the wall between portrait drawings of James Joyce and Terry McMillan. There was a photograph of another man high on the wall above the others. I knocked.

"Come in and sit down," Everett said, continuing to read *Sporting News*. "What do you need?"

"Your signature," I told him. "I want to take your Nonsense course."

"What year are you?" Still he didn't look at me.

"I'm a freshman."

"Anybody ever tell you that you look like Harry Belafonte?"

"Never."

"I'm not surprised. Where's your card?"

I pushed my blue card toward him, and he looked at me for the first time. "Nothing like Belafonte," he said. He looked at my card. "Not Sidney?"

"That really is my name," I said.

"Or else it wouldn't be on the card," he said. "I like it. Do you play golf? And I don't mean miniature golf."

"I never have."

"Good. It's a stupid game. A damn waste of water, keeping all that lawn alive and green. What about lunch? Do you eat lunch?"

"Occasionally."

"Me, too. Come on, I'll buy you some of what passes for food on this campus. What do people call you?"

"They seldom call me, but when they do, they call me Not Sidney."

He looked at me. "That's too bad." Then he studied his desktop. "Tell me, do you see my glasses?"

"They're on your head." I pointed.

He nodded. "That's a good place for them. Think I'll leave them there. Come along, Mr. Poitier."

"May I ask who that is a picture of?" I pointed.

"You may and you have," he said. "That, Mr. Poitier, is Pinto Colvig, one of the great artists and thinkers of our time."

"I don't know his name."

"You might know him by another name. He was the first Bozo the Clown. A genius. Oh, there were a lot of Bozos after him, but there will never be another Pinto Colvig. Even his son Vance was no Pinto. And that name. Pinto Colvig. What restraint it must have taken to not simply use his real name."

Everett was shorter than me and walked with a slight limp, favoring his right leg, but he walked quickly, if not in a straight line. After the third time he grazed me with his shoulder, he said, "I'm a weaver. Can't help it."

"Did you hurt your leg playing sports?"

"Stepped in a gopher hole. A stupid thing to do. I wasn't looking. Now, I always look. Of course I'm speaking metaphorically. Whatever that means."

We found our way to the dining hall in the student center. We grabbed trays and collected food. I picked up a burger and fries while Everett filled a bowl with salad and another with cottage cheese. As we stood in line, he looked at my tray and his. "Can you believe they have us pay for this shit?"

"It looks okay," I said.

He nodded. "Maybe."

We sat at a round table by the wall of windows and looked out at the passersby. He held a cherry tomato on the tines of his fork and then looked at me. "Are you a sheep, Mr. Poitier?"

"No," I said. "I don't think so."

"Most sheep don't think they're sheep. I wonder what they think they are. Pigeons, maybe."

I ate a fry and looked out at the guys walking along.

"So, what makes you interested in my class?" he asked.

"Nonsense," I said, flatly.

"Good." He laughed. "Keep it that way. You do your part and I'll do my part and all will be right in Mudville. Or Atlanta. Or maybe even Jonestown."

"What will the class be like?" I asked.

"Who knows?" he said. "We'll learn something, maybe. We'll read some stuff, maybe a lot of stuff. What, I don't know yet. You guys will do some presentations, I suppose. Bore each other and, sadly, me to sleep. Probably be some papers to write. Not long papers. I couldn't take that. I'm not a detail person." He finally ate the tomato from the end of his fork. "Are you living on campus?"

The question caught me off guard. For some reason it had never occurred to me that I might live at school. "I haven't decided," I said.

He didn't pause. With his glass to his lips, he said, "Might want to make a decision on that one. The dorms fill up fast, I'm told. Don't ask me why. They look like prisons."

"Do you think it's a good idea?"

He shrugged. "There's a lot of frat idiocy on this campus." He looked at me and seemed to consider his words. "You might like it, though. Who knows? You should talk to other people about it. I'm not the person to ask. Where are you living now?" Before I could answer, "Don't tell me. I'm really not interested. Besides, it's a good rule to never trust anyone who tells you all their business right away. Mind if I have a couple of your fries?"

I gestured that it was okay.

He popped one into his mouth. "Been over to Spelman yet?"

"No."

"What the hell is wrong with you? That's why men come to Morehouse. The only good reason."

"I thought it was because of the storied history," I said, using a phrase I'd read in some brochure.

"Well, there's that. Whatever that is. What doesn't have a storied history?" Everett ate another couple of fries. "Well, I'll see you in class, Mr. Poitier."

But he didn't get up. It became clear that he expected me to leave. He pulled out a cigar as I collected my tray.

"Don't worry," he said. "I won't light it in here. They'll all have a fit. I usually don't light them at all anymore. I read a book about U.S. Grant, and he had tongue cancer from these things. He felt as if he were swallowing razor blades at the end. I've never swallowed a razor blade, but I imagine it's awful."

"See ya," I said.

"Don't be a sheep, Mr. Poitier. Be anything, be a deer or a squirrel, a beaver or a gnu, but don't be a sheep."

"Okay."

"Be a gecko or a platypus. Be a panther or a sparrow, but not a sheep. Promise me that."

"Okay."

I walked away and out of the building. People moved by me like animals and in fact they were, as am I, but they seemed so far away. Or at least I did: I felt like a study by Muybridge. Occasionally I sensed the gaze of someone on me, as if I were being watched, and I imagined them wondering, as I walked too quickly, whether my feet were ever off the ground at the same time, like a horse trotting.

A strategically placed phone call to Gladys Feet and the promise of a few more dollars got me a room in Brazeal Hall and a roommate. It also got me a clearer sense that Gladys Feet was flirting with me.

"Perhaps we could have lunch again," she said.

"I don't know why that would be necessary."

"I thought you might give me a sense of how you're adjusting to campus life. I'd love to hear how you think we might improve things." In a softer, slightly deeper voice, she said, "We could meet well off campus."

"No, thank you." I hung up.

My roommate was the kind of guy who was considered cool on campus. In other words, my opposite. And he was none too happy to see me show up, as he believed that he would be living in the moderately tight space all alone. His name was Morris Chesney, and it's fair to say that he hated me from the moment he laid eyes on me. He was not quite as tall as me and this stuck in his craw. He had loose curly hair that he loved to run his fingers through, all the time. His eyes were green, and, from his generously offered reports at least, the Spelman girls loved them. When I arrived with my one bag, Morris had to abandon a closet; however, it was clear that all of his stuff would not fit into one, so I suggested, like a simp, that he take some space in mine.

I said, "Really, Morris, I don't have many things. You're welcome to use this side of my closet." I made the gesture in the spirit of getting along, being college buddies, elementary generosity. And so he proceeded to store his dirty gym shorts and sweat socks in there. To have called Morris Chesney passive-aggressive would have been a glaring understatement, as much as any understatement can glare. To have called him an egotistical, self-centered, not-terribly-bright asshole with a mean streak a mile wide would have been fairly accurate.

The room was what one might expect, essentially a cell. On the walls that were a color I called cholera were posters of musical groups the names of which I had heard in high school only in passing. Lots of guys in silky white suits who looked as cool as Morris Chesney — all either running their fingers through their hair or looking like they had just done so, and scantily covered curvy women in impossible, though not altogether uninteresting, poses.

Morris laughed when I told him my name. "What kind of stupid-ass name is Not?" he said.

"My name is Not Sidney."

"Excuse me, Not *Sidney*. I'll say you're not Sidney."

What was meant as an insult would have been a glancing blow at best, if I had cared. But what Morris Chesney had done was articulate what no one else ever had. He had said what probably everyone else meant to say but couldn't come up with, or wouldn't. He had pointed out to me that not only was I Not Sidney Poitier, but also that I was not Sidney Poitier: a confusing but profound and ultimately befuddling distinction, one that might have been formative or at least instructive for a smarter person.

Still, I responded to his intended insult with, "But you are every bit Morris Chesney."

This stung him though he had no idea what I meant, and he really couldn't have because I didn't know what I meant, however much I believed it. This started an application of what would become a familiar, though not unwelcome, silent treatment that lasted two whole days.

Not surprisingly, which is the understater's way of saying *of course,* Morris Chesney's friends saw fit to dislike me as much as he did. From the first day, they would litter the room with themselves and trash and stare at me. Sitting there in a clump like that they reminded me of the bullies that used to beat me up on the playgrounds when I was growing up, but now I was unafraid, perhaps a foolish condition in any situation. One asked me what my major was and I said I didn't know. Then they all laughed. Then he asked how I came to be in an upperclassmen's dorm and I offered a lie, said the others were full. The answer seemed in some way to satisfy them, but did not make them happy.

Morris Chesney belonged to a fraternity. Natch, as my mother would probably have said. He asked me that third day, at the end of the silent treatment, after his cronies had left, if I might be interested in pledging. I had no idea what he was talking about and I think what I said was, "What are you talking about?"

"How would you like to be an Omega?" he asked.

"?"

"You really are a nerd, aren't you?" he said. "I'm asking if you want to join my fraternity, Omega Psi Phi."

"Why would I?" I asked, but not in a snide way.

"We have great parties for one thing. Bitches will sleep with frat men, especially Omegas. And business connections after college. One brother got a job making six figures right out of school."

"What would I have to do?"

"Not much."

That sounded so much like a lie that I wanted to believe him. This was when my life again became essentially a wildlife film, in the way that it worked itself out as something of a vast morality play, where the strong survive and the maintenance of social conventions seems the most certain and steadiest hedge against the harsh and unforgiving environment.

The mammals in the fraternity employed a kind of moral biology. If ugly and cruel, it was at least consistent. I showed up with Morris at the frat house, not a dorm but a hovel where they met to drink, and, I was told, have wanton sex with any willing and drunk woman. The members wore black robes and held staves. Candles, black and white, burned in every corner. And there seemed to be a constant humming, like chanting, but I couldn't hear or see that any of them were making the sounds. It all made for bad music. They talked rather nicely to the seven of us standing in that poorly dressed living room, and then, after we seven agreed that we would be pledging, they shouted and made as if to punch us. They did punch one guy who failed to flinch with appropriate fear. After that he flinched as well as the rest of us. Morris Chesney was one of the bigwigs, strutting around in his dark glasses and red beret and casting an especially mean eye at me.

A tall man whom we were instructed to refer to as Big Boss addressed us as a unit. He said, "You are going to cross the sands. You are not yet black enough to be Omegas, but you will burn under the sun on this, our terrain. If you are man enough you will make it across and be made right." He turned to Morris. "Isn't that right, Big Brother Chesney?"

"Right you are, Brother Benson."

This hazing business wasn't going to get started too quickly. I knew that. Too harsh too fast and the lot of us, dumb and smart alike, would have called it quits. No, they wanted us to invest some energy and time. They were simply what nature had made them, small bullies. And yet, there I was, more fool me, because I wanted the *college* experience.

I could see immediately that Morris Chesney wanted me to fail, a blind man could have seen that, but not too quickly, because as long as I was pledging and was subject to their commands I was essentially out of our dormitory room. I was required to wear a red T-shirt, the same one at all times, without washing or rinsing it, though I was allowed to bathe every other day.

At the first meeting of Professor Everett's class, he walked by me, observed my red T-shirt, smiled, and said, "Baaaa."

Ted was equally unimpressed. He said, "A fraternity? Hell, why didn't you just go to LSU or some damn place? Have you ever seen a badger? They're kinda like little bears."

I had a vague understanding of their disappointment, but I wanted the full cliché college experience. In fact, I even attended the convocation in King Chapel, red T-shirt and all. There a short round vice president of something or other stood to address all of us, at least all of us who attended, and that turned out to be a small fraction of the student body. His name was Dudley Feet and so had to be in some way related to Gladys Feet. How many Feet could there be? There were at least two. He rose to the lectern and cleared his throat for about ten minutes, cast an eye about, no doubt counting the empty seats that so greatly outnumbered the scattered attendees.

He said, "Men, special men, men of our race, men of our future, our future men, our future, manly men, men men, Morehouse men, we gather here today to celebrate a mission, a mission that has produced the likes of the Doctor Reverend Martin Luther King Junior and Edwin Moses, Maynard Jackson and Spike Lee, Howard Thurman and Samuel L. Jackson. These men are more than graduates, they are alumni. This is more than a college, it is an institution. We gather here today on this the beginning of a new academic year to join our spirits and minds together, to move them in one fluid and forward motion toward that great good that is our mission and legacy here at Morehouse. We are called the Harvard of the South, but we here at Morehouse know that Harvard is the Morehouse of the North. You will be tested here on these grounds, tested for what life will throw at you. I ask you to recall the Book of Psalms, sixty-six, ten through twelve: 'For Thou has tested us O Lord; Thou has tried us as silver is tried. Thou didst bring us into the net, Thou didst lay affliction on our loins, Thou didst let men ride over our heads. We have gone through the fire and through the water; Yet Thou has brought us forth to a spacious place.' We ask what it means that silver is tried. It means that silver was tried, and it was not as good as gold. That's what that means. And you wonder what the psalm means when it addresses the affliction that has been laid on our loins and I will tell you what it means: it means leave those girls alone and you know the ones I mean or else men will ride over your heads. We will cross the desert together, our naked toes sinking luxuriously into the hot loose sand, our naked backs darkening beneath the hammering of the eternal sun, our sweat mixing, our blood boiling and becoming one, our voices lifting into one great instrument, our manhood rising into one massive thrust against the oppression that rides us!" Feet was sweating now, though the only rise he had gotten out of his audience was a shifting to become more comfortable and the exit of two students who had wisely seated themselves by the door. "I am pleased today to present our guest speaker. You all know him. He has done much to uplift the race. He was the first black man on television to carry a gun. He is a gentleman, an actor, a comedian, an author, and above all else, an educator. You all know him from television, but we know him as a friend. Students, Doctor William H. Cosby Junior."

There was an enthusiastic welcome. In fact there was more applause than seemed possible from the audience that I had roughly counted. And when I looked again, the empty seats had been filled, including the one next to me, which had been filled with a smiling Morris Chesney. The smile was a bad sign. After only a week in college I was able to deduce that much.

"Sit on the floor," he said.

"What?"

"Big Brother Morris says sit on the floor, you pimple."

I stood, folded up my chair seat, and dropped my stupid ass to the sticky floor. Why? Because Big Brother Morris had said so, and I had entered into this social system willingly for some reason and felt strangely compelled to abide by its rules. I sat, my sight just cresting the level of the seat back in front of me.

Cosby fumbled with a fat unlit cigar and adjusted his dark glasses. "You men think I'm going to take it easy on you. You think because you're in college and sitting here in khakis and loafers that I'm all right with you. You think that because you're not bopping your heads to rap music while sitting here that I'm going to embrace you. You're wrong. You're all pathetic. You're pathetic until you're not pathetic, until you do something strong and good and not until you do that. You think because you probably won't be clad in an orange jumpsuit for stealing a piece of pound cake that I feel all warm and fuzzy about you. I sell Pudding Pops for the white man. I don't know why I'm saying that, but I am. I make myself sick, but the white man is not to blame. He didn't put the gun in the hands of the black kid down in juvenile hall. No, his missing father put it there. Pound cake. I'm on television. Black girls have babies by three or four fathers and why? Pudding Pops! That's what I'm saying. Some of you are probably wondering how I can stand up here, call me high and mighty, talking about how I can stand here when I'm being sued for having babies with a woman other than my wife. Well, hell, I can afford to have babies. Pudding Pops! If you don't know who your children's friends are, then you're not doing your job. Some of you have probably fathered children already. Babies having babies. Pound cake. Did you know that black girls graduating from high school outnumber men seventy to thirty? Where are these educated, fine young women going to find suitable partners? That's why I have some babies on the side. Pudding Pops! Pants down around their cracks. What's wrong with them? There's something wrong with these people. When you put your clothes on backwards, there's something wrong. Fifty percent dropout rate. Where are the parents? What kind of parents will you be? That's the test. What kind of parents are you now? I've been on television since nineteen sixty-two. I kissed a Japanese woman on screen in nineteen sixty-six and managed not to have a baby with her. I want to thank you for having me here today, and I want you to know I will be more than happy to sign copies of my book, *Fatherhood,* which is on sale just outside at an attractive discount. Believe me, you need to read it. Thank you."

Everyone stood to applaud. I didn't know why. However, I saw it as an opportunity to get up off the filthy floor. Morris Chesney kicked me when I started to rise.

"Did Big Brother Morris tell you that you could get up?"

"No, Big Brother Morris."

"Then keep your sorry ass down there on that floor."

I looked down past the row of trousered legs to my right to see the filthy red T-shirt of another pledger, the smallest and meekest of us, Eugene Talbert. He was seated on the floor as well. I realized that though he was eight inches shorter than me, we were the same size.

I wouldn't say that I had custodial, protective, or even particularly warm feelings for Eugene Talbert, but I wouldn't say a lot of things that are true. He lived in DuBois Hall with many other freshmen, so I didn't see him except for shared hours of humiliation and torture at the hands of the Big Brothers. He was from New Jersey, I knew that much. I also knew that he was a chemistry major with little or no interest in chemistry. He wanted to be an Omega as his father was an Omega, as his uncle was an Omega, as his brother was an Omega. They were all chemists and loved chemistry and worked in labs making flavor additives and enhancers for the fast-food industry. They were all tall. Small Eugene told me all of this while we stood side by side with pails of sand suspended up and away from our bodies. We were standing in a room with maroon, flocked wallpaper cleared of furniture while the Big Brothers watched a Spike Lee film in an adjacent room. Eugene was sweating profusely; his eyes were starting to roll back into his head. I told him to take deep breaths, to try to get into a zone, to visualize something peaceful, quiet, a place he loved, which was all bullshit. I was still holding my load up because I was stronger than the little guy. He collapsed and Big Brothers Morris and Maurice came slowly walking in, heads bobbing or nodding, I didn't know the difference. They laid into Eugene without pause.

"Goddamn! What the fizzy fuck is wrong with you, EUgene?!" Morris shouted or maybe Maurice did; it didn't matter which one. That was how they said his name, EUgene.

"I think little EUgene here thinks we just give instructions to smell our own breath!"

"Thinks we're kidding!" The Big Brothers had a habit of echoing each other.

"Seems he thinks we didn't mean for him to keep the pails in the motherfucking air! What should we do to you, you little maggot?!"

"What should we do?!"

"I don't know, Big Brothers!" Eugene barked out.

"Do you really want to be an Omega, EU-fucking-gene?"

"Yes, Big Brother!"

"Then, tell me, you tiny worm, why did you drop those pails, the ones we told you to keep in the air?"

"My arms got tired, Big Brother."

"His arms got tired."

"Your daddy's an Omega, isn't he?"

"Yes, Big Brother!"

"But you don't really want to be one."

"Yes, I do, Big Brother!"

"No, you don't!"

"I do, Big Brother!"

"You'd do anything to be an Omega?"

"Anything, Big Brother!"

"Would you let Big Brother Maurice punch you in the face as hard as he can with a fist full of quarters?"

"Yes, Big Brother!"

I stood there like an idiot holding up my pails of sand, watching them do that to little Eugene, watching them break him down. I hated myself for watching, for continuing to hold my load, for simply being there. When Maurice punched the small man my stomach turned, the hairs on the back of my neck rose. I watched the blood gush from Eugene's nose and though my strength didn't fail, my pails did lower. I concentrated my stare at Morris, one brow jacked up, leaning into it. Maurice was rubbing his knuckles, looking orgasmic after his blow, and Eugene was crumpled into a ball, blood from his nose everywhere. Morris caught me staring and opened his mouth to say something, but he turned out to be the most susceptible subject I had yet to encounter. I Fesmerized him so quickly that I was uncertain how to proceed. But his eyes glazed over in the textbook manner. Inside his head, he had fallen back on his heels and was awaiting my instructions.

I leaned close and whispered so only he could hear. I said, "Dismiss us and meet me in our room."

He let us go. The befuddled Maurice said, I believe, "What?"

I didn't say anything to Morris that evening. I just let him wander about the room in his haze.

I went to Everett's class the following morning at eight, in my filthy red T-shirt and with red eyes. He didn't bleat as he walked by my chair that morning, but walked about the room, his eyes closed as much as open, playing with a stick of chalk. He delivered his lecture like that, as if talking to himself, but not.

"I suppose what we're talking about in this class is art. If it's not, then I'm lost, but of course I'm lost anyway. At least I've been lost before and it looks just like this. Let's consider art as a kind of desacralization, perhaps a sort of epistemological discontinuity that is undoubtedly connected or at the very least traceable to an amalgam of very common yet highly unusual sociohistorical factors. In this, the end of our rapid expansion into mass-media pop-industrial urbanization, all of which changes daily, not only in and out of itself, but transforms the texture and the intertexture of daily life and discourse, we find the degree of expansion or unfolding modified and tested by the parallel distension and unfurling of moral and ideological attitudes, even those and perhaps especially those of religion and traditional repositories of the so-called and so-seen sacred."

The students looked at each other, shrugging, scared, frantically trying to carve out something to stick in their notes. I knew that he was uttering gibberish, but what wasn't clear was whether he knew it. I don't think he did. There was no snide, sidelong glance at me or anyone or even an imagined mirror. It was just his voice attached to his head. He droned on like that for nearly twenty more minutes, until finally I raised my hand. I was, after all, paying considerably more than anyone else for this so-called, so-seen education.

"What does this have to do with nonsense?" I asked, grasping the levels of my question as I asked it.

"Precisely," he said. Then he looked at his watch. "It shouldn't matter where you are, the cat's in the kitchen, the dog's in the car. There's an elephant singing plinkidee czar, and the old man is strumming the same old guitar." He looked out the window. "Dismissed."

I walked out with my classmates and listened to their awe. "He's brilliant," one Spelman woman said. "I wish I knew what he was talking about," from another. "He'd be cute if he weren't so fat," the third and last woman of the class said. A couple of upperclassmen seemed equally impressed. I then began to doubt myself and decided to stop by Everett's office to see if I could be made to understand.

And so I did, around lunchtime again, and on this occasion I found him napping over an open book in his lap. I knocked on the doorjamb.

He opened his eyes and looked at me. "Mr. Poitier."

"Hello, professor."

"What can I do for you?"

I sat in the chair next to his desk. "I didn't understand a word of your lecture today."

"What are you, stupid?"

"I don't think so," I said.

"I don't think so either," he said. "Listen, Mr. Poitier, I'm going to hip you to the truth. I'm a fraud, a fake, a sham, a charlatan, a deceiver, a pretender, a crook."

"You mean, it's all meaningless?"

"I didn't say that."

"Would you say that?" I asked.

"No, I wouldn't say that either."

"Then you were saying something in class."

"Technically. My mouth was moving and I was making sounds." He paused and looked at my face. "You know what I see when I look at you?"

"No."

"I see Sidney Poitier."

"But . . ."

"I know, I know, you're Not Sidney Poitier and also not Sidney Poitier, but in a strange way you are Sidney Poitier as much as you're anyone." He opened and reached into the box on his desk, grabbed a cigar, pointed it at me. "You think I'm joking, pulling your leg, but I'm . . ." He stopped. "Have you ever played squash with a hard ball, Mr. Poitier?"

"I've never played squash at all."

"Shame."

"Can you explain to me what today's lecture was about?" I asked.

"Precisely. Now if you'll get out of my office and close my door, I'll be able to sit by my open window and enjoy my cigar without the smoke police getting wind of my activity, if you catch my drift."

I walked to the door.

"Do you want to know what I think, Mr. Poitier?" When I nodded, he went on. "I think you should read Althusser and Habermas. I've never read them myself. Well, I've tried, but I didn't get it. Something about ideology functioning to obscure the real conditions of existence or some such shit. That's what somebody told me. Anyway, you read it and then maybe you can explain it to me."

"You haven't read it?"

"And I don't plan to try."

"Then why should I?"

"Call it an assignment. Or simply don't do it. Then you could either tell me you haven't read it or lie and say you have. You could even make up what it means. It won't affect your grade either way. By the way, you have an A for the course."

"Already?"

"You all have As. Grades are nonsense. I'll give you whatever grade you want, but A is such a nice letter."

"What if I don't learn anything?" I asked.

"Well, tough titty. That's not my problem, is it?" He waved. "See you on Thursday."

I returned to my dorm room to find Morris still sitting on the edge of his bed. He was confused and looked tired.

"Morris," I greeted him.

He didn't look up.

"Are you ready for your instructions?"

He raised his eyes to me and his head followed.

I had thought long about what I would have him do, but everything seemed, well, obvious. I really had no desire to see him debased like Eugene Talbert. I didn't particularly dislike Morris, and if I had, I thought, that would have been even more reason to not give in to his influence and kind. I said, "Morris, I want you to start a recycling campaign on campus. I want you and the Big Brothers to try to get the other fraternities to collect all the bottles and cans and keep doing it. You are to admit all the pledgers and apologize to them for your childish cruelty. You are not to admit me. You're to tell me and everyone else that I am not Omega material." I was pacing to the window and back, thinking and talking. "Is all of that clear to you?"

Morris said it was.

"Recycling, Morris. I want you to be all about recycling."

"Recycling."

"When I say 'dismissed' you will have no memory of this conversation, but you will carry out your instructions."

He nodded.

"Dismissed."

He stood and walked to his desk, arranged his papers. He picked up a soda can and moved to toss it into the waste bin, but stopped. He looked at the can in his hand, then shoved it into a plastic bag. He dipped into the bin for a previously discarded juice bottle and put that into the bag as well.

I was driving and Ted was sitting in the passenger seat of my new used Buick Skylark. It was baby blue and Ted was asking why I'd bought it.

"I mean, it's a pretty color, but Nu'ott, you've got a lot of money," he said. "But I suppose if it runs."

"I like it."

"That's all that matters. Don't you just hate when you buy a new phone number book and you have to copy all those dang-blasted numbers from one to the other? I hate it even though I hire someone else to do it for me. My damn toenails need trimming, again. I am glad to see you're not wearing that red T-shirt anymore. It was beginning to smell."

"It smelled before I put it on."

"I read in the paper about some massive recycling campaign at your college," Ted said. He waved to someone he knew on the street, but they failed to recognize him since he was in a Buick and with me.

"Yeah, it's pretty cool."

We were on our way to a drugstore so Ted could buy condoms. "Jane prefers that I take care of these matters," he'd said when he asked me for the ride. Now he was looking in his wallet. "Just seeing if I have any cash with me. I don't. Do you have any? May I have a ten?"

"Do you mean *borrow*?"

"No, I mean have. I'm pretty sure I'll forget to pay you back."

I gave him a ten.

"Do you prefer latex or lambskin?"

"I don't know."

"Some of them feel like you've slipped your puppy into a garbage bag. So many choices, too. These rubber companies try to make you feel insecure and guilty. Guilty if you don't buy the one 'for her pleasure.' Our pleasure is pretty much taken for granted. I suppose the fact that we're buying them at all establishes that as a given. Do you have any?"

"No."

"Give me some more money," he said.

"Why?"

"I'm going to buy you some. My treat."

"It's my money."

"Nonetheless."

And so Ted bought me a box of condoms that I embarrassedly shoved into my jacket pocket. He sat there reading over his box as we drove home, saying a couple of times, "Amazing things."

As is inevitably the case, someone from my former life showed up and recognized me. It was a guy with whom I'd gone to high school. I could remember his face and I didn't recognize his name and this apparently offended and angered him. When he said his name, which still I can't recall, it sounded like a name that one might remember and it was that strange notion and feeling to which I attended—that a name sounded rememberable. He became insulted. He went back to DuBois Hall and apparently told all the freshmen there what a loser I had been in high school, and suddenly college was very much even more like high school. He told them that as far as he knew I was a dropout and had been in a sex scandal with a white teacher and he wondered how I'd gotten into Morehouse. He told them it was probably because I used to live with Ted Turner and was probably his houseboy toy or something. And so I was shunned more or less. Not a new experience, but disappointing nevertheless. Eugene Talbert heard all the stories, but focused on the part about Ted. He came right out with it.

"I heard you lived with Ted Turner."

I said nothing. I was sitting in the cafeteria and had not yet picked up my ham sandwich.

"How rich is he?" He sat down across from me.

"I'm trying to eat."

"Take me to his house," he said.

"Why?"

"Because he's so fucking rich. I just want to see what that kind of money looks like."

I took a bite and stared at him.

"I have a fascination with wealth."

He didn't want to meet Ted because he was smart or dumb or because he was quirky or successful, but because he had money. The little bullied fellow shrank in front of me.

"Sorry," I said.

"Aren't we friends?" he asked.

I studied his face and saw nothing but face. "No," I said.

"But you stood up for me."

"My mistake. Then I didn't know you well enough to like you or not like you. Now I know you well enough. I'm glad you made it into the fraternity. You belong there."

"So, you won't take me."

"No, I won't take you."

"You're not Omega material. I can see that now."

I nodded.

"You're just a white man's toy," he said. As he said it he reached over to pick up a plastic bottle that had been left on a table and slip it into his book bag. "You're not black enough to be an Omega."

I nodded. "I'll see you around, Eugene." I wrapped my sandwich in a napkin and walked away wondering if I might have any virtuous feeling from my show of restraint. I can't say that I was completely unaffected by his attack. An attack always feels like an attack, and I had to wonder if he was uttering some truth besides my not being Omega material.

Everett talked on and on about a thing being self-identical, but failed at any turn to make a drop of sense. He laughed over his assertion that contingency was necessary for the existence of necessary truth and laughed harder as he blabbed on about truth as a "pliable vacuum of manipulated fragments of no whole entity." The Spelman student who had said Everett might be attractive if not for his extra weight was staring devotedly at him. I watched her follow him with her eyes around the room. As always, in an attempt to understand something, I raised my hand.

"Yes?" he said. "Mr. Poitier."

"I'm sorry, but are you saying that a thing cannot exist without its opposite also existing?"

"I don't know," he said and looked truly puzzled. "Am I?"

"Is there an opposite to existence?" My question felt unbelievably stupid in my mouth.

"Precisely," he said. "Dismissed." Even though we were only halfway through the period.

As we walked out, the woman whom I had been watching walked after me. "Mr. Poitier," she said.

"Hello, Ms. Larkin," I said. That was all I knew of her name as Everett always called us Ms. and Mr.

"I liked your question," she said.

"I'm glad you did. I don't know what I asked him and I certainly don't know what was 'precisely' about it. Tell me, do you know what he's talking about?"

"Not a word. Isn't he fabulous?"

"I guess." I looked at Ms. Larkin's soft features. Her red hair was pulled back tight. I noticed for the first time that she looked white, but that was true of many black people. I assumed she was black because she was attending Spelman. I felt stupid even wondering about it.

We walked toward the student center, not talking. I was thinking about class and then I realized I was thinking about class, though I was hard pressed to know what I was thinking about the class. I did know that somehow I felt as if I had been tricked into thinking that existence was a thing instead of an attribute, and then I wondered why I was thinking like that.

"Well," Ms. Larkin said as we reached the doors of the center. She said "well" as if we'd actually had a conversation.

"What is your first name?" I asked.

"Maggie."

"I'm Not Sidney."

"I know," she said. "Everyone knows." She pulled open the door. "See you Thursday morning."

That *everyone knows* was deadly. It cut through me. Yet I was not sure that she meant any harm by saying it. I had the sense, or at least wanted to think, that she was merely stating a fact, albeit a disheartening, if not disturbing fact.

I came across Professor Everett having coffee in the commons. He invited me to sit down and so I did.

"You're distressed," he said.

"I don't know if I'd say distressed."

"You don't have to. I can see that you're in a deep distression."

"Is that a word?"

"Doesn't matter. You know what I mean. That's all I require of language."

I was about to disagree, perhaps strongly, when I caught him staring outside through the window.

I looked to see Maurice and other frat guys dressed in black jackets, combat boots, and dark glasses stomping their way along the sidewalk. They would stomp with the left foot twice, once with the right, slide the left toe, and fall onto the right, and bark all the while like dogs. And every few steps, one would dash out of line to collect a discarded can or bottle.

"That's strange," Everett said.

"What part?" I asked.

"All of it."

When I returned to my room I found it filled waist-high with plastic bags filled with bottles and cans. Morris was arguing with the brute Maurice. Since I had not given Morris the suggestion to act civilly toward me, he did not.

"What are you looking at, maggot?" he said.

It wasn't a question, so I didn't attempt an answer. I waded through the containers to my desk.

"What are we going to do with all of this shit?" Maurice said.

"You tell me," Morris said.

"You're the one who started this. 'Let's recycle, let's be green,' you said. Well, the clubhouse is filled with bottles too and so is my room."

"Let me think," I said.

That notion struck me as funny in some way that made me feel bad about myself, and so a self-pitying laugh sneaked out before I could catch it.

"What about you, Poitier?" Morris said. "You got any ideas?"

"Yeah, keep your things on your side of the room."

"We should have left all these motherfuckers in the garbage cans where we found them," Maurice said. "Crazy fucking idea. Recycling, my ass. We don't even have a truck. You got us driving these cans to the recycling place in two cars. Man, that's crazy."

I opened my book bag and pulled out a bottle of juice I'd started earlier, swallowed the last couple of ounces, and tossed it into the waste bin. Morris walked over and retrieved it, put it on his pile.

Maurice watched him. "Dude, I don't know what the fuck is wrong with you. I'm getting out of here. I'm going to my room and throw every motherfucking can I got back in the trash."

I surveyed the room and realized that my stupid suggestion was compromising the quality of my own living situation. I Fesmerized poor Morris once again and instructed him to end the collecting madness and to drive the cans and bottles to the nearest recycling center.

And that's what he did. Nonstop for two days, back and forth in his Corvette. I have to say that I felt a little bad, but only a little. I discovered that I too had a bit of a mean streak—a realization that left me both saddened and relieved.

❖

It came as most dreams, while I was asleep:

My mother encouraged me to buy bubble gum at the convenience store and sell it at school. I was in fifth grade. I bought the balls for a penny apiece and sold them for a nickel. My transactions were conducted behind the cafeteria before school, and all went smoothly until a teacher got in line. She took me to the principal, who in turn called my mother. He was quite surprised to find out that my mother was upset only because I had been interrupted during the conducting of my business.

"Is there a rule against a child selling candy on school grounds?" she asked.

The principal was dumbfounded. "I don't know," he muttered. "It's disruptive," he haltingly said.

"Disruptive of what? Show me the rule in the governance."

"I can't say there is a rule, per se."

"Then my son will be allowed to continue his business?"

"What will I get out of this?" he asked.

"A percentage," she said. "How does 5 percent sound?"

The principal looked at me. "If he can answer a question."

"Shoot," my mother said.

"Explain supply-side economics," the principal said.

My mother laughed.

I looked at his face and then hers.

"Tell me, honey," she said. "And don't forget to talk about the proper indicators and about inflation."

I of course said nothing.

"Tell him!" my mother shouted.

"Tell me!" the principal shouted.

I started to cry.

"Is that sweater made of wool?" the principal asked. He touched my shoulder and cocked his head oddly to the side.

"It is," my mother said.

"Doesn't it itch?" he asked.

"Yes, it does," my mother said. "But it itches him, not me."

"And so that makes it all right?" he said.

"Yes, it does," she said.

I began to itch and then to scratch and that made me itch even more. I scratched until I knew I was bleeding under the sweater.

"Don't worry," my mother said to me. And then she said nothing else, but sat in a chair against the wall.

The principal opened my wrinkled paper sack of gum balls and began to toss them, underhanded, to my mother, who clapped her hands like a seal and barked. She caught them in her mouth and seemed to swallow them. I shook my head, concerned about my mother swallowing the big purple, red, and yellow balls, but what came out when I opened my mouth was, "My profits!" I stood straight, looked left and right, wondered where those words had come from. I watched my mother swallow another yellow ball. I wanted her to stop, and again I opened my mouth and out came, "My inventory!" I slapped a hand over my mouth.

"Not Sidney," the principal said.

"You must build," my mother said, as if finishing the principal's sentence. "Build is what . . ."

"You must do," the man said.

"Not Sidney?" my mother said, the voice more my mother's than it ever had been in life.

"Yes?" I said.

"Wake up."

And so I awoke to find myself sweating and frightened and unsure why. It had not been a terribly scary dream as dreams go, and yet I was terrified. But I had scratched my arm raw in a place.

Everett was doing push-ups in his office when he called for me to come in. He stopped and faced me while sitting cross-legged on the floor. "I used to be able to do seventy of those."

"How many can you do now?"

"Six."

"That's not very good," I said.

"It beats none. Why are you in my office?"

"May I ask you a question?"

"You just did, and I might point out that you did so without asking. What does that tell you?"

"I don't know."

"You're troubled, Mr. Poitier."

"No so much troubled as confused."

"Then you're not troubled at all. And if you're confused, then I've done my job and so I don't have a problem. Yet here we sit, me on the floor with my leg going to sleep and you in a chair."

"Is this whole course some kind of object lesson?"

"That's good. I'd never considered that. You're a lot smarter than me. I have no problem with that. Some people are thinner than me, some taller, some uglier, cuter, faster, and many smarter. That's the way it all shakes out."

"I don't feel very smart," I said.

"What does smart feel like? If it feels like an orgasm, then I'm going to start studying right now. Me, I'm only slightly above average. It fits me."

"Some of the students think you're brilliant."

"Yeah, well, like I said."

"What did you say?"

"How many push-ups can you do?"

"I don't know. Fifty maybe."

"Probably more," he said. "Have you had lunch?"

"No."

"Well, you had better go grab some before they run out of whatever it is you eat. And close my door on your way out." He said as I was halfway out, "Oh, and one more thing, don't imagine that you have limitations."

"Don't I?"

"I'm sure you do, but don't imagine it. Good day."

At the next class meeting, Everett informed us that we would be taking an essay examination that day.

"You said 'no tests,'" one of the women said.

"This is an examination," Everett said.

"That doesn't make sense," she said.

"Well, be that as it may." He passed around the exam. "There are three questions, and I urge you to divide your time unevenly on them, as they are of equal value. Since one hundred is not divisible by three, there is no way for you to achieve a perfect score. Unless of course we decide that ninety-nine is a perfect score, and I wouldn't mind that at all."

The examination:

1) Imagine a radical and formidable contextualism that derives from a hypostatization of language and that it anticipates a liquefied language, a language that exists only in its mode of streaming. How is a speaker to avoid the pull into the whirl of this nonoriented stream of language?

2) Is the *I* one's body? Is fantasy the specular image? And what does this have to do with the Borromean knot? In other words, why is there no symptom too big for its britches?

3) How might it feel to burn with missionary zeal? Don't be shy in your answer.

We students looked at each other with varying degrees of confusion, panic, and anger. And like idiots, we set to work. At least they did. I read the questions over and over and after the numbers 1 and 2 on my paper I wrote, *I don't know.* After the number 3 I wrote, *Awful,* then added, *damn it.*

Podgy Patel was tapping my desk with the eraser of his pencil. He looked around the dorm room, then at me sitting on my narrow mattress. He said in his lilting singsong accent, "You know you don't have to live like this."

"I choose to live like this." I looked at his chinos and red sweater. "Thanks for not wearing a suit."

"Casual Friday," he said.

"It's Thursday."

"At home it is Friday. Or Wednesday maybe. I cannot remember which way it goes."

"What's up, Podgy?"

"Your money continues to grow, but it would be growing much faster if you made an investment."

"Why should it grow faster?" I asked.

This agitated him slightly. "Mr. Not Sidney, money should be allowed to grow as fast as it can. This is my business. I am your advisor, and your money wants to grow faster."

"I don't know anything about investing."

"Of course you don't. That is why you have me, Podgy Patel. That is why I am here."

"Thank you. So, what do you want me to do? Buy stocks or something like that? I trust you. Just buy whatever."

"No stocks. Stocks are no good. Chimp change."

"Chump change."

"That, too. No, I don't like stocks. I think you should buy a television network. A cable network."

"Excuse me?"

"A television network."

"I heard you, but I don't understand you, or at least I think you're nuts. You mean like Ted's network?"

Podgy nodded. "Yes, like that, but not so big. I have one in mind, and it will not cost you much. It is called N-E-T."

"What's that stand for?"

"I believe it stands for Negro Entertainment Television. I say so because there are many many black people on all the time."

"Why would I be interested in that?" I asked.

"Are you not black?"

"I don't know the first thing about running a business, much less a big business, much much less a television network. I couldn't run a doughnut shop. Hell, I couldn't run a lemonade stand."

"Ah, doughnuts. Those Krispy Kremes sell themselves."

"Then maybe I should buy one of those."

"Oh, no. The boom of that franchise has peaked and will soon crumble. Pardon my pun."

"N-E-T," I said.

"The infrastructure is in place. All you have to do is own it. You simply show up for meetings now and again and listen to how things are going. You can participate however you like."

"You make it sound easy."

He laughed his high-pitched giggly laugh. "When you have so much money, everything is easy."

"You'll be involved?"

"I am a financial advisor. Nothing more."

I reached over and took the pencil from his hand. "And the new head of my network. Pay yourself what network heads make." I thought about the whole business. "N-E-T. Net. I like that it spells *net*."

"It is a very nice word."

Ted was pleased to hear of my bold move into the media business. I was surprised, however, to learn that not only had he not prompted it, he'd known nothing of Podgy's advice to me. We were sitting in a Church's fried-chicken restaurant. We'd entered at his insistent, whining request. His lips, his face, and fingers were shiny with grease.

"Jane would shit her yoga pants if she saw me eating like this," he said. "I no doubt will later."

"Nice image, thanks."

"Sorry about that."

"Why are you eating this stuff?"

"A media mogul." He nodded. "You'll do great."

"I won't be involved in running the thing," I told him. "I decided to put Podgy in charge."

Ted poked at some chicken skin with his finger. "I don't believe Podgy knows anything about running a company."

"He knows more than I do."

"I wonder if the skin is good for you. I can't imagine it is. It tastes good, I know that."

"If the network fails, it fails," I said.

"That's the spirit. How are classes?"

"Fine. Most are boring, predictable, and nondescript. And then there's Everett. He's a nut. No one knows what the hell he's talking about."

"Must be a genius," Ted said.

"He's an idiot. He admits to being a phony."

"What network is it?" he asked.

"N-E-T."

"The black soul station," he said. "I actually thought about buying that once. Then I figured I'd be stepping out of my comfort zone. As if that ever stopped me before."

"I'm out of mine, I can tell you that."

"I wonder how astronauts go to the bathroom? And how much do they eat? Can you get fat in a weightless environment?" He chewed more chicken, then laughed to himself. "Not to sound racist, which, being American I no doubt am, you'd better watch Podgy. Next thing you know you'll have shows on the air called Punjabi Profiles and Getting Down on the Ganges."

"You're right, that is kind of racist."

"Your point being?"

"Well, I wouldn't mind if he did program stuff like that."

"I think I left the front door unlocked at the ranch in Montana. People always think of blue as a cool color, but the hottest part of a flame is blue, so blue is actually a hot color."

Everyone in the class was confused, even angry. I too. We had been handed back our surprise midterm exams, and to a person we had received failing grades. This was bewildering, especially in light of Everett's assurance that we would all get As for the semester.

"You failed the test," Everett said. "That's all I can say. That's all I need to say."

"You said we were getting As," a big guy in the front row said. "This is not an A."

"Had you been that astute on the exam, you might be looking at a different grade. However, for your observation, you now have a D. Does that make you happy, Mr. Winston?"

"Only slightly," Mr. Winston said.

"That it makes you happy at all forces me to lower your grade once again."

"How do we raise our grades?" I asked.

"Now, that is the question to ask," Everett said. "Mr. Poitier has hit the screw on its head. That is the question. How? Pray tell, how?"

"This is bullshit," another guy said and seemed to pull together his things to leave. "I'm dropping this motherfucker."

Everett smiled at him. "You're willing to give up an A in an upper-level course because you failed an exam?"

The student fell back into his seat, looked around at the rest of us, then back at Everett. "I'm just saying I'm confused. Is that it? Is that all you're trying to do, confuse us?"

"Not all," Everett said. "Not all. Class dismissed."

"What if we don't come back?" Maggie Larkin asked.

"Then you won't know if I'm here waiting for you, will you?" Everett looked out the window at the sky. "On that rather shrill

note, which is very close to a C-sharp, I'll say again, and with a clar-
ity unheard of in the hallowed halls of academe, class dismissed."

"He's crazy," Maggie said to me as we stepped out of the building
into the autumn air.

"He's boring, that's what he is," I said. "May I ask if you find me
in any way attractive?"

"You may ask," she said.

"Do you?"

"I do."

And so began my first relationship. Maggie Larkin was from
Washington DC. Her father was a lawyer, her mother a physician
in training only. Her older sister had graduated from Spelman and
was in law school at Georgetown. She spoke proudly of her family,
and I never mentioned mine, as there was none. To her questions
about my past, I told her I'd come to Atlanta after the death of my
mother. She asked me why, and I deflected the question by telling
her that I needed to get away from Los Angeles, which was true
enough, and lied to her about an uncle with whom I lived until his
death. When she asked me where I got my money, I told her that
I had worked three jobs to save up for college. I lied stupidly and
clumsily, and I am afraid with little gusto as my story was anything
but detailed. Though not well thought out, my answers for some
reason went unchallenged, though I could sense a raised eyebrow.
We kissed and rolled around on the little bed in her private dorm
room. I soon was spending most of my time with her. We sat beside each other in Everett's class, which we continued to attend
despite his insanity and lack of coherence, but our being together
at least made it more bearable. Everett even noticed us once as
we made eyes at each other, and I believed he nodded approvingly.
The man unnerved me, but his nonsensical rambling became a
sort of entertaining white-noise sound track to everything that I
pretended or perhaps hoped would entify, crystallize, or coalesce

at some point into something vaguely useful or at least coherent, however shapeless.

Thanksgiving came around, and Maggie haltingly invited me to DC to meet her parents.

"Do you think it's a good idea?" I asked. "I mean, isn't it a little soon? You seem a little nervous."

"You're nervous," she said.

"I'm scared to death. Aren't you a tiny bit nervous?"

She nodded. "My family is slightly class conscious," she said. "A lot class conscious. Hell, they're snobs."

"I see."

"They expect me to be with someone whom they consider to have a pedigree. It's not enough for them that he be a doctor or a lawyer or a CEO, his parents have to be as well."

"I see. I have no parents."

"Oh, but Not Sidney, I don't think like that. Honestly, I don't know how they'll be. I just want you to be aware that they might, I emphasize *might,* try to make you feel uncomfortable."

"Then why should I go?" I asked.

"Because I want you to."

That, I found to be the most interesting and persuasive argument she could have offered.

That night Maggie and I had awkward but sweet and finally probably unsatisfying sex, but we held each other afterward, feeling closer than we'd felt before we'd started. I considered that a very good thing and found myself more relaxed, all the more for the absence of oral sex; even then the thought of it conjured disturbing recall of Beatrice Hancock's incisors and canines. We lay there, her head was on my chest, a campus lamp was burning outside her second-floor dorm room. There were voices in the hall, Friday-night joking and chortling. I felt suddenly a part of the college world, and then I laughed at myself, knowing how untrue that was.

The phone rang, and Maggie turned over to answer it. "Oh, hi." She pulled the sheet to her chest. "It's late. I know. I'll be in DC for Thanksgiving. You too? I guess I'll see you then. I can't talk now. It's late." She hung up the phone.

I didn't ask any questions, just let her head fall back onto my chest. I breathed in the fragrance of her hair.

"Sorry about that," she said.

I said nothing.

"That was Robert. He's like my brother. We used to go out."

"Where is he?"

"He's at Dartmouth." She dragged her nails along my shoulder. "He'll be in DC over break. You'll get to meet him."

"That'll be nice."

In a fine example of returning to the well, Gladys Feet called and arranged a lunch with me downtown. She didn't look the part of the corporate porn star that day, but a regular porn star. She wore a short skirt and a tight sweater and high heels, and if not for the absence of knee socks and her being black instead of white, she could have been Beatrice Hancock. At least I felt the same vibe. We sat not far from the bar in a hotel restaurant.

"How are classes, Mr. Poitier?"

"How much do you need and what for?" I asked.

"No foreplay or anything?"

I have to admit that her sexually charged attempt at a joke gave me pause, and as I paused I imagined that that was the desired effect. She wasn't trying to put me at ease with a bit of humor, but to put me on notice, to cast up a flare, to warn me that there was a fellatio somewhere looking for me.

"Is Dudley Feet your husband?" I asked. A pail of icy cold water on her fire, I thought.

"Yes, he is." Her eyes did not move away from mine. "Why do

you ask? He's not a good husband. He's inattentive and he cheats. The latter I could live with. Why do you ask?"

"Feet is not a common name," I said.

"Tell me about it. My maiden name is Birdsong."

"That's beautiful," I said.

She shot me a look that for the first time let me see her as an interesting person. She then turned her attention to the menu.

"I'm sorry," I said.

"It's not that he's an awful man." She was weeping now. "But my life is awful. I'm just so lonely."

"Ms. Feet, please, don't cry."

"Gladys," she said.

"Gladys. I'm sure your husband loves you."

"Who gives a fuck whether that little-footed monkey loves me or not. I'm not thinking about him. I'm thinking about me. I have needs."

Her voice carried. I looked around to find a few pairs of eyes on us. As was my custom, I was embarrassed. "I'm sorry," I said, again, like the imbecile I was. "I'm sure everything will be okay."

"Oh, what do you know? You're just a boy."

"I'm not quite a boy," I said, feeling oddly defensive. She was probably correct, but I bristled.

"Just because you're rich doesn't give you license to speak."

"That's true."

"Just because you're extremely handsome and look like Sidney Poitier, who most women would pay good money to sleep with, doesn't give you the right to say anything."

"That's true, I guess."

"You are very handsome," she said, her tone shifting.

I looked around for our waiter.

"I apologize about this. I'm sure you're every bit a man."

"Don't worry about it."

"It's only that when I'm around you, I have these . . . these feelings. I feel all tingly on my arms and thighs. Do you know what I mean?" Her voice was low now; one might say sultry, one might say crazy. If cigarettes had been allowed inside and if she had had one, she would have lit it. "Do you like older women? I mean, women my age? Not old, but older than you?"

"I suppose. My mother was an older woman and I liked her."

"No, I mean, are you attracted to older women?"

"You're very . . ." I stopped, thinking that I might have flattered myself into a corner or worse. "Can you just tell me how much money the college needs?" I was sweating. My shirt felt sticky.

"What about my needs?"

"All I have is money, Ms. Feet."

"Gladys."

"Gladys. Really, all I have to offer is money."

"I don't want money."

"I was afraid you were going to say that." Whereas at one point in our relationship, back when everything was about money, I had felt, if not in control then on equal footing, I was now lost, confused, in over my head.

"Would you come upstairs with me and rub my temples?" she asked.

"Upstairs?"

"I got us a room."

I wish I could say that I said something clever, pulled back her chair, and escorted her up to the room where I left her alone at the door. I wish that I could say that I said something cool and aloof and excused myself gracefully from the table and hailed a taxi as the sky began to drizzle. But I can say neither. I knocked my chair over as I stood too quickly and sprinted suspectlike from the restaurant as if I was on fire, like a seven-year-old little boy confronted with his first kiss, like the coward I was. Gladys Feet would have to go up to her room alone and imagine me or Sidney Poitier; it apparently didn't matter which.

"And here I was going to invite you over to my place for Thanksgiving," Everett said.

"Really?"

"No."

We were sitting in the student center. He picked at a muffin.

"I'm sure you'll have a fine and memorable time in Washington. Young Ms. Larkin seems very nice. I think she's quite bright, though I'm not a good judge of such things."

"Her old boyfriend will be there," I said.

"He has to be someplace. Why does that make you nervous? He's the old boyfriend."

"What if she still has feelings for him?"

"Better to find out sooner than later."

Of course he was correct, but I was finding little comfort in that fact. "It's just that I like her so much."

"You're rapidly becoming a boring fellow," Everett said. "Have you had sex with her?"

"I believe that's my business."

"I'll take that as a yes."

"I really don't think we should be talking about this," I said. I looked out the window.

"Okay, okay, relax. Don't get your no-doubt-patterned bloomers in a clove hitch."

I drummed my fingers on my thigh, upset that I was not relaxed, but said, "I'm relaxed."

"What about her parents? Are you nervous about meeting them?"

"Extremely."

"Well, don't tell that you've seen their baby naked. That's my best piece of advice."

"Thanks a lot."

"And be yourself."

"Who else would I be?"

"I don't know. You might decide all of a sudden that you're Sidney Poitier. You're not, you know. Though you do look alarmingly like him. Tell me, whom do I look like?"

I looked over his facial features. His sad but alert brown eyes were too close to his face. His lips were strangely thin. His large nose looked like it had been broken several times. I could think of no one he resembled. "I don't know many actors," I finally said.

"What about Roscoe Lee Browne?"

"I don't know who that is."

"Come on, you know Roscoe Lee Browne. He was all over the television. Maybe he still is. He was in *The Cowboys* with John Wayne. I don't much like John Wayne, but Roscoe Lee Browne was great. Anyway, you'd know him if you saw him," he said. "I know you would. What about Bill Cosby?"

"You look nothing like Bill Cosby," I said.

"Thank the lord," Everett said, "if only there were such a thing. But seriously, you have to know that you look more like Sidney Poitier than Sidney Poitier ever did. Have you ever seen *In the Heat of the Night?*"

"No."

"A beautiful love story, that movie. Let me hear you say, 'They call me Mr. Tibbs.'"

"They call me Mr. Tibbs," I said.

"No, say it as if a crab is biting your ass, as if someone is peeling an unpleasant and undesired memory from your core, as if you're feeling a little bitchy, as if you might be gay but even you don't know."

I said it again.

"Uncanny. You ever do drugs?"

I shook my head.

"Huh. That's too bad, but hardly surprising." He stood, looked out the window at a Spelman girl in a short skirt and then down at me. "Enjoy your break. And remember, be yourself. Unless you can think of someone better."

CHAPTER 4

Maggie and I could not manage seats together on the flight to Washington, and so I sat in 23B watching her head bob and turn in apparent bemusement and laughter with her neighbor in the nineteenth row, a guy who might have been an upperclassman at Morehouse, but I never found out. I couldn't even find an escape in a nap on the relatively short flight because of the constant washroom trips of the woman in the window seat. About the fourth of five times she offered an apology in the form of a quick explanation by whispering, "UTI." I didn't know what she meant, but it sounded awful and I found complete and sudden compassion for her, even though she would not trade seats with me because she didn't want to give up the window. And so I was in a bad mood when we landed at National Airport, though, as was my wont, I did not let on to Maggie. One might ask then what was the point of the bad mood, and I can only answer, the satisfaction of personal suffering.

The cab driver kept craning to glance back at me in his mirror. "I know you," he said. "Are you from Nigeria?"

"No."

"I know you. You look like that Sidney Poitier."

"I hear that. Thank you."

"You are not him, are you?"

"I'm not him, no."

"Where are you from? You look Nigerian."

"I'm from Los Angeles," I said. Somehow that didn't feel true. "That's where I was born."

From the taxi window Maggie pointed from the 14th Street

125

Bridge out over the Potomac. "Do you know anything about boating?"

"I've sailed," I said.

"Daddy will like that," she said.

The house was large, a midsixties' split-level with a three-car garage and an expanse of lawn that seemed somewhat ridiculous. The taxi left us out in the holly-hedge-lined driveway. I carried my bag and the heavier of Maggie's two as I followed her past the beige Cadillac to a side porch where she unlocked the door. We stepped into an anteroom, what might have been called a mudroom in a farmhouse. It was a room that might have been bright and cheery if not for the heavy red drapes covering the windows on either side of the door. From that room I could see into the kitchen and beyond that into what I would learn later was the breakfast room. The walls were painted red, the tiled floor of the kitchen was red and white, the refrigerator and stove were red.

"My mother loves red," Maggie said, almost as an apology. "So, this is it. Where I grew up."

"Wow," I said, not a big *wow*, but a polite one.

"Who is that in there?" a woman called from another room. "Could it be? Could it be? Is that my Maggie? My shaggy Maggie?" A woman in her midsixties came around the corner and hugged Maggie, then stepped back. "Lord, look at you, miss college girl. Still pretty. But don't they feed you children down there?"

"Oh, Violet."

"Don't tell me. You lost weight."

"Violet," Maggie said. "This is Not Sidney."

I put my hand out to shake, but it was left hanging there. "Pleased to meet you," I said.

"Not Sidney goes to Morehouse."

"Hmmm," she said.

"He's my boyfriend."

"I see," Violet said. "You have family here in Washington?"

"No, I don't"

"Not Sidney will be staying with us," Maggie said.

"I'll make up the guest room, I suppose. And see if I can get another steak from the butcher." She muttered to herself as she walked off. "Nobody tells me a damn thing around here. Guest."

"Who is that?" I asked.

"Violet," Maggie said.

"I got that much."

"She's been with us forever. She lives in the apartment downstairs."

"Is she a relative?" I asked.

"No. She's like family. She takes care of things. She cooks and cleans, stuff like that. She took care of my sister and me when we were little."

"She's the housekeeper," I said. The word servant seemed more correct but less appropriate.

"No, she's Violet."

"She seems nice," I lied. "She didn't seem to know I was coming. Seemed kind of upset about it."

"I guess I forgot to mention it."

"Do your parents know I'm here?"

"Must have slipped my mind to tell them. But they won't care. They're going to be thrilled to meet you. They're going to love you. Come on, let me show you the rest of the house."

We left our bags in the foyer, and Maggie led me through the crimson-carpeted downstairs. The expanse of red was, if not disorienting, unsettling, and I found it difficult to take a step without staring down at it. In the dining room was a long, elaborately ornate table with an enormous arrangement of impossibly colored silk flowers in its center. The room was dark; the large windows were covered by Venetian blinds, which, though open, could only let in so much light past the white curtains and the red drapes, which were belted by gold cords. At the center of the coffee table that was as wide as the gold sofa was a collection of variously sized blown-glass swans filled with red-colored water.

"Like I said, my mother loves red."

I nodded. "Well, she certainly doesn't seem to be shy about liking it," I said. The quality of the silence that followed made think I'd been a bit disrespectful, and so I added, "Shows strength."

"That's where the Christmas tree will go," Maggie said, pointing at the corner near the fireplace.

"What does your mother do?" I asked.

"She heads a conservative think tank."

Maggie might as well have said it in Russian for all the words meant to me. I didn't say *what?* but I thought it and I'm sure it showed on my face.

"My mother testifies before Congress and goes on television all the time talking about conservative issues. She's trying to get rid of the welfare system because it keeps black people down and to stop gay rights because it endangers the family structure and keeps black people down and to abolish affirmative action because it teaches special preference and that keeps black people down. That sort of stuff."

I nodded.

"You'll love her," Maggie said without a lot of conviction.

"I'm sure I will."

Maggie showed me up the spiral staircase to my room at the end of the hall, so I could get cleaned up and, as she put it, rest for a spell. The upstairs was considerably less red than the downstairs, but no less troubled by many knickknacks, figurines, snow globes, shot glasses, and small bells. The bells gave me a shudder as I recalled my experience with Beatrice Hancock. The guest room, my quarters, was a stable to an array of stuffed animals, small and not so small, mostly bears, but also two lions, a pug dog, a giraffe, and what I took to be a lemur.

I sat on the bed and felt suddenly like I ought not. The spread was gold in color, stiff and shiny, smooth as if it had never been touched. I stood and stepped away. I went into the bathroom and looked at the many-colored soaps on the sill of the sink. There was a shower, but no tub. Violet had put a stack of clean towels and a cloth on top of the hamper by the door. The was a knock on the door, and I stepped back into the bedroom to find Maggie entering.

"How is everything?"

"Great. It's a very nice room."

"You're comfortable?"

I nodded, picked up the stuffed pug. "Your mother's?"

"All over the house. She grew up dirt poor and never had a doll or a stuffed animal and now she says she's making up for it."

"What about you? Did you have a favorite stuffed animal when you were little?" I set the dog back down unto the bed.

"A bear," she laughed. "Named Teddy. Pretty boring, huh?"

"I don't know. Apparently a lot of people named their bears that."

"What about you?" she asked. "Any animals?"

"Not that I can recall. For some reason I don't think my mother would have approved."

Maggie sat on the bed and I sat next to her. "What was she like? Your mother, what was she like?"

"Intense," I said. "Smart, I believe. I'm pretty sure she was smart. Intense, certainly."

"How old were you when she died?"

"Eleven."

"And that's when you moved to Atlanta? You told me you went to live with an uncle."

"That's right," I said.

"I heard a rumor that you lived with Ted Turner."

"That's crazy." I felt bad for lying to her and I in fact had no idea why I was. It felt especially bad to be lying when she had so plainly articulated what was true. "No, I lived with an uncle, my mother's younger brother. He died last year."

"Oh, I see."

I heard voices out of the room and then footfalls on the stairs.

"Is that my baby up there?" a woman said. "My baby come from college?"

"We're in here, Mommy," Maggie said.

"And not alone, I understand, not alone," Maggie's mother said as she turned into the bedroom. She was a tall woman with no shoulders, and though her clothes were not made of metal, it seemed to me she was wrapped in foil. She glittered, but maybe not in a good way. She was wrapped in gold necklaces and bangles. Surprisingly, however, she wore no red.

I stood and glanced back to see if I had rumpled the bedcover. It seemed I hadn't, but still I smoothed it.

"Mommy, this is Not Sidney."

My name, as it did with so many, gave her pause, and I could see the thought bubble over her head, *Then what is his name?*

"Not Sidney," I repeated. I reached out and shook her hand. "It's a pleasure to meet you."

"Not Sidney," she said.

"Not Sidney," Maggie said, "this is my mother, Ruby Larkin."

"Ms. Larkin." I let her hand go and it hung there in space.

"Not Sidney goes to Morehouse."

"Not Sidney," Ruby Larkin said. She cocked her head to the side and regarded me. "That's a very interesting name."

I nodded. "My mother was eccentric."

"Was?"

"Not Sidney's mother died when he was eleven," Maggie told her.

Ruby Larkin looked blankly at me for a second, then said to Maggie, "Well, you two get situated. Daddy will be home in an hour or so."

"Okay, Mommy."

Mother kissed daughter's cheek. To me, she said, "Not Sidney," turned, and left us alone. To get situated.

Maggie informed me that we would be grabbing a bite out, eating light, and saving ourselves for the coming *feast,* as she called it, of the next day. I didn't remember Thanksgivings with my mother. I did remember that she found the day somewhat ridiculous as she railed on about how the soon-to-be-removed Indians were actually saving the starving and stupid Pilgrims and not having some warm and fuzzy picnic. The truth lay somewhere in the middle of those two depictions, I was sure, and though her reaction had not left me with bad feelings about the holiday, I found it difficult to generate a lot of enthusiasm.

Maggie left me so that I could get ready to go out, though I didn't know what getting ready really entailed. I showered, standing with raised goose bumps under a nearly icy spray as I'd grown tired of waiting for the water to heat up. I put on fresh clothes, but after seeing the attire of Maggie and now her mother, I thought, as I buttoned and zipped, that my clothes were more clean than fresh. Then, as I sat on the ladderback chair near the window I discovered that one could hear conversations quite well through the listening device that was the heating vent. Mr. Larkin was no doubt home, and Ruby had a few words to say about me, beginning with:

"He's just so dark, Ward."

"Well, how dark is he?" Ward Larkin asked.

"Black."

It hadn't occurred to me, but now it did that the Larkins were all very light in complexion. It hadn't dawned on me that I should have noticed or cared. More fool me, I guess.

"Well, what's his name?" Ward asked.

"That's the other thing," Ruby said. "His name is Not Sidney."

"Then what is it?"

"That's it. Not Sidney. The word *not* and Sidney."

"Hmmph. Some kind of ghetto nonsense, no doubt."

"I don't like him. He acts all nice. But you know what nice and a nickel will get you."

"Nothing costs a nickel anymore," Ward said.

"Exactly."

"I'll check him out. What's his last name?"

"I don't know," Ruby said.

"I'll get it from Maggie."

"Are they eating here tonight?" Ward asked.

"No, they're going out. I'll go let Maggie know you're home." I could hear Ruby less clearly now as she, I assume, was leaving the room. "Ward, it's just that he's so dark."

I pulled my white socks over my black feet and laced up my sneakers. Maggie came in and observed the expression on my face, an expression that though I'm certain I cannot describe, must have conveyed a bit of terror, some disgust, and a dash of get-me-the-hell-out-of-here.

"Daddy's home. Ready to meet him?"

"You bet."

Maggie led me down to the red-carpeted first floor, through the living room, and to a set of double doors. The doors were dark wood and ominous enough looking, but then she asked again, "Are you ready?"

I wondered now if I was ready, and I don't recall responding at all when she pushed open both doors. She pulled me into the room that was paneled with dark hardwood like the door and was washed in yellow lamplight. The severed heads of once-large animals covered the walls. There was an actual bearskin rug, the head of which nearly tripped me as I stepped fully inside. Leaning on the edge of his oak desk with the window and late afternoon light behind him, Ward Larkin cut a distinctly unimpressive figure.

"Daddy, this is Not Sidney."

"Welcome to our home," Ward said, and though he didn't say it, I heard the word *boy*.

"Thank you for having me." I shook his hand and paid particular attention to the fact that his grip was overly firm and that he was slow to let go.

"What's your last name?" he asked.

"Poitier."

"Like Sidney Poitier."

"Just like that," I said.

"Any relation?"

"None that I know of." I looked around at all the heads, reminding myself that they were called trophies. At the leopard, the moose, the lion, the water buffalo, the boar. I settled on the boar and asked, "Did you kill all of these animals?"

A bit of a hush fell about the room, and Ward cleared his throat before saying, "No, I didn't." He turned and moved around to the other side of the desk.

"Which trophies are yours?" I asked.

"Hunting," he said with sort of a laugh.

His laughter put me briefly at ease. "I think hunting is stupid, too," I said. "I just thought since you had all these heads . . ."

"Daddy's not against hunting," Maggie said.

I felt ambushed, as no doubt did others in that room. I imagined my head filling the narrow gap between the tiger and the yak.

"No, young man, I believe hunting is a demonstration of man's primacy in the order of nature."

"It probably is," I said, trying hard to sound just slightly more cowed than sardonic.

Still, Ward cut me an unfavoring glance. "I've never myself been hunting. I have a bad leg. As well, I have no desire to visit Africa. Do you?"

I'd never thought about it and I certainly didn't see the question coming and so I said, "I've never thought about it."

"Let me ask you this, do you consider yourself African?"

These were not difficult questions, but they were confusing. However, I was not so young, naïve, and stupid that I could not spot a classic case of self-loathing. "Well, somebody in my family line was from Africa." I made a show of looking at my brown hands.

"Hmmph. Young man, let me just say this, I'm one-sixteenth black, an eighth Irish, two-fifths Choctaw, one-thirty-second Dutch, a quarter English, and a ninth German."

I didn't, nor did I want to, do the math, but it was clear that he was ten-tenths crazy.

"Do you know what that means?" he asked.

I said nothing.

"It means that I'm nothing but an American. I'm no needy minority. Do you understand?"

"I suppose."

"Well," Maggie interrupted, "Not Sidney and I have to get going. We won't be out late."

"We'll chat later," Ward said. "Just the two of us."

"That went well," I said, once Maggie and I were well away from her father's study.

"Daddy can be a little intense," she said.

"Really? Let me ask you something. Do your parents have a problem with dark-skinned people?"

She was noticeably irked by my question and said, looking away and out the kitchen window, "No, they don't."

"Then I guess it's just me they don't like."

"Don't be silly, they've only just met you."

We put on our jackets and exited the same side door through which we had entered. Maggie fell in behind the wheel of the beige Cadillac. I buckled my belt as she adjusted the seat.

"Big car," I said.

"Mommy's old one," she said. "They kept it so that my sister and I could use it when we're home from college. Since Agnes has come back to Georgetown for law school, she has her own car."

"Your sister's name is Agnes?" I asked. "Are your parents Catholic?"

"No, why?"

"Your names. Margaret and Agnes just seem so Catholic to me."

"No, we attend the Methodist Church." The way she said it made me feel unsettled, and it turned out the feeling was rightly placed as she then said, "You'll like it. We're going to service Sunday morning."

I didn't complain. I didn't know enough to complain. I'd never been in a church. My mother had specified in her will that there be no church or religious *crap,* as she put it, associated with her funeral. I stared ahead through the windshield at the oncoming traffic.

"So, where are we going?" I asked.

"We're going to my friend Lydia's house. She and I grew up together. We're like sisters. More like sisters than Agnes and me."

It crossed my mind to ask and so I did, "Does she know that you're bringing me along?"

Maggie's failure to respond could as easily have been her turning her face to me and roaring, "Nooo." Still, I took no offense, however much I might have been starting to worry. I looked at her profile as she drove the monstrous car through one of the circles. She was almost pretty and I liked that, though I was unsure whether it was the *pretty* or the *almost* I more admired.

"It's okay that you didn't tell her," I said, trying to be reassuring, but knowing that I was being a bit sarcastic. "You didn't tell me about her either."

"It just slipped my mind," she said.

Slippery place, your mind, I thought, but said, "The traffic's not too bad." Then I asked, "What made you choose Spelman?"

"It's a good school."

I nodded.

"Why do you ask that?"

"I don't know, just seems as if your parents might have a problem with a traditionally black college."

"What are you trying to say about my parents?"

"I'm not trying to say anything about your parents," I said. "You mention that your mother is opposed to affirmative action."

"What's that have to do with Spelman?"

"Nothing, really." I looked at the fingers clenched on the steering wheel. "Nothing at all. It was a stupid question."

"Yes, it was."

I sought to change the subject and recalled Maggie's comment about her father and boating. "So, does your father sail?" I asked.

"Does my father what?" She was on the defensive or the offensive, I was unsure which, if in fact there is a difference.

"You mentioned that your father would like the fact that I know a little bit about sailing. So, I assumed that he sails."

"No," she said, softening. "Daddy doesn't sail. He's afraid of the water, but he likes the idea of it. I know he would love to talk to you about it."

"So, we're going to Lydia's," I said.

"Yes. A few other friends will be there. Robert will be there. I mentioned Robert. He's at Dartmouth."

"The boyfriend who was like a brother," I said.

She said nothing.

I wanted to say that it all sounded rather Faulknerian to me, but I decided that was mean and perhaps unfair, but I was at least momentarily tickled by something. I suppose my private amusement somehow showed on my face, as I noticed Maggie staring over at me.

"What's funny?" she asked.

"Nothing."

Thanksgiving week was unfurling as a highway of decidedly bad turns. I could feel Maggie's growing regret at having invited me home, or more precisely over my having accepted that invitation. However, on some level, or even a particular level, my presence was serving a desired end, namely to upset her parents. She had to know, and I'm certain she did, that even the simple matter of dark skin would be a cause of consternation for her parents. I came to imagine them as Ward and June Cleaver. I recalled my mother happening upon me watching that television show one afternoon. It launched her into such a fit of hysteria that I was afraid she might become pregnant again.

"How dare they put that propaganda on the television?" my mother barked. "But of course that's what the box is for, isn't it? Here is my black son sitting here in his black neighborhood watching some bucktoothed little rat and his washed-out, anally stabbed, Nazi-Christian parents."

"There's a brother, too," I said, being six or so and not really understanding the tirade.

"Oh, a brother, too. I see him there, an older lily white acorn fallen so close to the tree. Turn that crap off. No, leave it on. Study the problem, Not Sidney. Soak it in." With that she marched off to make cookies.

Sadly, even my innocent satirical private and lame joke soured quickly as I played out the possible meanings of all the words; *Beaver* was an unfortunate way to refer to Maggie.

"What are you thinking?" Maggie asked while we sat at a particularly long red light.

"I was thinking about the faces of the animals in your father's study," I told her. It was a lie, but one of my better or at least quicker ones. My mind did then move to the poor dead beasts. "They all look so . . . so . . . surprised."

"I never liked that he has them," she said. It sounded like an attempt to settle into my camp or at least on my side of the river. Then she said, to obliterate that naïve notion, "But they're already dead. He didn't kill them. And you shouldn't be so judgmental."

"I didn't mean to be."

"My father has gone through a lot to get where he is. From dirt poor Alabama to Yale."

"That's impressive," I said.

"It's very impressive. My father is one of the biggest and most successful lawyers in DC."

"Wow."

The family home of Maggie's sisterlike friend Lydia was little different from Maggie's own. Except that the décor was more pronouncedly gold than red, and the accents were blue, every bit as garish, yet somehow as ugly. Lydia was sitting in an overstuffed chair when we entered without knocking. Two other women were seated on the sofa. All three rose, and the four women hugged and squealed in a way that seemed like fun, but made for harsh music.

"This is Not Sidney," Maggie said. "This is Lydia, Jasmine, and Sophie." She pointed to each woman in turn and I nodded to each, making eye contact only to have it broken by them. The women, all similarly sized and lightly complected, paused as they regarded me, leaving a tiny empty space in time that led me to my antecedent remark about their skin color. I was becoming, sadly, irritatingly, horrifyingly observant of skin color and especially my own.

"Let's sit down," Lydia said.

We did. I sat between Lydia and Maggie on the sofa, and the other two women sat across on a love seat.

"Where are you from?" Lydia asked me.

"I live in Atlanta," I said.

"But Not Sidney's from Los Angeles," Maggie said.

Sophie sat up. "I love LA."

"Well, I haven't lived there since I was eleven."

"And you're at Morehouse," Lydia said.

I nodded.

"What's your major?" from Sophie.

"Philosophy, I guess. It's not clear."

"Are you in college?" I asked them.

"Tufts," Jasmine said.

"Smith." Sophie.

I looked at Lydia.

"Howard," Lydia said, flatly.

"That's here in DC, right?" I asked, more to make conversation than anything else.

"Yes."

"So, tell us about Atlanta," Jasmine said to Maggie.

"There's not much to tell. Spelman's okay. Classes are okay." Maggie smiled at me. I wondered how Maggie's answers were influenced by my presence. I imagined them asking about the guys at Morehouse and Maggie telling them how many cute ones there were or weren't.

But before the conversation could fail to get going, the doorbell chimed. Maggie knew, Maggie's friends knew, and I knew that, according to the rules of bad drama, according to my evening's apparent and particular adherence to a steady and predictable awkwardness, Robert was at the door. Brotherlike Robert, five eleven, trim and fit, handsome and appropriately shaded stepped into the room. I could picture the insane mothers of these insane women sneezing out dating advice between sessions on the stair machine and the treadmill, "Light not white, girl, light not white."

Robert shook my hand and seemed friendly enough as he gave me the once-over. I suppose I was doing the same. He paused at my name.

"Then what is your name?" he asked.

"My name is Not Sidney," I said.

"Not is a part of Not Sidney's name," Maggie said.

"Knot, with a k?" he asked.

"Not with a k," I said.

"That's what I said," he said.

"N-O-T," Maggie said.

"Sidney?"

"Not my name is not Sidney. My name is Not Sidney. Call me

Not Sidney." Though he was the one being dense, I was the one in the middle, feeling stupid, trying to explain the unexplainable. And for no good reason.

We sat and the children's song ran through my mind, "Fly's in the buttermilk, shoo, fly, shoo."

They talked and laughed about old times. I learned that Robert was a business major, a member of some fraternity, and already had a summer internship lined up with Stanley Morgan or Morgan Stanley. Then Lydia brought up the old days in *Jack and Jill* and they all laughed.

"What's *Jack and Jill*?" I asked.

"It's a club, an organization," Jasmine said. It was a rather uninformative and mysterious answer.

"It's a club for children," Maggie told me.

"What kind of club?" I asked.

"A social club," Robert said. "For cultural and social enrichment. It was started in nineteen thirty-five in Boston."

"Nineteen thirty-eight in Philadelphia," Maggie said.

"I stand corrected."

"Who gets to be in it?" I asked.

They looked at each other. "You have to be sponsored by someone who is in it or who has children in it or was in it," Sophie said.

"And then you have to meet other criteria," Robert said.

"What criteria?" I asked. "Is it for black children?"

"Yes," Jasmine said. But it could have been any one of them speaking, as they had all blurred together for me, even Maggie.

"What criteria?" I asked, again.

"There's a whole selection process," Maggie said.

I could see I was getting nowhere, so I shut up.

"So, do you play any sports?" Robert asked me.

"No," I said.

"Robert's on the lacrosse team and the swim team at Dartmouth," Lydia said and watched me closely.

"I'm not a very good swimmer," I said.

"Do you play golf?" Robert asked.

"Never have."

The room was fairly quiet, but not in an interesting way. Sophie finally said something to Jasmine who said something to all of them and then they were chatting again and, this time, with no pretense that I was to be kindly included. Instead, I was kindly excluded and I felt somewhat happy about that. I had a sneaking realization, however incapable I was at articulating it, that my presence was essential to them, not in some singular, specific way, but in a broad and pervasive and insidious way that none of them would or could understand or acknowledge.

On the way home as Maggie drove the luxury coffin of silence, I watched the streetlights reflect off her fair skin. She was lovely and monstrous, but also sad as I knew she had invited me home as a wedge to use between herself and her parents. However, she had no mallet to give the wedge even a light tap, and so it (I) lay there on its (my) broad side. We managed our way into the house and into our separate rooms without so much as a grunt or hiss, though the hiss was implied. In my quarters, I showered, trying to rinse off whatever had been dumped on me. I felt, remarkably, okay and somewhat better for the steam. I was drying off with a stiff towel when, startled by a woman sitting on my bed, I covered myself.

"I'm Agnes," she said.

"Not Sidney."

"So I hear."

"I'm naked."

"So I see."

"Why are you in here?"

"I hate my sister," she said.

"She's not in here," I said.

"That's right."

"What do you want?"

"I want to have sex with you."

I understood everything she was saying and yet still I said, "I don't understand." My jeans were lying uselessly on the bed beside her. I pulled the towel tighter. "She's your baby sister, you're supposed to look out for her."

"I suppose one of us should," she said.

"I honestly don't believe she'll be terribly upset." I was recalling the events of the evening.

"Oh, she'll be upset." Agnes stood and stepped toward me. She wore a powder blue flannel gown that looked comfortable, if not alluring. She was slightly shorter than Maggie and in a strange way prettier, perhaps because of an oddness in her features, a too-high forehead and a hawkish nose. More than Maggie, her face seemed to have a story, or at least wanted a story.

She brushed against me, laid her head against my chest, and then quickly pulled away the towel. She and I were impressed as we looked down at my erection. It was one of my penis's better efforts.

"Well, well," she said.

I was in no position to deny my arousal, however confusing it might have been to me.

Agnes latched on with a fist, then lowered herself, finding me with her mouth. It was agreeable, the sensation. In fact, I am ashamed to say, I was surprised to feel that either Agnes was quite good at it or I was as invested in upsetting Maggie as she was. I caught a glimpse of us in the standing mirror, and the image was a bit of Gothic porn. I looked so much like Sidney Poitier that I was momentarily distracted, until I remembered that Sidney Poitier would never have appeared in a scene like this one. I closed my eyes, stood there, and had a remarkably relaxed and floatingly nice time, during which I dreamed.

I dreamed it was 1950 and that I was a young doctor with a Bahamian accent and that no one believed I was a doctor and yet I was given a patient, a white man who called me *nigger* and tried to spit in my face. He had been shot and the bullet was near his heart and he went into cardiac arrest and the other doctors, all white and believed to be doctors by everyone else, stood around and told me it was my call. I attended to the heart attack, asking for adrenaline, compressed the chest, but the chest wound was severe and the man died.

My elderly white mentor patted me on the back and said, "What could you do? Nothing, that's what."

Into the scene walked a man with a skeletal face who said he was the brother of the dead man and wanted to know why he had died. All the white doctors and nurses and my elderly mentor turned and pointed to me and said, in unison, "The nigger killed him. That nigger killed him."

"That nigger?"

"Yes, that nigger."

"Wait a minute," I said. "There was nothing that I could do. Ask my elderly mentor."

But when I looked, my mentor was gone and there was a white female nurse standing there and she said, shaking her head, "And I never liked the way he looked at me."

"You killed my brother, nigger," the skeletal man said.

"He was already dead," I said.

Outside in the street I could hear chanting, like a riot starting or wanting to start. I could hear the voices of dark faces like my own demanding to be left alone. And then the white man pulled out a gun. I could see that he was handcuffed, but he had no trouble aiming the pistol at me.

"I'm going to kill you, nigger," he said. "And all your kind out there in that street."

"He was already dead," I said. I looked around for someplace to run, for some door or window, but there was nothing, no way out.

I watched his finger slowly squeeze the trigger.

All of this while sister Agnes sucked on my penis and knew that the whole time I was dreaming, and it felt good the whole time I was terrified that I was about to be shot. I wondered what kind of mind had such a dream while having oral-genital relations and this scared me more than anything. Still, I could not shake myself out of the dream. As the pistol fired off the round, so too did my penis. Time stopped, my breathing stopped.

I awoke naked and alone in my too-soft bed with the stiff sheets and impossibly pressed bedspread. I sat up and slowly remembered my encounter with Agnes and wondered how it would play out. I had a fleeting, quickly dismissed thought that Agnes wasn't so terrible, at least at a certain thing. I walked to the window and looked out at the morning, at the turned leaves still half filling the trees. Then I heard their voices. Again, through the vent I was hearing Ward and Ruby.

"Get in here," Ward said, "and shut that door."

"Did you find out something?" Ruby asked.

"I had Mitchell make some calls. I told him get in there and dig deep. He was on the horn all night."

"And?"

"And he's rich."

"So, he's got a little money," Ruby said.

"He's got a lot of money."

"How much?"

There was a rustling of pages. Then I sneezed.

"What was that?" Ruby asked.

"What was what?" Ward cleared his throat. "Here it is. It seems the boy owns a television network. NET."

"Nigger Entertainment Television?"

"He just bought it. Paid cash for it. He's somehow involved with Ted Turner, but none of this is clear. What is clear is that he can buy and sell everyone we know a couple of times over."

"But he's so dark," Ruby said.

"He's fucking rich is what he is." Ward paused. "I knew there was something about that boy I liked."

"He's so black."

"We might have to overlook that. You know, he does look quite a bit like Sidney Poitier."

"He does that," Ruby said. "But our little girl. She's so fair."

"So, be nice to him."

"I'll try," Ruby said.

"And tell Agnes to be nice to him."

Ruby laughed. "You know I have no control over Agnes."

"Well, talk to her."

I was, to say the least, stunned, not only by the highly objectionable nature of their conversation and thinking, but by the unsettling fact I had been set on a course for matrimony. A snake of ice slithered up my too-dark ass and lodged itself at the base of my spine.

"Agnes, get in here." It was Ruby, and I was still hearing them through the vent. "Sit down."

"What is it?" Agnes asked.

"We want you to be nice to that boy upstairs," Ward said.

"Why?"

"Just be nice, that's all," Ruby said.

"Something's up," Agnes said.

"He's your sister's boyfriend," Ruby said.

"They're serious?"

"They will be," Ward said.

"What's going on?" I could feel Agnes sitting on the edge of whatever leather seat she'd chosen as the solemn and mocking faces of nature stared dead-eyed at her from every wall.

"He's rich, okay?" Ruby said.

"Really rich," Ward said.

"Why should Maggie get him then?" she asked.

"Shut up and don't be that way," Ruby said.

"They're not even serious. She just brought him home to mess with because of his dark skin."

"Doesn't matter," Ward said. "Be nice."

There was a knock at my door and before I could cover myself, Violet came in with some clean towels.

"Lord, have mercy on my soul," she said, threw the towels on the floor, and backed out, slamming the door. Just as quickly the door reopened, and an obviously upset Maggie walked in.

"I have a feeling Violet didn't like the look of my penis," I said.

My words seemed to have no meaning for her as she said, "Was Agnes in here last night?"

Having been generally no good at lying in my life and being apparently too stupid to give it one more try, I said, "Yes."

"What did she want?"

"I'm not sure."

"What did she say?"

"She introduced herself and I think she said she wanted to upset you and I think she has."

"That bitch," Maggie muttered. "That crazy bitch. What else? What else happened?"

I looked out the window.

"You didn't," she hissed.

"I didn't do anything," I said. I believed this to be pretty much true. I hadn't kissed or inserted anything or even fought her off. I'd done nothing. I could not even say that I had had sex with Agnes, only that she had had sex with me. Perhaps if I had moved a muscle instead of having a muscle merely move, I might have remembered a bit or detail of the encounter. But all I was left with was the general impression that Agnes was pretty good at blow jobs.

Maggie stormed out of the room.

I dressed and walked down the stairs to the kitchen where I found Violet beating eggs in a bowl. I asked her if there was a phone I might use.

"Long distance?" she asked.

"Collect," I said.

"You can use the phone in Mister's study. Just the phone. Don't be touching anything else."

It seemed that none of the Larkins were around, but I knew they were. I cautiously walked into Mister's study and parked myself behind his massive desk. It felt like a blind from which I might draw a bead on any of the twenty prey that lined the walls and floor. I placed my first call to Ted.

"So, how is DC?" he asked.

"Fine," I said. "I'm calling because I needed to hear a friendly voice. I want your opinion on something."

"Shoot."

As I looked at the head of the rhinoceros (how could I have missed it before?), it occurred to me that I didn't know how to approach this subject with Ted, the whole thing about skin color. "I don't think Maggie's parents like me," I said.

"Hell, that dynamic is as old as butter," Ted said. "Did you know that India eats more butter than any other country? My mama always swore by butter. Never did turn to margarine. Turns out she was right, too. That margarine is bad for you. What's the weather like up there?"

"It's cool."

"Don't worry about her parents hating your guts. It's natural. They're almost required to hate you."

"Thanks, Ted."

"Well, I'm off to Montana tomorrow, so I won't see you when you get back. Just try to relax."

"Okay. Bye." I hung up and placed my next call to Professor Everett. I got his number from directory assistance.

"What's going on?" he asked.

"Professor Everett, these people are crazy," I said.

"Listen, you're calling me collect, so don't call me Professor Everett. At least not all the time."

"What should I call you?"

He thought about it, then said, "Call me Sir."

"Are you serious?" I asked.

"Of course not. I want you to call me Dave."

I didn't say anything.

"Seriously, call me Dave. I want you to call me Dave. I could ask you to call me Bill, but what sense would that make?"

I was terribly confused by now. "Why do you want me to call you Dave? That's not your name."

"So what? I like it. It's got that . . . that . . . that American thing going on. Dave, please call me Dave."

"Okay, Dave."

"See, that wasn't hard. Not, why the hell are you calling me during my precious Thanksgiving break?"

"I needed to hear a sane voice." I couldn't believe I was saying this to Everett, of all people.

"Then I'm glad you called. What's up?"

"These people hate me," I said.

"What people?"

"Maggie's parents. I heard them talking through the vent, and all they could talk about was my skin color."

"First, why were they talking through a vent?"

"I just heard them through the vent."

"Your skin color? What about it?" I could hear Everett leaning back and lighting his cigar.

"They think I'm too dark."

"Too dark for what?"

"For them. For their daughter."

"What does that mean?"

"That means they're a bunch of fucked-up people is what it means. It means that I don't want to be here."

"Well, if you know that, then why are you calling me? All I can do is tell you that your assessment is correct. What, do you want me to fly up there so that we can present a dark wall of solidarity?"

"And then I found out that they found out that I'm rich, and now that's all they care about, my money."

"You're rich? How rich are you, Mr. Poitier?"

"Very rich."

"I need three hundred and fifty dollars," he said. "Just kidding. I say you sit back and have some fun at their expense. I just want you to remember one little thing though."

"What's that?"

"You are a bit on the dark side. Not that I care, but a fact is a fact."

"What are you saying?"

"Have you ever known me to say anything? Well, anything that matters? Listen, just remember that nothing puts you at an advantage like knowing what someone is thinking when they don't know you know what they're thinking. Do you know what I'm telling you?"

"No, not exactly." I paused and thought for a second. "You're telling me to give them hell?"

"That's right. Happy Thanksgiving."

Once off the phone with Everett I sat back and stared at the carcasses around me. Talking to my professor had not been a waste of time, as usually it was, but I was certainly less clear about how I was to exploit the situation than he was. I surveyed the desktop and tried to take it in without feeling that I was snooping; perhaps I was trying to get a sense of the man, perhaps trying to avoid dead eyes. There was a pen-and-pencil set centered on the outside edge of the leather blotter. The pen and pencil were set as two mats on the deck of a brass schooner. The engraving at the base was thanks for support from the Lions Club. There was a leather checkbook set off to one side, but I didn't touch it. And there was a miniature brass golf bag that contained pens shaped like gold clubs. I was holding and examining the putter when Ward walked in. I quickly put the pen back into its slot. "I'm sorry, Violet told me I could come in here and use the phone," I said.

"Of course you may, son," he said. "Of course you may."

"Thanks."

"Calling family?"

"A friend."

"Not a girlfriend, I hope." He laughed and tossed a nervous glance over his shoulder as he closed the door. He sat on the leather sofa against the far wall and beneath the water buffalo.

"That would be awkward," I said.

"Where is your family?"

"I don't have any," I said.

"None?"

"Not that I know of."

"That's too bad."

I nodded.

"Well, I'd like you to think of us as your family, of this as your home. What do you say?"

"Thank you."

Maggie opened the door, poked her head in, and then stepped fully inside. "What's going on?"

"Your young man and I are just sitting here having a chat, a little man talk," Ward said. "We'll be done soon."

Maggie backed out of the study.

"Maggie's remarkable, isn't she?" he said.

"I guess so."

He looked around his study. "This room makes you nervous. It has that effect on many people. You wonder why I have these heads. Well, I think they give the place a kind of warmth."

"They're dead," I said.

"Yes, but they were once alive, weren't they? I find them comforting. I find this room comforting. It's filled with memories." He pointed at the bearskin rug. "It seems like just yesterday that Maggie was a baby lying bare-bottomed on that fur. Imagine that."

"I imagine her as an adult," I said. I knew it was an inappropriate utterance and in fact it wasn't true; I wasn't imagining Maggie at all.

Ward's reaction was immediate, but he contained himself. He cleared his throat and said, "Really?"

All of a sudden, I understood my position of power, and I was heeding Everett's suggestion that I have "fun," as he put it. "Yes," I said. "I especially like the idea of that rich dark brown fur set against her beige, almost yellow skin."

I had, in a manner of speaking, undone Ward Larkin. Though it was not visible to the naked and untrained eye, the man was trembling. Either from anger or fear or both, perhaps on a molecular level, but the trembling was real and physical, not psychic, not metaphoric. He had followed me into his own den, his own territory, and found me more than a mere lifeless head on his paneled wall, more than frightened prey. Even more was that he had found me armed, armed with the weapon that any human fears most, something he wanted. He was, I realized, so taken with my wealth that I could have pulled out my tallywhacker and handled it while we talked. But I didn't. I didn't for a host of reasons, the main one being that I was afraid.

"Maggie tells me you like boating?" I said.

He let out a breath. It could have been relief, it could have been merely breathing. "I do," he said.

"I like sailing," I told him. "I love the salt air and the spray. What kind of boat do you have?"

"I don't own a boat."

"I see." I looked at his desk. I was still seated behind it in his swiveling chair. "I see you like golf." I pointed to the brass bag of club pens.

"I do."

"I've never played," I said. "Seems like a boring game. What is it you like about it?"

"It's a very difficult game," he said.

"If you say so."

Maggie poked her head back into the room. "Are you two done yet?"

"Yes," Ward said, "we are."

In the car, on our way to pick up much-needed cranberries for Violet, Maggie regarded me suspiciously. "So what was going on in there?"

"We were just talking. You know, I think your father likes me."

"What?"

"I think we hit it off."

She watched the road.

"Does that surprise you?" I asked.

"No, not at all."

"Maggie, tell me, why did you invite me here?" I asked. I really had no interest in trying to punish Maggie and I really didn't consider it my place to even entertain the notion.

"I like you," she said.

I saw no reason to challenge that. In fact I hardly doubted it. Still, I didn't imagine that was the reason for my presence. I was making some kind of peace with my place in the rebellious daughter/ overbearing parents tragicomedy in which I'd found myself.

She said, "I didn't want you to be lonely on Thanksgiving."

It was a lie, a patronizing one, that didn't sit particularly well with me, and I found myself disliking Maggie and perhaps feeling a little sorry for myself. I looked over at her and found that, oddly, as my dislike took shape and grew, she seemed prettier. That minor observation meant little to me except insofar as it was an observation.

"So, why didn't things work out with you and Robert?" I asked.

Maggie was caught off guard by the question and also by the relaxed tone with which it had been posed.

"They just didn't."

"Why?"

"Like I said, we're like brother and sister."

"I don't know what that means," I said.

"I love him but I'm not in love with him."

I studied her face as she pulled into the grocery-market parking lot. "He seems like a nice enough guy," I said.

"He is," she said.

"Nice enough?"

"Very nice."

Not caring was a comfortable place to sit. Comfortable enough for me to let the matter go. Comfortable enough to resolve to not actively pursue the having of fun, but to remain aloof and simply watch.

My mother had been, if not disdainful then suspicious of holidays; she thought that they were all either some form of corporate extortion, religious indoctrination, or governmental propaganda. Thanksgiving fell into the third category—one big glorious lie to put a good face on continental theft. Then she would point out that the turkey is not a noble bird. She didn't dislike the holiday as much as the Fourth of July, but she disliked it plenty. The upshot for me was that I never experienced a so-called traditional Thanksgiving family dinner with the bird, cranberry stuff, and all the trappings. Ted had steadfastly maintained any boundary that might have confused our relationship with some suggestion that I was an adopted member of the family. And as for my staff, the women who cared for me through childhood, well, they were employees and they had families and lives of their own. So, in a rather peculiar and perhaps anthropological way I was looking forward to Thanksgiving dinner with the Larkins.

The dining-room table was fantastically long or at least it seemed so to me. Heavy. Wooden. And it was set for ten. There were two arrangements of plastic flowers, roses and something imaginary, that seemed to have little if anything to do with the occasion, and in the center of each arrangement was a silver reflective globe, what people put in their gardens and called gazing balls. From any spot a glance at a ball would yield a fish-eye view of most of the room. The tablecloth was red and the napkins were thick gold paper with a border of turkeys. I was standing alone next to the china cabinet watching Violet in the kitchen. I could hear Maggie and Agnes going at each other upstairs someplace, but I had no idea and every idea what it was about. Ward and Ruby were visiting in the living room with the first guests to arrive. Violet came to the table with a stack of plates.

"Can I do something to help?" I asked.

"No."

"Why do you dislike me, Violet?"

"I don't dislike you," she said. "I don't care enough about you to like or dislike you."

"Thank you for clearing that up. Let me ask you something. Most of the people in this house seem a bit crazy. You might be one of them. So, here it is. Do you have a problem with my skin color?"

"What are you asking me?"

I did not beat around the bush. "So, you think I'm too dark for precious little Maggie?"

"Now I dislike you," she said.

"So, you care."

She put down the last plate at the head of the table. "As a matter of fact," she said, then without saying another word walked back into the kitchen.

I followed her. "As a matter of fact what?" I asked.

"Listen, boy, Mister and Missus have worked too hard," she said.

"Too hard for what?"

"To have a black boy like you come around Miss Maggie."

"Listen to yourself, Violet. Mister and Missus and Miss Maggie. This is not the antebellum south and you're not a house slave."

"Why, you nigger," she said.

"Violet, you and I are pretty much the same color," I said.

"No, we're not," she snapped. "I'm milk chocolate and you're dark cocoa, dark as Satan."

I was stunned. Saddened perhaps, somewhat frightened, but mostly just stunned.

Maggie came into the kitchen, surprisingly cheerful in a dark blue dress that made me somehow think of the Pilgrims. "Everything smells great, Violet. What kind of pie this year?"

"Pumpkin."

"You haven't had pie until you've had Violet's," Maggie said to me.

Maggie took me by the hand and led me out of the kitchen and away from the burning gaze of Violet into the living room to make introductions. I was presented rather ceremoniously to Reverend Golightly, his wife, and their grown son. I nodded to each one in turn and was sickened that I had been so influenced by my experience in this household that I caught myself gauging the skin tones of the guests. Large Reverend Golightly was the color of coffee with a generous helping of cream. Slightly more cream had been added to Mrs. Golightly. Thirty-year-old Jeffrey was an albino. Jeffrey was also mentally challenged. He shook my hand too vigorously and for too long, prompting the Reverend to say, "Let go, Jeffrey." When he did let go he smiled a genuine smile and became the first person I'd liked in days. I sat in a straight-backed chair next to him.

"So, how do you like Washington?" Reverend Golightly asked me.

"I find it interesting," I said.

"We haven't had a chance to do much," Maggie said. "We arrived just yesterday."

"Well, you must take him to the Mall," Mrs. Golightly said. She sipped from her little glass of sherry. "The monuments, the Smithsonian, all of it. Maggie, you must take him."

"I will," Maggie said.

"I like Lincoln," Jeffrey said. "He freed the slaves."

"A lot of good that did," Ward said.

The rest laughed.

It was all so absurd. I expected the walls to wiggle in and out of focus and change color at any second. Yet I couldn't seem to rise to leave. Big fat Reverend Golightly, a mound of yellow Jell-O on the davenport and human stick-figure wife stuck into the cushion beside him stared at me, smiled. And there was Jeffrey, whom I liked immediately — sweet, innocent Jeffrey, completely lacking pigment and outside the bizarre game altogether.

Then Agnes came into the room wearing a red skirt, the hem of which was as far from her knees as her knees were from her red pumps. Maggie was immediately furious and gave me a look before stomping out. I sensed that I was expected to follow, so I stayed.

The Golightlys, Reverend and Mrs., cleared their throats. Jeffrey simply stared at Agnes's legs and said, "Legs."

"You look nice," Ruby Larkin said, with unsubtle sarcasm. She nudged Ward with her elbow. "Doesn't your daughter look nice?"

"Yes, nice," Ward said.

Ruby stood and walked toward the door to the dining room. "Agnes," she said. The *come with me* was clearly implied, and so Agnes complied. Ruby closed the pocket doors behind them.

We sat in an awkward silence that was interrupted by the loud voice of Agnes saying, "It's just a skirt."

"You're right about that," Ruby snapped back. "It is *just* a skirt, just barely a skirt."

Jeffrey looked at me, smiling, and repeated, "Legs."

"That will be enough, Jeffrey," Reverend Golightly said.

Jeffrey sat back straight in his chair, gave me a covert nod, tapped a finger on his leg, and mouthed "leg" to me.

We sat at the table. Ward sat at the head. At least he called it the head of the table. His exact words were, "I'll take my usual place at the head of the table." If that were so then I understood Ruby to be sitting at the foot. I sat in the center of the table, Maggie to my left and Agnes across from me. Jeffrey was at my right. Mrs. Golightly was on Ward's left, and there was an empty chair on his right. That chair was for Robert, who had not yet arrived. There was an empty seat beside Agnes that was supposedly for Violet and the Reverend Golightly was on the end beside Ruby. All of this matters little except for the fact the Agnes was near enough to me to attempt a game of footsie and far enough away to mistake Jeffrey's foot for mine. Agnes wasted no time. Jeffrey paid no attention to the candied sweet potatoes, green beans, and dressing being heaped on his plate by his father, but sat there with his eyes rolling up into his head so that only the whites showed.

"What's wrong with you, Jeffrey?" Reverend Golightly said. "What are you doing with your eyes?"

I looked across at Agnes and offered a weak smile that I think led her to believe that I was enjoying the foot rubbing.

Ward Larkin carved the enormous turkey on a side cart beside his station at the table. He did so ceremoniously and placed the meat on a platter being held by Violet, still wearing her apron.

"I love this," Ward said. "I feel like the king of a pride of lions." I imagined the large feline head on his study wall.

"Jeffrey has a preference for dark meat," Mrs. Golightly said. "He'd like a leg, I believe."

"A leg for Jeffrey," Ward said.

Jeffrey's knee was bouncing wildly beside me, and there was a faint rumble of a moan in his throat. I could see the concentration in Agnes's eyes, and every time I glanced at her, made eye contact, she became more focused on whatever it was she was doing to what she took to be my foot.

"I forgot the cranberries," Violet said.

"Agnes, run into the kitchen and get the cranberries, please," Ruby said.

"They're on the counter," Violet said.

"Send Maggie," Agnes said.

"You're closer to the door," Maggie said.

"Yes, you're right there," Ruby said.

Agnes gave me a sidelong glance, more side than long, and broke tarsal connection with the albino. Jeffrey whimpered. At least I thought I heard a whimper. Just as quickly as he had been transported he returned; his eyes fell back to center as his attention turned to the food on his plate. I believe Agnes worked her foot back into her red high heel and after that rose and walked into the kitchen with some indignant stomping.

Agnes returned with the cranberries, and all plates became full. Ward took his seat, and the Reverend Golightly cleared his throat to announce the saying of the Thanksgiving prayer.

It was not until this moment in my life that I realized that I did not believe in a god. My mother had talked quite insultingly about Christians and Christianity, and I had listened well enough to know what she might say about a number of things, including the forthcoming prayer, but I had never, I guess, cared enough to contemplate the question or, in my case, the lack thereof. At any rate, the most striking thing to me at that moment was the fact that Violet did not sit but stood by the kitchen door, her hands reverently pressed together in front of her closed eyes.

Golightly began. "Jesus, our Lord God Savior Jesus, Godalmighty, Jesus God, thank you for loving us, one and all, each and every one, and providing this bounteous, munificent, and glorious meal as we bow our undeserving heads in the face and light and brilliance of your magnificence. Thank you, Jesus Lord God, for the presence of our beloved family and cherished friends, our visitor, and the help."

I glanced at Violet, since my eyes were open and saw no reaction in her face or posture.

"And about this meal, dear Savior God Jesus, thank you for this succulent turkey, this big juicy bird, for this cornbread, and these candied yams with little marshmallows sprinkled on top slightly browned, and these mashed potatoes, and this creamed spinach, and these green beans, and this beautiful dressing full of walnuts and raisins." The Reverend's reverence was growing as he made his way through the side dishes.

Across the table, eyes closed, Agnes had renewed her pedal activity, making Jeffrey distracted from his plate and the prayer. His leg was bouncing again, but his hands remained still on either side of his plate.

"We want also to thank you, Jesus God, for our good health and the right to live in this great country of ours, where free men are free to live freely, free to live where they choose, next to whom they please and away from those they choose not to be near. Thank you for our fine homes and our nice clothes and for money. Thank you for our lineage, our good blood, and our distance from the thickening center."

I was certain the food was barely warm anymore and even more certain that Jeffrey was about to finish up. His colorless lips parted.

Jeffrey spoke. "May your stuffing be tasty. May your turkey stay plump. May your potatoes and gravy have nary a lump. May your yams be delicious and pies take the prize and may your Thanksgiving dinner stay off your thighs." With that, he pressed his eyes even more tightly shut, and he had, I'm certain, a rather satisfying climax. He said, "A-men," nodding, then shaking his head.

"Amen," Reverend Golightly said, staring angrily at his son.

At first only I was aware of Jeffrey's experience, but I looked across at Agnes as she became aware of her successful though misdirected efforts. I then looked to my left at Maggie, who had become aware of Agnes's attention to me, but was unaware of her bad aim. Maggie shot me the evil eye and then began to eat, tearing into her turkey while glaring at her sister.

Violet, who had yet to even graze her seat with her bottom, went to answer the front-door chimes. It turned out to be of course Robert. He was dressed, I must say, beautifully, though not to my taste, in a rust-colored suit and a dark yellow turtleneck sweater. He looked like autumn.

Maggie made a fuss over him and guided him to the chair beside her as he made his apologies for being late. While Maggie, Robert, and Ward caught up at their end of the table, Jeffrey talked to me.

"Something did happen that made me straight and now I have fallen, but I'm clearing my plate," Jeffrey said.

"That's nice," I said.

"I feel somewhat sticky, messy, undone, and still eating dressing is oh so much fun," Jeffrey said. He then held up his turkey and said, "Leg."

Agnes nibbled on in a sort of stunned silence, her eyes locked onto her plate. Ruby knew that something had or was happening, but she didn't know what and so she tossed glances at Agnes as she pretended to be enthralled with Reverend Golightly's monologue about something to do with the dwindling income/tithing ratio, his mouth full all the while. Jeffrey was simply happy, chewing and greasy-faced happy. Violet was in the kitchen.

The almost restful drone of separate conversations was broken by Ward as he barked out, "That's dreadful!" When we all looked his way, he said, "Robert has just told us that Dartmouth is using a quota system."

"Pathetic," Ruby said.

"Yes, it is," said Reverend Golightly. "Would you pass the potatoes over this way, please."

"It all goes to undermine real achievement," Ward said. "Robert gets in by his hard work and good grades and then they just let anybody in." He looked at me. "What do you say about this, Not Sidney? About affirmative action?"

I sipped my water and felt remarkably not nervous. "How do you know that their grades are not as good or better than Robert's?" I asked.

Silence fell on the table like a bad simile. Even Violet stopped making noise in the kitchen. The only sound was the smacking of Jeffrey's greasy lips.

I looked at Robert's wide-open face. "What's your GPA, Robert?"

He reddened. "I don't see what that has to do with anything," he said.

"It might," I said. "How do you know that affirmative action didn't get you into the college? No, really, what are your grades like?"

"My father went to Dartmouth," he said.

Maggie gave me an angry look.

Ward's eyes darted about. "Not Sidney has a point. But this is a Thanksgiving dinner, so let's eat and enjoy ourselves."

"I'd still like to know what Robert's grades were like in high school," I said. "I don't understand why he's afraid to tell me. I guess I'd also like to know if anyone at this table has benefited from affirmative action or something like it. Where did you go to law school, Mr. Larkin?"

"Yale."

"How many black students were there at the time?"

"There were three of us," he proudly said.

"And you three had better grades than all the rest of the black students who wanted to go to Yale?"

Ward was angry, nervous, and, I think, afraid of me.

"My mother never went to college," I said. "She couldn't get in. But she invested well and now I'm worth scads of money. My mother studied in her kitchen. I wonder what she could have become if she had gone to college."

"I'm sure your mother was a very special woman," Ruby said, perhaps sarcastically, I wasn't sure.

"My point is, she didn't want to be white. More importantly, she didn't want to be not black. I'm sorry," I said. I looked at all of them, especially Maggie. "You were kind enough to invite me here. I don't know why, but thank you, anyway. You people almost had me hating you because of the color of your skin, but I've caught myself. You should know that from the guest room a person can hear every word spoken in the study, and I heard you mention my unfortunate darkness."

They turned red, sort of.

"I know that you love the fact that I'm rich. In fact, Maggie didn't know that, but Ward and Ruby did." Using their first names shocked them slightly more. "So, I don't hate you because you're light. I dislike you because your *help* has yet to sit down and enjoy any of her own cooking. I like Jeffrey here because he knows how to enjoy carnal pleasure without broadcasting it. I like Agnes because she has no qualms about performing oral sex on a dark-skinned member for the mere purpose of undermining the confidence of her sister."

"You bitch!" Maggie said and threw a handful of green beans at Agnes.

"Young man, I think that's enough!" Ward said, becoming again the man of the house.

"I suppose you're right, Mr. Larkin," I said. "I'll go pack." I rose and left the table.

No one came into my room while I collected my stuff and pushed it into my little duffel. I in fact didn't know where anyone was as I walked down the stairs and through the far side of the kitchen; everything was so quiet.

Violet was standing near the stove. She handed me a paper sack and said, "You might get hungry later."

"Thank you," I said.

CHAPTER 5

Some part of me (whether generous or not, I don't know) tried to convince the rest of me that there was something to be learned from the color-challenged Larkins, or at least that some perverse fun had been had. But the rest of me was not accepting it, and so the flight back on the evening puddle jumper was nothing more than sad and tedious, though welcomed. I felt some vague regret as I considered that Maggie might actually have held a few sincere feelings for me, but now I would never know. There was never any future, I thought, and I laughed at the thought because, of course, there had been no suggestion of a so-called future. Still, I was sorry, if at the same time mildly satisfied, that I had caused them more family turmoil than was normally theirs. I certainly had not contributed significantly to the intense family sickness.

Off the airplane in Atlanta I was met by a rather animated and giggly Podgy Patel. I was more than a bit surprised by his presence and so I asked, "How the hell did you know to be here?"

"It is very simple," he said in his singsong accent. "I make it a habit to track your credit-card transactions."

"I'd like you to break that habit."

"As you wish. But who would have picked you up?"

"A taxi," I said. "A bus."

"Now, you are just being silly."

"Why are you so giddy, Podgy?"

"Oh, for good reason, very good reason. Our network is a big success, a major success. We are making money foot over fist."

"Great, more money."

"I detect sarcasm. Am I to understand that you want no more money?"

"Does it really make a difference?"

"All the difference in the world," he said.

We were walking through the parking garage. I turned to him and looked at his smiling face. "Really, Podgy, it's just that I feel I have too much money."

"You are not very American," he said.

"I suppose not."

"Then perhaps you should give some of your money away. You should give much away and not much would be different, as you say. It is actually a very lucrative practice. It is a wonderful write-off, charity."

I watched as he unlocked the car doors. "Thanks, Podgy. I believe that's a really good idea."

"You will find, however, that it is harder to give away money that one might imagine. Very much harder than it seems." He started the car. "Shall I drive you to your dorm at the college?"

"Please."

As we drove through a pleasantly deserted Atlanta I considered my previous venture with philanthropy, my gifts to the college. They had not been donated in the spirit of giving, however, since they were more payoffs or bribes, and they had gotten me no more than a college admission I didn't really want and a standing invitation to diddle the very sad Gladys Feet. I had spread no joy to anyone and certainly had been left with none. I was headed back to campus to pack up and leave and where I was going was anybody's and especially my guess. But first I would call Professor Everett to see if he could offer any good argument for my staying put. Why I held his opinion in any regard was beyond me, but I did.

Everett answered, sounding tired but awake. I put the question to him with no warning. "Why should I remain in college?"

"You've got me," he said without a pause.

"That's the best you can do?" I said.

"How much money do you have?"

"More than I know what to do with," I said, honestly.

Everett sighed. I could hear him lighting his cigar. "I suppose you could remain in school for the sex. I hear there's a lot of it. Or not."

"What about an education?"

"Hell, you can read. You know where the library is."

"You're a professor," I said.

"If you say so."

"If you were me," I said, "would you stay in school?"

He said nothing.

"Well?"

"I think you should come over to my house so we can talk head to head or face to face, however it goes. And bring some doughnuts, the kind with the sprinkles." He told me his address, and before he hung up he said, "You know, we mustn't judge people by what they drive."

"What does that mean?" I asked an empty line.

I drove my car over to Everett's home, a narrow two-story brick house with an enclosed front porch. He held open the screen door for me as I walked past him into the foyer. I followed him into the living room, such as it was. There was a low yellow, floral-print sofa in the middle of the room facing a windowless wall against which sat a small television on a wooden table. On the screen two men boxed.

"Do you like boxing?" I asked.

"Hate it."

I looked at the television. "Why are you watching it?"

"Because I love the sublime violence of it. In a way. It's a lot like doing drugs, if you know what I mean. And even if you don't. What bullshit I'm spouting."

I handed him the doughnuts.

"How thoughtful," he said. "You shouldn't have. I can't accept them, though. I'm watching my weight, before anyone else does.

You have them, enjoy them. They have sprinkles. Now, what's this business about dropping out of school?" He sat on the sofa.

"Why shouldn't I?" I sat beside him.

"Don't you want a degree?"

"I never really thought about it."

He shook his head. "That's a damn good answer. I wish I'd said it. I wish I'd thought it. I will the next time." He took his cold cigar from the ashtray and stuck it in his face. "Now that you've thought about it, do you want one?"

"Not particularly."

"Well, there you have it."

"There I have what?"

"What do you get after four years of college?" he asked.

"A degree."

"And you don't want a degree. So, there you have it. Go sailing or skiing or something."

"What about an education?" I said.

"Listen, if you want to stay in school, then stay in school, but don't ask me to tell you what to do. Truth is, I don't know or care what you do."

"Is that true, that you don't care?"

He paused to think it over. "Pretty much. Eat a doughnut. It will make you feel much better. It will make me feel better if you eat one."

"For some reason, maybe because you're a *professor,* I thought you'd try to talk me into staying."

"It's a bitch, ain't it? The things we assume." He looked at his watch. "Hey, it's ten o'clock. Time for some real entertainment." He walked over to the television and changed channels. "Now, this is genius."

A man's white-turbaned head appeared on screen, disembodied and floating against a blue field, slowly, from one corner to the other. The head wore a white turban and sang in what I took to be Hindi. The title grew large enough to read: *Punjabi Profiles.*

"Absolute genius," Everett said. "Listen, Poitier, you'll get your education. Hey, you're already a smart guy, smarter than most, better educated than most of my so-called colleagues. Don't get me wrong, I believe in higher education, but you'll find your way. I don't worry about you. Doughnut?"

"Why do you teach?"

"Money."

"That's it?"

"I'm no good at anything else," he said.

I wanted to tell him that he was no good at teaching.

But then he said, "As if I'm any good at teaching. But you know what? Who the fuck cares? You know what I mean? Still, I can teach you two or three things, among them how to perform a tracheotomy on a squirming and unwilling patient, but you probably don't believe that."

I sat quietly for a few minutes while we watched an Indian music video. I thought about my visit to Maggie's home, about the Larkins, about the dinner. "Why are people so fucked up?" I asked.

"Maybe you do need college, Poitier," Everett said. "You want to know why people are so fucked up? Son, that's about the only question I can answer with even a small measure of authority. It's because they're people. People, my friend, are worse than anybody."

I was not certain whether I was troubled more by his answer or by the fact that he had called me son.

Everett, as usual, had been of no help whatsoever. He insisted as I left that I take the doughnuts, sprinkles and all. He said that they would kill him, but he'd be happy to know I was enjoying them. I took the doughnuts and ate them as I drove back to campus and my dorm. The place was so empty, so quiet and dead, that there was a sudden and strange appeal to it, but I refused to be seduced. I would have liked to talk with Ted, but he was off at his ranch in Montana doing something with buffaloes. And what would he have said to me anyway except, "Why is it that the buffalo's head is so disproportionately large?" or something like that. I'd always wanted to see Turner and Everett meet, imagined it a little like Perry Como performing with Ornette Coleman. I resolved as I walked across campus to again attempt my drive west. Only this time I would stick to the interstate system, the homogeneous tangle of the ribbons that made up the fifty-first state. I would observe each and every traffic rule and avoid people whenever possible. I realized that I could simply board a plane and fly to California, but being there wasn't the point, getting there was what I was after. I didn't know anyone there or what I would do and so the drive would afford me time to formulate some kind of plan. Also I still harbored the young, romantic, naïve, and stupid notion that a cross-country trek would be a valuable learning experience, a rite of passage. That night I packed up my Buick Skylark and headed west once again, my heart pounding, my palms sweating against the plastic of the steering wheel, a thermos of coffee beside me next to a sack of my newest addiction, doughnuts with sprinkles.

The Georgia that surrounded Atlanta had lived up to its billing on my first migratory attempt. I made the short drive to the state's edge in a quick dead sprint and fell into the next state, which turned out to be Alabama. Of course, I knew it would be Alabama, but still I don't think anyone is ever quite prepared for Alabama, though I imagined it appropriate and decent preparation for Mississippi; *decent* is a term the connotation of which I am here unable to articulate.

My chosen route seemed simple enough. I would take Interstate 85 to Interstate 65 to Interstate 10 and that would take me to Los Angeles. There were no turns involved. How could a person get lost? I got lost. I was somewhere in Alabama, in the dark, and it turns out that night in Alabama is darker than night anywhere. I recalled the song "Stars Fell on Alabama" and thought, no, they didn't. I was further disheartened by a sign telling me I was near a town called Smuteye. Look at the map. And then of course my Skylark began to shutter and make a new unfamiliar, though not terribly alarming sound.

I managed to roll into a lonesome and unlit gas station on a dirt road. The dark sign hovering over the pumps read *Rabbit Toe's Filling Station*. My car's wheels tripped a bell that might as well have been a siren for the way it split the still night air. But nothing and no one stirred. A dog barked far off in the distance and though that reminded me of life, it did more to make me fear death. I was at once terrified that there was no one there and that at any moment someone would appear. And someone did.

An extremely tall, extremely thin, extremely washed-out, and extremely white man walked out of the darkness beside the building and into the white glow of my headlights. He bent at the waist and peered through the driver's-side window and said the scariest thing I could imagine. He said, "Boy, you must be lost."

"I must be," I said. "Can you fix my car?"

"Can but won't"

"May I use your garage to try to fix it myself?"

"You may not."

"Are you Rabbit Toe?" I asked.

"That's what they call me."

"It's not your name?"

"That's what they call me," he repeated.

"Why do they call you that?" I asked.

"I don't know."

The belts of my engine were squeaking and squawking. I spotted some WD-40 on the rack with the oil by the pumps. "I'll take some of this," I said.

"It's for sale," he said.

I handed him some money. "Keep the change."

He nodded.

"Well, thanks for nothing," I said.

"You bet." He gave me a hard stare.

I started the engine and the sound was not there. I made it another few miles and the noise again started up. It was just about
sunrise and I found myself off the dirt road on a dirt drive in front
of a small house. Three women were trying to build a fence around
a chicken coop. Another older woman spied my approach, crossed
herself, and looked up at the sky. I thought I could read her lips
and I thought she said, "Thank you, God, for sending me a black
buck."

I got out of my car and opened the hood to look stupidly at the
troubled engine. The oldest of the women walked over and stood
behind me.

"Your car is not running?" she asked.

"I'm afraid that's true," I said. "Would you mind if I worked on
it here? I think the belts are loose, but I can tighten them. Do you
mind?"

"No, we don't mind." The other women had come to stand
with her. "Our roof needs to be fixed."

"Really?"

"It leaks when it rains. And you will fix it?"

"I don't know how," I said.

"It's simple," she said. "We have a book that explains it."

"Well, I suppose I could try."

"You will do more than try. You will do it." With that she
marched off and left the other women to stare at me. I offered a
smile and glanced back at my engine.

The battered service manual for my Skylark suggested that the
job of tightening the belts would be simple and fairly quick. In
fact it said, "This adjustment is simple and quick," the rather clear
subtext being that any idiot could do it. I read this recognizing that
I was not just any idiot. I put the car manual aside and picked up
the book that had been given to me by the old woman, *How to Roof
a House.*

She stood over me while I read. "It is clear?" she asked.

"Yes," I said. "I'll do this, but then I'll have to go."

"We will see," she said.

I climbed the ladder to look at the roof. It was a simple flat roof that required only that I remove the bad surface, replace the bad wood, roll out the new roofing paper, and paint the seams with tar. It would take awhile, but I was happy that I at least understood the project.

I called down, "It's a big job."

"But you can do it." It was not a question.

"I can do it."

It was thankfully November, so, though the air was insanely humid, it was not insanely hot. Nine hours later, just as the sun was setting, I finished the roof. I was dirtier than I had ever been, smellier, more tired, and yet I felt a kind of vague peace. I washed up at the outdoor spigot at the side of the house. The water was cold, but I didn't mind. I dried my face and underarms with a stiff white towel that one of the women had set down near me.

The oldest came and said, "Come, you eat with us."

"Don't you want to see the roof?"

"You have fixed it. That is all that matters."

Clean and wearing a fresh shirt I stepped into the building to find the women dressed alike in what might have been habits and sitting around a rectangular table; the oldest was at the head. She finally introduced herself as Sister Irenaeus. She introduced the others as Sisters Origen, Eusebius, Firmilian, and Chrysostom.

"Really," I said, somewhat astonished. "My name is Poitier."

"Poitier," Sister Irenaeus said.

"Poitier," the others whispered.

"Where are you from?" I asked. I had been trying to place Sister Irenaeus's accent.

"We are from North Dakota."

It was hardly the answer I was expecting. "You're a long way from home," I said.

"We are indeed. Have a seat, Poitier."

I sat in the woven-cane chair opposite Sister Irenaeus. The room was quiet and damp and dim, and lit by two brass standing lamps. There was a dark, heavy wooden buffet against the wall behind Sister Irenaeus, and to the left of that was a book stand supporting what I was certain was a very large and tattered Bible.

"I didn't know you were nuns," I said.

"We are not Catholic," Sister Irenaeus said. "We are of the Church of the Ever-Holy Pentecost of Our Savior Jesus Christ of Nazareth."

"I'm sorry," I said.

"We are all children of God," said Sister Firmilian, who was by my estimation the prettiest of them. Then and now, thinking this made and makes me shudder.

"We say grace," Irenaeus said.

They all put their hands together and for some reason I did as well.

Sister Irenaeus cleared her throat. "Dear Jesus, thank you for this day, this bread, our roof, and our new big man, and he is a black man just like William J. Seymour and his one eye, but his eye was open to only you, Jesus, only you, and so you have sent him to us to help us in our mission, our quest to bring your word of love to every breathing human creature that walks the face of your beautiful Earth and, Jesus, this road is difficult, arduous, but not hard as you have kissed the trail we travel with your divine lips, full, Godly lips, so that our feet might tingle with the joy of your love with every step, O Jesus, our Jesus."

And with that Sister Origen, the stockiest and shortest of the five, began to tremble, and inside I felt myself take a step back. Sister Origen's mouth opened and her tongue fished around in the air and sounds came out, though I found them incomprehensible, but strangely clear. She said, "Ailalossolg si eht eugnot nekops yb em nema nema nema nu sam msitpab yb yloh tirips ninzela lump zaba zabalee zabael yliem si devol ehs si enim bleedle peetle leetle little zaba za zalee." She went on that way for what seemed like four or five minutes. Then she shook her face violently and was done and the sisters said, "Amen," and sat. I sat too and watched as they passed around a loaf of sliced white bread. I took a slice and pushed the basket back to the middle of the table.

"This is supper?" I asked.

"Yes," said Sister Irenaeus. "You may have a second portion if you like. You are a big man."

"So I understand. I'll be leaving in the morning," I said.

Sister Irenaeus shook her head. "I don't think so."

I didn't know what to say, so I said nothing.

"God has sent you to us."

"He didn't mention it to me."

"He wouldn't."

"He might."

"He wouldn't."

"Tomorrow, you build a fence," she said. She closed the door and I found myself outside, alone in the dark. The sky was very clear and I could see Cassiopeia and Orion and maybe Canes Venatici, but I was never too sure about that one. I lay back on the hood of my car and stared upward for a while.

I would have tightened my engine's belts then, but frankly I was too exhausted. I was still hungry after what had passed for supper, but luckily I had one doughnut left. Finally I crawled into the backseat of my car and drifted into a fitful, dream-racked sleep.

The wind blows steadily across the rolling Texas prairie. A rust-muddy river flows some hundred yards away, marked on either side by cottonwoods with white seeds floating all about. I am standing only a few yards from an old man who is tossing pieces of bone onto the wrinkled surface of a spread-out blanket. No, wait. There is no wind, just a stillness of arid air. Monument Valley. Spires of red rock rise into the cerulean sky, a blue bluer than blue. An old man, gray haired and weathered, tosses bones on a tattered blanket. Other men, younger men, watch.

"We go on," the old man says.

One of the younger men turns to me. "You know that DeChenney and his army ain't gonna let us go. They want us back to work their land."

"Buck," an older man says, "we's a-goin' on. If Old Deke says we go on, then we go on."

"All right then," I say. I take off my Stetson and wipe my brow, stare out across the plains at the mountains in the distance. "Be ready by the time I get back here tomorrow. Be about midday."

"We be ready, Buck."

"Good. And you're going to have to pare down some. Those mules gonna have to pull you a long way."

"All de way to de green valley," he says.

I nod. I step away, nodding at the women who were cooking over the fire, tip my hat. I mount my bay quarter horse and rein him in a tight circle and then trot, no, canter off away from the camp and not on a bay but on a palomino, flaxen mane and tail full of the wind.

A shake of the head. A clearing. I am saying again:

"All right then." I push up the brim of my Stetson and look at the unforgiving western sky. Then I look at the mountains in the distance. Lavender hills capped with snow. "You all be ready," I say. "I'll be back tomorrow around midday and you all just be ready. You hear me?"

"We be ready, Buck."

"You see all this furniture and these heavy trunks. You gotta pare down something fierce. These same sad mules gonna have to pull you all the way over those mountains."

"All de way to de green valley," he says.

"Why are you talking like that?" I ask.

"Sorry, Buck."

I step away and acknowledge the women who are cooking at the big fire. I tip my hat to them and smile. They giggle at the sight of my smile. I mount my palomino and ride off; his flaxen mane and tail are full of the wind.

I ride through a stream and through a canyon as my horse kicks up a steady red cloud. I approach a cabin, a homestead. I am looking for my woman, Bes. But something isn't right. The farm is too quiet. The cabin is too quiet. There are the usual animal sounds—chickens, pigs. The cow is standing where she always stands. Bes's brother and his wife and children have been living here too, and there's no sign of them. One of them is always outside. The cabin is small, two rooms, and it gets crowded inside, but where are they? I dismount some distance away and lead my horse to a teamless buckboard next to a sycamore. Bes steps out into the shadow on the porch, stands there. A breeze moves her blue gingham dress. Her yellow dress. She slowly raises her hand to wave, a stiff wave. I wave back, knowing that something is bad wrong. I slip off the leather keep from the trigger of the pistol holstered on my hip. I study Bes's eyes. I look closely at the windows of the cabin, at the barn, at the smokehouse. The chickens walk about in front of Bes. Then she runs, and a white man behind her starts shooting his pistol at me. No, he pushes Bes to the side, she loses her balance, falls into the dust. He shoots, and other men shoot from the windows of the cabin, the smokehouse, and the open barn doors. I dive to take cover in the pig corral, sliding through the mud to the far side where I kick out the bottom fence rail and roll out. Bullets whiz by my head, and I can't see where to shoot back. I spot Bes running to the trees, her skirts full of the wind, and I wave for her to keep going, to get clear. The faces of the white men are fierce, evil, full of hate. I run and slip and slide and squirm to more cover and still more cover as the bullets ricochet by my ears. I get to my horse and dash away, hunched low over the saddle, a cloud of dust pluming behind me. Soon, the white men have found their horses and are chasing me and though I can't see them, I can feel the posse's hooves drumming the ground. I ride into the night. No, I've ridden hard for a couple of hours. My horse is slick and foamy with sweat. He is walking now. I've ridden him so long and hard.

At a watering hole I see a man bathing, wearing nothing but a hat. He splashes around in the pool on skinny brown legs while I admire his chestnut horse, no, black horse. The animal is hobbled next to the man's camp, his clothes are laid out on some big rocks next to a dead fire. I remove my saddle and the sweat-drenched blanket from my palomino and quietly approach the black horse. He becomes nervous, whinnies, and I put a hand on his neck to settle him down.

"Who's that up there?" the man calls from the water.

I draw my pistol and point it at the man's chest as he climbs naked up the hill toward me.

"Excuse me, brother, but there seems to be a misunderstanding here. That horse, the one you're putting a saddle on, belongs to me." He holds his hat over his private parts.

"We're trading," I say. I nod over to my palomino.

"A trade usually requires agreement, wouldn't you say?"

"I don't have time for agreement. My horse is a good one. You'll find that out once he's rested."

"I'm sure that's true, brother. So, why don't you sit here for a while and have some coffee and let him rest?"

"Don't have time."

"My name is Jeremiah Cheeseboro and I'm a man of the cloth. Does that make any difference to you, friend?"

"Another day it might."

The man makes a move toward his clothes.

"That's far enough," I say and pull back the hammer on my nickel-finished peacemaker pistol.

"I was just reaching for my drawers," he says. "I'm feeling a little exposed out here in my altogether, if you know what I mean."

"You're doing just fine."

"So, you're just going to steal my horse," he says.

"Trade."

"You say."

"I say. Now, why don't you just walk on back down that trail and get in that water."

"I'm clean enough," he says.

"Go on."

"You're no Christian, brother," he says as he shuffles backward to the water and in. "Your deeds will catch up to you."

"Better them than the posse that's chasing me," I say. I climb onto the back of the black horse, give a final nod to the preacher, and then gallop away.

I'm seeing this from high above, like a god, only shorter, I suppose. That preacher from the watering hole is dressed in black, dusty from the trail, dismounting and tying my palomino to the post in front of a livery. The preacher is minding his own business, his big Bible under his arm, no, held to his chest. He makes his way down the side of the livery to the back door of a saloon.

He takes off his hat and bows to a young boy. "Son, I would be much obliged if you would see fit to take my two bits into this here establishment and procure for me a bit of the spirits."

The boy stares at him, dumbfounded.

"I want you to go in and buy me a whiskey."

"Why didn't you say that?"

"I'm sorry, lad. I'm afraid I overestimated your ability to comprehend simple language."

"What?"

"I didn't realize that you're stupid."

The boy goes inside and slams the door.

The preacher walks back to the street where he finds his horse encircled by dirty, dusty white men. "Is this here your horse?" a lanky man asks, stepping close and spitting tobacco juice onto the preacher's shoes.

"Messy," the preacher says.

"I asked you a question," the white man says. "I asked you if'n this here horse is yourn."

"Not exactly, brother, not. You see I was baptizing my body anew to the knowledge of the Lord when my own horse was stolen by a cowardly heathen, and that heathen left this wretched animal in the place of my own. He was almost lame when he was delivered unto me, but prayer, brother, good old prayer restored him to his present condition of health. My name is Jeremiah Cheeseboro, conveyor of the gospel, a shepherd of men's souls."

"Should we shoot him now or later?" asks a man standing on the other side of the palomino.

"I wouldn't shoot me at all," the preacher says.

The lanky man spits more juice onto the preacher's boots. "And why is that, Mr. man of the cloth?"

"Because it is clear to me that you are searching for the very heathen what stole my horse."

"Do you know where Buck is?"

"I didn't even know his name. Thank you for telling me. But if I find him, I'll be happy to inform you and your associates of his whereabouts."

The man looks at the other thugs. "I like you, preacher man."

"Thank you. I like you, too."

"If you do find out where Buck is, you ride on out to Rusty Gulch and tell Mr. DeChenney."

"DeChenney."

"You do that?"

"As sure as Moses floated to safety in a basket."

"Let him go," he says to the other white men.

They all step away and let the preacher mount the palomino.

The lanky man says, "Preacher, if'n I see you again and you ain't got no information for me, I'll have to kill you."

"I sincerely thank you for your overwhelming Christian generosity of spirit," the preacher says and canters away.

While I'm aimlessly riding around the vast and mysterious landscape, things are happening at the camp of the newly freed slaves. White men, eleven of them, no, fifteen of them gather on horseback at the edge of the dark woods.

The white men rein their horses in tight circles and then charge the camp, wildly galloping down the sloping meadow, hooting and shouting. Moonlight. Black doughnuts around rocks. Moonlight. Women scream. Moonlight. Children cry out. A few men take up their few arms and are shot for the trouble. Perhaps because of the darkness, perhaps because of their drunkenness, the marauders kill only three people — two men and a young boy. They wreck a covered wagon, upset it, and leave it ablaze, sending gray smoke into the purple sky. The white men take the strongbox. Women weep. Men weep.

At sunrise I approach the wagon train. From the ridge I can see the smoke rising from the burnt wagon. I kick the black horse and gallop into the camp. My hat blows off as I dismount while the black horse is still running. I don't ask what happened; I don't need to ask.

"How many were there?" I survey the damage — the three bodies covered from the neck down some yards away. The faces are ashen, unreal seeming. The dead boy looks younger the longer I study him.

"I don't know, Buck," one of the men says. "It was quiet and peaceful and then all hell broke loose. Nothing but the flash of powder everywhere and bullets whizzing every which way."

While I stand there listening and not listening, someone taps on my shoulder. I turn around to find that preacher from the watering hole. He doesn't say anything. I can see the anger in his clenched jaw and gritted teeth, and then he rears back and punches me square on the jaw.

I wake up and I'm confused; sunlight cuts through haze and my dusty back window. I come fully awake to the nudging and pointy-fingered prodding of Sister Irenaeus. She had the driver's-side door of my Skylark open and had pushed forward the driver's seat.

"Mr. Poitier, wake up," she said. "It is time to work. It's time for you to build our church."

"What are you talking about? I'm on my way to California."

"You have to build our church. That is why the Lord has sent you to us poor sisters."

"I really believe you misunderstood him," I said. "I don't know how to build anything, not even a doghouse."

"We don't need a doghouse. We don't have a dog. We need a church, and you have been sent to build it."

I moved her away and out of the car and followed her into the chill of the morning. Whether it was the previous day's hard work on the roof, I do not know, but I felt stiff, creaky, considerably older. I did not have on a shirt and my dark skin glistened; I could feel it glistening, and I became aware of my partial nakedness. I leaned back into the car and grabbed a T-shirt, pulled it on while she pointed with an open hand past the chicken coop.

"It will be built over there," she said.

Sister Irenaeus led me across the yard, past the chicken coop where Sisters Eusebius and Firmilian were trying to stretch and staple wire netting about twenty yards on to a large clearing. "Here," she said. "You will build it here, and we will help you."

I laughed. "Sister, I told you, I don't know how to build anything, much less a building. No, if you'll excuse me, I'll fix my car and get back on the road before you ask me to turn water into wine."

The other sisters had formed in a huddle behind us. They said nothing, neither to me nor to each other. I smiled weakly as I stepped by them and back toward the chicken coop. Sister Irenaeus and the others followed me back to my car where they hovered like bees making no sound, and yet I could feel them buzzing.

As suggested in my trusty car-service manual, tightening the belts was not so difficult. I used my lug wrench as a pry bar and stuck it between the alternator and the water pump. While I was tightening the bolt on the alternator bracket, contorting my body to keep sufficient pressure on the bar to keep the belt taut, I noticed the faces of the sisters under the hood with me, staring at my progress. I managed to get the bolt tight, and they all said, "ahhhh," as I pulled away.

"You are good with tools," Sister Irenaeus said.

"Nice try, Sister," I said.

I tossed my tools in the trunk and shut it, then fell in behind the wheel. I turned the key and the engine started and ran smoothly, at least as smoothly as it ever had. I decided that it was best to say good-bye from inside the car, that I might feel less guilt if I were already rolling away, as opposed to a more formal standing, hand-shaking farewell. Even then I laughed at myself, wondering why I should feel guilt at all. For what? Refusing to perform a task I was incapable of doing? I drove away. I leaned out the window and waved as I approached the bend in the dirt drive. They did not wave, but looked to the sky. The mere thought of them praying should have been enough to keep me driving and yet their faces were so innocent, so open, so, so stupid. I got to the highway and drove back toward Smuteye.

My stomach was twisted with hunger, and so I stopped at the sadly, but no doubt aptly, named Smuteye Diner. It was not a railcar, not even a large Airstream trailer, but a sad rectangle of a mobile home, set up on cinder blocks with a bent set of prefab metal stairs. I entered and sat at the counter.

A large woman turned to me and smiled. "Food?" she asked.

"Please," I said.

She pointed over her broad shoulder at the menu hand printed with a marker on a poster board.

"What's good?" I asked.

"It's all good," she said. "At least it's all the same."

"I'll have two scrambled eggs."

"Bacon or sausage?"

"Bacon, I guess."

"We're out of bacon," she said.

"Then why did you . . ."

"I was just joking," she laughed. "We got bacon, lots of it."

I was relieved and relaxed by her sense of humor.

"Why are you here?" she asked. "It's hard to get here and here ain't on the way to no place else. Believe me, I know. So, you're family to somebody here, which I doubt, or you're lost."

"I was lost. I think I know where I am now."

"You think so, you do?" she said. "You want coffee?" She was already breaking eggs one-handed into a bowl.

I didn't want to stop her. "Maybe later."

"Got lost in the night?"

"Late yesterday. I ended up fixing a roof for some crazy nuns or something. I guess they couldn't be nuns."

"Pentecostals," she said.

I nodded. The sound of the bacon on the griddle and the smell of it were making me hungrier.

"Those poor sisters," she said. "They come here from Montana or someplace because somebody left some land to their church."

"North Dakota," I said.

"What?"

"They came from North Dakota."

"What did I say?"

"Montana."

"Well, it don't make no difference no way. It might as well be Russia, it's so far away. Anyway, I suppose they'll be hitchhiking back there soon enough. You can't eat dirt."

"They want to build a church," I said.

The woman laughed a big laugh. She had a big laugh and it went with her big hair. It was a mountain of black hair with red streaks and big loop earrings stuck out of it.

"They might do it."

She smiled at me. "You liked them, huh?" She slid the paper plate of eggs and bacon in front of me. I studied the plate as the grease stained the paper around the edges of the food. "Toast will be right up."

"Thanks." I took a bite. "Good."

"If them sisters build anything, it'll be a miracle."

"I think they'll do it."

"You're as crazy as they are. What's your name, crazy man?"

"Poitier," I said. "Sidney Poitier."

"You do look just like him. But what's your name?"

"Sadly, that is my name."

"No shit?"

"No shit. What's your name?"

"Diana Ross," she said. "Got you!"

"That was good."

"You name's not Sidney Poitier, is it?"

What a question she had put to me without even knowing what she was doing, and so I answered truthfully the question she didn't know she was asking. "It is."

"Must be rough," she said. She scraped the griddle with a wide spatula. "Having the same name and looking so much like him."

"Not so rough. I'm better looking."

She laughed. "I like you. Where you on your way to?"

"Los Angeles."

"Sidney Poitier would be." She put a plate of toast in front of me.

"So, what's your name?" I asked.

"Well, it's not as pretty a name as yours. My name *is* Diana, but it's Diana Frump."

"Frump?"

"Frump."

"I like Poitier better," I said.

"Thought you might."

"Diana is a pretty name."

"Thanks for saying so." She poured ketchup from a big plastic bottle into smaller plastic bottles.

"Tell me what you know about the sisters."

"Oh, they come around here every so often. That bossy one gets on my nerves a little, to tell the truth. What's her name?"

"Irenaeus," I said.

"Yeah, whatever. And that's another thing, who the hell can say those names, much less remember them? There's Oxygen and Firmament and then the others. Anyway, they come round here looking for donations. I don't get many customers in the first place, and I don't want them bothered for handouts."

I nodded.

"They even asked me for money. Want to build a church. I ain't got nothing extra. Nobody around here does. I say, 'Why don't you get it from your main church office, whatever you call it?' and that Sister Iranus gives me this dumbass look like she'll pray for me. I don't say nothing. I'm a good Christian. I'm a Baptist. I should be the one praying for her. Hell, we got us a church."

The screen door opened, and a short man in a ball cap walked in. "Hey, Diana," he said.

"Hey, Dan."

The man sat next to me at the counter and said, "Hey."

"Hey," I said.

Diana put a cup of coffee in front of him. "We were just talking about the sisters."

"Those crazies?" he said. "Gonna build themselves a church. Out of what, is what I want to know."

"They might," I said. I didn't know why I said it.

"I don't see how," he said. "They ain't got no money. I wish they did. We could use some jobs around here. There used to be a paper mill up the road about a thousand years ago."

I put down my plastic fork and knife and wiped my mouth with my paper napkin and considered just how much money I had. I could finance this church myself. The thought of it was repulsive in some ways, since I found religion generally offensive and off putting; my mother had always been adamantly opposed to absolutely anything having to do with the notion of a so-called higher being. But my impetuous, abrupt, and inexplicable desire to assist the forlorn sisters had nothing to do with a god, religion, a sudden onset of a messiah complex or/and certainly not my own (perhaps, sadly needed) salvation. It had simply to do with a newfound and fairly ironic way to spend my ridiculously easy-to-come-by money.

"May I use your phone?" I asked.

"There's a pay phone on the side of the trailer over there." She pointed. "Next to the porta-johnny. It's the only phone I got. Need quarters?"

"No, thanks." I excused myself, nodded to Dan, and left the diner. The screen door slammed. The phone was not in a booth, but bolted to the vinyl side of the trailer. I placed a collect call to Podgy, and while I waited to be connected I studied the words, names, and numbers scratched into the wall.

I hate Farley

Jiggles Boatwright sucks for free

Call Janifer 234-756

Sheraff Purkins is a shithole

If you here reading this you fucked

Podgy accepted my call. "I need you in Smuteye, Alabama," I said.

"Who is this?"

"It's me. Sidney."

"I know no Sidney."

"Not Sidney," I corrected myself.

"Mr. Poitier?"

"It's me. I need you down here in Smuteye, Alabama."

"Surely, there is no such place."

"There is and I'm here."

"Are you in some kind of trouble?"

"No, I want you to build something."

"What?"

"A church," I said, not quite believing it. There was thick, awkward silence. "Podgy?"

"Who is this?"

"It's me, Podgy," I said, again. "Not Sidney."

"I will not come to a place called Smuteye," he said.

"I want to build a church for someone."

"I know nothing about building. You have money. Hire somebody. I am too busy with the network. I am producing a special about the rap music."

I looked at the phone in my hand. He was right. I had a checkbook. It was my money. I didn't need Podgy Patel holding my hand. "You're absolutely right, Podgy," I said.

"I know I'm right. Just as I know there is no Smuteye. You are too funny, Mr. Not Sidney. Now, if you will excuse me, I have to get back with my posse."

I drove back to the sisters' place and found them, frighteningly, much as I had left them, with their heads upturned stupidly to the sky. Of course my return could only be construed as prayers answered, and who was I to dispute this belief? After all, my complete faith in the nonexistence of their god notwithstanding, I was at a loss to explain my reappearance.

"We knew you would come back," Sister Irenaeus said as I got out of my car. There was an arrogance in her tone that made me immediately sorry I'd returned. Yet I did not leave. Inexplicably.

"I'd like to talk to you," I said. "To all of you."

They stared at me.

"Can we go inside?"

We marched up the one step, through the solid wooden door, and into the austere two-room building. I assumed the room in the back was where they slept. I gestured for them to sit and so they did. The windows were shut tight and so it was not only hot inside, but airless.

"So, you want to build a church," I said.

"You know that is true," Sister Irenaeus said. The others nodded.

"Do you have a plan for this structure?" I asked.

"We do." Sister Irenaeus looked over at Sister Firmilian and nodded. Sister Firmilian got up and walked to the writing table against the far wall. She opened the drawer, withdrew a paper, and brought it to me.

I looked at it. It was a crude sketch on lined, white-notebook leaf. Two angles were depicted—from above and from in front. The church was to be a rectangle with a pitched roof.

"What do you think?" Sister Irenaeus asked.

"I don't know how to build a church," I told them. "However, I have a lot of money." I let this sit with them for a moment. "And I'm willing to pay for the materials and labor to have it built."

All their eyes lit up.

"God has answered our prayers," Sister Irenaeus said.

Sisters Chrysostom and Eusebius immediately went into a state and started rattling away in tongues; their eyes rolled up into their heads and pretty much scared the living shit out of me. The other three carried on as if nothing was happening.

"As I was saying, I will pay for your church. But you're going to have to find an architect to draw something usable."

"You will do that for us," Sister Irenaeus said.

"No, you have to do it."

"God has sent you."

"No, bad judgment has sent me." I pulled out my checkbook

and started writing. "This is for fifty thousand dollars. This should get you started."

"I do not have a bank account," Sister Irenaeus said.

I looked at her.

"We have no money," Sister Origen said.

"You will take care of it for us," Sister Irenaeus said.

"No," I said, sick of saying it. "I'll find a bank, cash a check, bring you the money, and then I'll leave." With that I walked out, thinking that I should forget everything, but I'd told them I'd give them the money and so I would. I wondered as I fell in behind my steering wheel if there was a bank in Smuteye.

The sign on the one-story brick building set between a dry goods store and a defunct mortuary said *Smuteye Farmers Savings and Loan,* and I had no reason to doubt it. I parked diagonally in an unmarked space, only because the one other car there was so parked. It was across the street from nothing. The bank was quite naturally tiny: one old-fashioned teller's window with one old-fashioned teller, a man, and just one desk on the floor behind which sat an old white woman with a canister of platinum blond hair set upon her small head. Since the check I sought to cash was relatively large I went to the desk instead of the teller.

"I'd like to cash a check," I said.

"I see," she said without really looking up at me, though I knew that she had looked me over and was still doing so. "Well, have a seat and we'll see what we can do for you."

I sat.

"I don't believe you have an account with us."

"That's true, I don't have an account here. And it's a rather large check I'd like to cash," I told her.

"Hmmm. How large?"

"Fifty thousand dollars."

She whistled and I thought I saw a disbelieving smile behind her cat-eyed, horn-rimmed bifocals. "Hmmm. Is it a cashier's check?" she asked.

"No, it's my own personal check."

"I see." She showed no reaction. At least she showed no reaction that I, not knowing her, was able to read. She began to rearrange the items on her desk. She moved her stapler a few inches to her left, then her coffee cup of pencils and pens toward her a short distance. She fussed with the edge of the blotter. "The problem, young man. What is your name?"

"Poitier."

"The problem, Mr. Poitier, is that I don't know you."

"That's very true," I said.

"I've never seen you."

I nodded. I understood her position and her reservation completely. "Would it be possible for me to have the funds transferred here from another bank?"

"You mean a wire transfer?"

"Yes."

"You could do that. That would give us permission to dispense the money, but I'm afraid it wouldn't create the cash for us to dispense. You see, we don't have that kind of money."

"This is a bank?"

"A savings and loan," she corrected me. "Mr. Poitier, this is Smuteye, Alabama."

I nodded.

"The only reason I'm not stepping on the alarm under my desk, aside from the fact that it doesn't work, is that any fool can see that there's no money here in this godforsaken hamlet."

All of this was no doubt true, and I felt the requisite amount of pity for her and her community, but all I said was, "So, how would I go about getting my money?"

"I guess you could go over to Eufaula. Troy is closer. The bank in Perote might be able to help you. That's not far at all."

"Thank you." I started to leave, then asked, "Are there any ar-chitects around here?"

She pretended to consider my question. "I don't think so." I was impressed that she was able to say it without a hint of sarcasm. Neither did she show any interest in why I might need or want so much money in Smuteye.

I nodded.

As I drove those desolate Alabama back roads it became clear to me, through no feat of intellect, that my merely suggesting to someone that I'd like to cash a personal and out-of-state check for such a large amount would do far more than find a raised eyebrow as accompaniment to a resounding *no*. And like the Smuteye Farm-ers Savings and Loan, the local Western Union offices were not likely to have enough money to accommodate such a hefty wire. So I was left to wonder just how I would deliver the money I had promised to the sisters. I stopped at a truck stop, a lot full of big rigs and Confederate flags, and called Podgy from a pay phone. From where I sat I watched a fat trucker play a video game and watched another walk out of the washroom still brushing his teeth.

"Okay, Podgy, how can I get fifty grand down here to Smuteye, Alabama?" I asked.

"I will wire it to you."

"They don't . . . nobody here has that kind of money. Not even the Western Union office."

"You must go to a bigger city."

"Or you can bring it to me."

"I will not come to a place called Smuteye."

"Podgy," I whined.

"No." Then, away from the phone, he said, "Cool, I will be right there, my good dog."

"All right, Podgy. Find a bank in —" I looked at my map, "— Montgomery that can or will handle the transfer and let me know where it is. I'll call you in a few hours so you can tell me. What are you doing?"

"I am running your network."

"Good," I said. "Carry on."

"Awright, dog."

I hung up and rubbed my chin, found it stubbly. I bought a razor and some shaving cream in the little store and then walked into the giant washroom. There I shaved while truckers in undershirts brushed teeth and washed hairy pits. No matter how they scrubbed they looked nothing like Sidney Poitier, but I looked just like him and so they stared. They stared at Sidney Poitier's face in the mirror and I stared at it, too. The face was smooth, brown, older than I remembered, handsome. The face in the mirror smiled and I had to smile back.

It was very late afternoon when I arrived in Montgomery, and it was everything I thought it would be and less. It was a sad and depressed place, but it was clear it felt it had some chance of revival. People greeted me, waved, said hello, and were generally quite polite. I grabbed a bite in a diner in which every item on the menu was fried, ate a chicken-fried-steak sandwich and drank a very sweet iced tea. The banks were already closed, and I had yet to call Podgy to find out where I would collect my money. I had come to understand that my skin color and youth were an impediment to my being taken seriously, and so I thought I might overcome a bit of this appearance difficulty by at least dressing in a suit. I stopped at a JCPenney located in a mall on a giant circle of a road and bought one. It was black, the jacket snug fitting in the shoulders, the trousers tapering in the leg and slightly short at the ankle. With the crisp white shirt and the narrow black tie and black leather-soled shoes to replace my sneakers, I could have added dark glasses and been of the Fruit of Islam, but instead I was, I believed, nonthreatening, safe.

I checked myself into a motel, lay back on the too-soft bed, and called Podgy, and he told me the name and address of the bank that would be expecting me. I hung up and stared up at the particularly gross ceiling. I could have questioned my motives for helping the sisters, and the fact that I think it now must mean that somehow I did, but I don't recall doing so. I watched television and settled on my own network. Music video after music video, a gospel-music special, a stand-up so-called comedy hour, and *Punjabi Profiles.* I drifted in and out of sleep until I was moored in an awake state and looking back and forth at the lightening sky through partially closed blinds and paid programming about a very special mop. I remembered a troubling dream that I'd had. In it my new black dress shoes were far too small and this worried me greatly as I had someplace to be, but when I tried them in the morning they fit perfectly fine, oddly better than they had in the store.

At the First National Bank of Alabama, I straightened my tie and walked inside. The bank building was far larger than the one-room savings and loan in Smuteye. It was in fact grand. A uniformed guard stood near the glass and brass front doors, a line of tellers stood behind a grand carved wooden barrier, and an island of the same ornate wood dominated the center of the vast room. Behind the tellers, bank people did bank work and talked bank talk and walked bankly back and forth. I walked to the reception desk, signed the list, and sat in the waiting area.

The bank officer, a Miss Hornsby, who received me did not rise from the seat behind her desk, but said as I sat, "My, but you look just like Sidney Poitier. I mean just like him."

I nodded. "I'm Not Sidney Poitier."

"Of course you're not." She was a middle-aged woman who had probably grown up on a steady diet of Sidney Poitier. Her graying hair was dyed blond and her makeup did more to reveal cracks than cover them.

"No, what I'm telling you is that I'm Not Sidney Poitier."

"And I'm telling you I understand that fact."

I looked at my notes from having talked to Podgy. "Is there a Mr. Scrunchy here?"

She looked offended. "Yes, there is."

"May I speak to him?"

She was certainly offended. "I'll get him."

Extremely tall and bald Mr. Scrunchy answered the intercom call by walking over to Miss Hornsby's desk. "What seems to be the problem?" he asked.

"This man here, who has informed me that he is not Sidney Poitier, refuses to understand that I don't believe he is Sidney Poitier."

"So, you're Not Sidney Poitier," Scrunchy said.

"I am," I said.

"I've been expecting you. Why don't you come over to my desk, Mr. Poitier." Then to the woman, he said, "I'll take it from here, Miss Hornsby."

The stunned Miss Hornsby licked her painted lips and said nothing as I rose and followed Scrunchy to his office. Scrunchy walked with a slight limp, the rhythm of which I found it difficult to not fall into. I followed him into his office. One wall was a window that looked out into the bank. He walked around and sat behind his giant desk, and I sat opposite him in a chair somewhat lower than his.

"Mr. Poitier," he said.

I nodded. "Mr. Patel has arranged everything?" I said.

"He has, indeed. He wired the money this morning. If I may see some identification?"

I pulled my wallet from my hip pocket and removed my driver's license, realizing as I was doing so that it was bogus. I had never bothered to get a real one. He took it from me, glanced quickly at it, and returned it.

"I'm satisfied," he said.

"May I have my money?"

He signaled through the big window and across the room to

another man. "Of course you may have your money," he said. "It's an awful lot of cash to be carrying around."

The man came into the office, and he had with him a small green vinyl satchel that he placed on Scrunchy's desk. He was broad in the shoulders and thick in the belly, with sunken eyes and dark bushy brows punctuating his stern expression. He gave me the once-over and then walked out.

"Cheery."

Scrunchy pushed the bag across the desk toward me, and as he did I realized that he was frighteningly correct. It was a lot of money to be walking around with. The hairs on the back of my neck stood up.

"You should count it," Scrunchy said.

"I trust you," I lied.

"I'm afraid I have to insist that you count it. Liability and all that. You can do it right here. I should watch of course."

"Of course," I said.

And he did watch while I opened the satchel and pulled out ten-thousand-dollar bundle after ten-thousand-dollar bundle.

"It's all hundreds," the banker said.

"Of course," I said.

He watched while I counted to 100 five times, fanning through the bundles, having to stop and start over a couple of times.

"That's a lot of money," he said as I finished.

"Yes, it is."

"Well, if that's all," he said and turned his attention to a stack of pages on his desk.

With the money back in the bag, I stood to leave.

"Be careful, Mr. Poitier," he said without looking up.

I felt like an idiot walking out of the bank with the money. More, I felt like a sitting duck, a dead duck, a chump, easy pickings, a babe in the woods, dead meat, a victim waiting to happen, a complete and utter fool. In the bright sunlight I was immediately concerned with what or who was behind me, beside me, waiting for me. I hoped Podgy had not babbled anything to Scrunchy about Smuteye, so at least no one would know where I was going. I could hear him saying in his singsong way, "I must wire the money because I cannot bring myself to go to a place called Smuteye. What kind of name is that anyway?"

I suppose there is no need to mention how terrified I was as I fell in behind the wheel of my car. Though I was not savvy or talented enough to spot them, I knew they were there—the watchers, the robbers, the highwaymen, snaggletoothed spawn of aging grand dragons. I drove my shaking and stupid suited self to the edge of town and beyond, into deep Alabama. It was still early in the day. At least I had that going for me and then I imagined it would be going for them as well, as I was fairly easy to spot—my black face behind the wheel of my yellow Skylark. I drove past the suburbs and onto the highway and, when there were no cars in front of me or behind me, I pulled off onto a little dirt lane and from that into a firebreak, out of view from the road, There I sat, for hours, waiting and hoping that I was waiting for nothing. Cars hummed past on the highway, and I didn't know who they were or where they were going, only that they kept going. I fell asleep.

Night fell and I awoke to find it unwanted and all over me. I once again recalled the song "Stars Fell on Alabama" and again thought that was never true. This night was even darker than the last one. I moved to start my engine and then I heard it—singing or chanting. I reached up and removed the cover from my dome light, then removed the bulb. I opened the door and felt my way about twenty yards to the edge of a clearing. As if waiting for me to arrive, a torch was put to a tall cross, and it lit up darkness some two football fields from me. I watched the hooded heads walk around doing hooded things and making hooded speeches that I could not hear. The only thing that was certain was that I wasn't going anywhere at that moment. The white-clad idiots hadn't spotted me, and unless I decided to do something stupid like light a cigarette or shout out to them, they weren't going to. They prayed and sang and yakked, and then some two hours later they began to clear out in a single-file queue of glowing headlights. I waited until the last pickup was gone, and, not until I thought the cross was cold and only then, did I go back to my car, start it, and leave.

CHAPTER 6

It was just before daybreak when I pulled into the yard of the sisters. There was no one up, not even the chickens. I waited in my car, put my head back, and drifted off to sleep. I dreamed I died. I didn't know how, but I was dead and yet I was staring down at my dead face on the ground. I awoke to see my face in the outside rearview mirror. I looked dead enough. I glanced over the yard and saw a blue pickup truck that I hadn't seen in the darkness. The house door opened, and Sister Irenaeus emerged smiling and clapping her hands. She called back for the others, and they came out equally full of glee and good cheer. They must have smelled the cash. They danced around my car chanting some nonsense or other; two of them were lost in tongues. It all made for awful music as I worked my stiff limbs free of the car.

"Do you have our money?" Sister Irenaeus asked.

I didn't like the way she said *our* money, but I responded, "Yes."

Just then a man walked out of their quarters. A short, wide-shouldered man with a matching broad face and a shag of stringy white-blond hair. He had bad skin that somehow looked okay on him.

"This is Thornton Scrunchy," Sister Irenaeus said.

Well, of course he is, I thought, and nodded hello.

"He is our architect," she said.

"I didn't know you had an architect." There was something different about Sister Irenaeus. The other sisters were still prancing around like loons. But Sister Irenaeus was standing near me, with Thornton Scrunchy. Scrunchy's blue eyes were piercing, but only because of their color, I thought. In fact, he seemed to have the glassy-eyed look of an alcoholic or at least of someone who was drunk. There was a toothpick sticking out the corner of his mouth.

He shook my hand. "So, you're Mr. Poitier. Mr. Poitier. Mr. Poitier. The sisters have told me all about you."

"You're an architect here in the town of Smuteye?" I asked. "Smuteye, Alabama?"

"Well, that's a yes and a no," he said, "Mr. Poitier." He seemed to like saying my name. "You see, I'm a man of many professions. It's so kind of you to help the sisters out. They're such good souls." He turned to Sister Irenaeus. "We're going to build us a church, ain't we, Sister?"

"Praise the lord," she said.

Scrunchy stared at my face. "You look just like that Sidney Poitier, the Hollywood actor."

"I know," I said.

"But you're not Sidney Poitier."

"I am."

He moved the flat toothpick from the left side of his twisted lips to the right side of his twisted lips.

Remembering the Scrunchy from the bank in Montgomery, I asked, "Are there a lot of Scrunchys in Alabama?"

"Alabama, Georgia, Mississippi. There are Scrunchys all over, Mr. Poitier. Whether we're related, I can't tell you, but there's a mess of us. We Scrunchys have been around forever. I heard tell we was on the *Mayweather.*"

"*Mayflower,*" I said.

"You have our money," Sister Irenaeus said.

"Some of it," I lied.

"How much?" Scrunchy asked.

I looked at him.

"Well, we need to get moving on this thing."

"So, do you have some plans drawn up?" I asked.

"I do," he said. "Been working on them all night. They're right here inside on the big table."

I followed him to the door. I looked to Sister Irenaeus, but could not read her face. It was no surprise; I didn't know her well enough to read the most obvious expressions. "Sister, when did you find this guy? Where did you find this guy? Why did you find this guy?"

"You said we needed plans. He has drawn the plans," she said. "He made the blueprints so that we can build our church."

Inside the house country music was playing. I looked to the corner and saw a stack of 45s on an old turntable. Patsy Cline was singing. I recognized her voice, but the song I did not know. It was a lament, or so I thought, but with all the dancing and howling in tongues, I couldn't really hear. On the table was a rolled-up sheet of white paper, about two feet long. Scrunchy unfurled and held it open with his soft-looking and meaty hands.

"Well, here it is," he said.

I looked. The drawing was just slightly more detailed and skilled than the little piece of paper I had been shown earlier. It was a crude pencil sketch of a rectangular building with a pitched roof and a steeple on one end, and beside it was a floor plan that showed there was nothing to it but four exterior walls. There were no measurements or marks indicating windows or doors or any other architectural symbols. I looked at them in turn.

"These aren't blueprints," I said. "They're not even blue. This is a sketch and a bad one at that."

"Well, son, this is just a start. I just got hired yesterday. The sisters have been asking me to help all along, but they didn't have any money."

"And now we do," Sister Irenaeus said.

"Not yet," I said.

"You know how it is," Scrunchy said. He nodded to me as if I knew what he was talking about. "People are always coming to me and asking for plans, then they look at them and go build it themselves."

"Do you have a state license?" I asked.

"I'm not a contractor," he said. "Ain't that something, the way them gals blather on like that?"

"God has sent you with our money," Sister Irenaeus said.

"Well, he sent me with some of it," I said. "He sent me with a thousand dollars to get Mr. Scrunchy here going on the blueprints."

"That is all?" she asked.

"For right now," I said. I watched her shoulders sag and observed the disappointment on her face. "I'll get it."

The other sisters had caught on that not all was well and had stopped chanting and howling and dancing and merely looked at us from across the room. They stood there with their shoulders waiting to sag.

I left them inside and went to my car. I opened the satchel in the backseat and tore the band from a stack. I took ten hundreds and looked at the forty-nine thousand remaining dollars. It was bad enough that some people driving around believed I had this and worse that in fact I did. I took the thousand dollars back inside.

"This is all?" Sister Irenaeus said.

"For now," I repeated.

Scrunchy took the bills and fanned them through a count. "This will work for my retainer. You will be able to pay me for the rest of my services?"

"How much will it cost, the rest of your services?"

"I would say about five grand, I mean, a thousand more for a complete set of expertly rendered and delivered blueprints," he said. He glanced at Sister Irenaeus and smiled.

"I can get that much," I said.

"You said fifty thousand dollars," Sister Irenaeus said.

"That's a lot of money, Sister," I said. "I couldn't get it all at once." In my mind loomed the fact that I had in a matter of twenty-four hours met two people named Scrunchy. If that was not an incredible coincidence, then the pock-faced man in front of me was well aware that I had the balance of the fifty thousand dollars in my possession, stashed somewhere, if not on me. So, I added, trying to sound confident, savvy, like anything but the clueless idiot that I truly was, "I'd be a fool to travel with that much money on me at once."

"I suppose you would be, son," Scrunchy said. He turned to Sister Irenaeus. "Well, Sister, I guess I'll go get to work on those blueprints." Then again to me, "You take care now." He walked out, got into his truck, and drove away.

"Do you trust that guy?" I asked Sister Irenaeus.

"I do," she said. "Where is the money?"

"It's coming."

"We must build the church," she said.

"I understand that, Sister." I looked at the faces of the other women. They seemed more confused than disappointed or put out. Now, their shoulders sagged. "I'm going to grab a bite at the diner."

I walked out to my car. They didn't follow. I drove away and stopped just beyond the bend in the drive, still hidden from the road. I got out, took the satchel from the floor in the back, and concealed it under some brush at the base of a twisted and memorable tree. I kept a thousand with me. As I fell in again behind the wheel I observed my face in the mirror. I looked so much older, felt so much older, stiff, and beleaguered. If I hadn't known better I would have said I had a gray hair.

At the diner, I found Diana Frump shaking her ample rump under her white waitress dress to country music on the jukebox. A couple of men were watching her and laughing. She stopped when she saw me.

"And he's wearing a suit," Diana said. "Looking sharp there, Mr. Poitier. Who died?"

I'd forgotten I was wearing the suit. I must have been a sight after sleeping in the car in it. "I might think I did," I said.

"Come on in, Sidney," she said. "Have a sit-down."

I sat at the end of the counter. "A party?" I asked.

"Yep," she said. "A party because work's coming to Smuteye. I heard tell that them sisters got money to build their church. That means construction, that means construction workers, that means customers for me. A party. What can I get you?" She walked to the other side of the counter.

"A burger," I said.

"Cheese?"

"Okay," I said.

"Ain't got none." She laughed. "Just foolin' with you." She slapped a fist of meat on the griddle. "Yeah, them sisters found somebody to foot the bill. I guess praying ain't such a bad gig."

"Some fool," one of the men said. He was wearing a John Deere cap. "But I'll take the work."

"You know somebody named Scrunchy?" I asked Diana.

"Thornton Scrunchy?"

"Yes."

"Never heard of him," she said, then laughed again. "Just foolin' with you. Yeah, he lives around here. Owns some land. I hear a lot of land, over by the river. He had something or other to do with the paper mill way back when." She studied my face for a second. "Why?"

"Is he an architect?"

"Elroy, is Scrunchy an architect?"

"Thornton Scrunchy is a lot of things," said the man in the cap. "An architect? I don't know."

"He ain't no architect," said the other man, a fat man. "I reckon he's a Baptist jest like the rest of us."

The screen door opened and slammed shut, and I turned to see a policeman of some kind standing rigid, in dark glasses and a Smokey Bear hat that wore him. He was a skinny, young man with a bad shave. He rested his right hand on his sidearm, a large-caliber revolver, and rested his eyes on me.

"Hey, Horace," Diana said.

"Diana," he said.

I looked away from him and at my near-ready burger sizzling on the griddle. Diana watched the man behind me, seemed nervous as she flipped the patty once more. I felt the deputy approach me, hover at my shoulder.

"What's your name, boy?" the deputy asked.

"This here is Sidney Poitier, Horace," Diana said.

"Not the Sidney Poitier," Horace said.

"No," I said. "Not Sidney Poitier." I knew it was a bad idea to say that as soon as I opened my mouth.

"Why don't you step out and put your hands on that counter for me," the deputy said.

I turned to look back at him. "What did I do?"

"I think you know what you done," he said.

I supposed that was true of all of us, and in a strange way I found it a reasonable utterance.

"Now, I ain't gonna ask you again." He released the leather keep on his holster. "Hands on the counter and spread them legs."

"What's this boy done?" asked the man in the tractor cap.

"I think I done caught myself a murderer." The deputy seemed ready to giggle he was so excited.

"You don't say," said the fat man.

I leaned against the counter as instructed, and Horace kicked my feet into a wider stance. He then frisked my torso, under my jacket, and then moved down to the pockets of my trousers. He found the lump of cash in my front pocket.

"What do we have here?" he said. He pulled the wad of bills out, looked at it, and whistled. "Boy, howdy!"

"What is it, Horace?" asked tractor cap.

"A ton of money." The deputy leaned closer to me. "This here is a lot of money for a nigger to be carrying around."

I cleared my throat and said, quite without good judgment, "One, I'm not a nigger, and two, that's not that much money."

"Oh, I got me an uppity one," the deputy said.

"He's uppity, all right," tractor cap said. "Tell by that suit."

"How much money he got?" from the fat man.

"Ten crisp one-hundred-dollar bills," the deputy said.

Tractor cap whistled. "That must be close to a thousand."

"Pretty close," I said.

"Shut up, boy."

I shut up.

The deputy reached out and took my left wrist and pulled it behind my back, slapped a cuff on it, and then said, "Put the other back here." I did and I was cuffed. "Don't you try running now."

"I won't run," I said.

"Okay, let's go." Horace put his hand in the center of my back and shoved me through the screen door and across the gravel to his battered squad car. He opened the back and muscled me down into the seat. He let out a rebel yell and said, "Have mercy. I done caught myself a crook."

I tried to get comfortable against the ripped vinyl, but my hands were tied behind me and my suit coat was bunched up. I pressed my face against the cool, dirty window and looked at my Skylark as we rolled away. Just down the road from the Smuteye Farmers Savings and Loan was the Smuteye Police Station.

Deputy Horace rooster-strutted into the crumbling station house with me in tow. "I got him, I got him," he said in a singsong. When the big-haired dispatcher asked him who, he said, "The killer, the killer." I wondered as I observed the woman sitting at the ancient radio set whom and to what would be dispatched in Smuteye. Horace pushed me through the first room and into the dank back where the cells were. He opened a barred door and roughly shoved me in. I stumbled, but I didn't fall. I sat on a metal bed that was attached to the cinder-block wall and looked up to see a filthy white man sitting on the bunk opposite me.

"Nice suit," he said.

"Got it in Montgomery," I said.

"Good place to buy a suit. What are you in here for?"

"I don't know. You?"

"Stealing," he said.

"Stealing what?"

He shrugged. "I steal a lot of things. It's kinda what I do." He studied me for a second. "You ain't from around here."

"The suit give me away?"

He laughed. "Funny nigger." Then, "Naw, just the fact that I ain't never seen you before."

The arrest in the diner and drive in the cigarette smoke–soaked squad car and the hustle back to the dingy cell all seemed unreal enough that I felt simply lost. Now, sitting in the cell across from my fellow prisoner, the reality of the situation settled on me. I began to shake. I held out my hand and looked at it.

"Scared?" the man asked.

I nodded.

"At least you ain't no fool."

I was in fact terrified. It was a ghostly kind of fear, a kind of distant growl or rumble in the ground. I was in jail and being accused of murder. I had a notion that I could just get up and walk out, but I knew that was just a way to get myself shot. And I didn't want the last words I heard in life to be, "I got me one." My stomach felt empty and icy and hot and crowded all at once. My stupid foot tapped with a mind of its own, and I stupidly watched it.

"What's your name?" he asked.

"Poitier."

"That French or something?"

I nodded.

"My name is Last."

"Last?"

"Yeah, last face you'll ever see." He laughed hard.

There was commotion in the front of the station. I lay back and looked at the ceiling. Horace came to the door and told me to get up. "Come on, boy, the Chief's here, and he wants to see the killer I caught."

"Who is it that I'm supposed to have killed?" I asked.

"Woooeee, don't you talk pretty, boy," the deputy said. "Just get your black ass up and out here."

The bald, wide Chief was sitting in his office trying to get a drawer open. "Horace, didn't I tell you to fix this here drawer?"

"Yes, sir."

"Well, did you fix it?"

"Not yet." Horace pushed me in the middle of my back farther into the room. "Chief, here's the prisoner."

"You a killer, boy?" the Chief asked.

"I've killed no one," I said.

"See how he talks, Chief."

"Shut up, Horace."

"Just where were you yesterday morning?" the Chief asked.

"I was in Montgomery."

The Chief bit his lower lip and looked up and out the window. "Anybody see you there?"

"A banker named Scrunchy."

"Horace, did you ask the prisoner any questions?"

"No, sir. But I ain't never seen this boy before. And he had all this money on him, just stuck down in his pocket." The deputy pointed to the wad on the desktop in front of the Chief. "That's close to a thousand dollars."

The Chief counted the money and frowned at Horace. "Pretty close." He looked at me. "This here is a lot of money, boy."

"Not really," I said.

"Whoa, he say 'not really.' You hear that, deputy? He say 'not really.'"

"I heard it, Chief."

The Chief picked up my wallet, opened it. "Not Sidney Poitier," he said, looking at my license. "That your name?"

I nodded.

"Where you from, boy?"

"Like the license says, Atlanta."

"Atlanta," he repeated. "Big city. What you doin' here, boy?"

"Passing through. And don't call me boy."

"What do they call you in Atlanta?" he asked.

"They call me Mr. Poitier."

"Well, *Mister* Poitier, you can go on back to your room now while I call me a fella named Scrunchy in Montgomery. What bank was that?"

"First National Bank of Alabama."

"You do a lot of business with banks, do you?"

"Some."

"Take him on back there, Horace." The Chief gave me one last disdainful glance. "Then I want to see you in here, you hear me?"

"I hear you, Chief."

Deputy Horace took me back to the cell and I sat on the same bunk and looked across at the same face. "So, what's your name?"

"Why, I'm Clark Gable."

"Pleased to meet you."

"You can call me Billy."

"I'll do that."

"So, they say you killed somebody," Billy said. He was sitting way back on his bunk, his back against the wall. I noticed that he had one boot off.

"That's what they say."

"Well, I don't believe it," Billy said. "You don't look like you could kill nobody."

I understood this to be intended as an insult, and the thought occurred to me that I should take it as one as a matter of decorum, but I didn't. I looked at him looking at me. "You're right, I couldn't."

"Hmmm. So, who did you kill?"

"I don't know yet," I said. "I take it you live around here. What do you do? To pay the bills, I mean?"

"A little of this. A little of that. Now and then. Off and on." He ran a hand through his greasy hair. "Steal."

Horace came back to the cell door. "Okay, boy, on your feet. Chief wants to see you again."

I followed the deputy back into the Chief's office. Horace pushed me to the chair in front of the desk and gestured for me to sit. The Chief was chasing a fly around the room with a swatter. He missed again.

"I suppose you can do better," he said as he sat.

"Did you call the bank?" I asked.

The Chief called into the outer office. "Horace, get your sorry ass in here right this second."

Horace entered and sheepishly walked over to stand by the window. He looked at his shoes.

"I want you to hear this, Horace," the Chief said.

"Yes, sir," Horace said.

"Well, *Mister* Poitier, I called the bank in Montgomery, and I talked to this Scrunchy, and it turns out he remembers you."

"Therefore?"

"Therefore?" the Chief repeated, leaning back in his chair and looking at me with his head tilted. "Therefore? You hear that, Horace? Therefore."

"I told you he talks fancy. Don't he talk fancy?"

"Shut up, Horace," the Chief said without looking at the deputy. "Therefore, *Mister* Poitier, you couldn't have killed our dead man. And you know something? I don't like you."

I said nothing. I glanced over at Horace. He seemed amused. His ugly face seemed ready to break into a giggle.

The Chief looked at Horace, too. "And I sure as hell don't like you right now, Horace."

Horace straightened.

The Chief looked at me while holding the wad of bills in his hand. "You still ain't told me where you got this money."

"I got it from the bank. It's my money."

He looked at it in his hand, then pushed it across the desk to me along with my wallet.

"So, I can go?" I said.

"I don't think just yet. I need you to take a look at our dead man and tell us if you know him."

"Why?" I asked.

"Because I don't know who he is," the Chief barked.

"Well, I don't know anybody around here."

"That's good, that's good. Because the dead man ain't from around here. If he was, I would know who he is. He's got that in common with you. That and the fact that he's a black boy."

"I don't know him," I said.

"You might know him. It's possible. You never know. Just do me this favor, *Mister* Poitier."

I didn't want to look at a dead man, and yet in some way I knew I had to. I looked out the window behind Horace at the late afternoon light. I remembered the money hidden under that tree. I felt cold with fear.

"Do you know another guy named Scrunchy? His name is Thornton, and he's from around here? A strange-looking man." I thought of the banker. "I mean, how many Scrunchys are there?"

Horace blurted out a laugh. "Hell, boy, you can't turn around in these parts without bumping heads with a Scrunchy."

His answer, not surprisingly, did not make me feel better. I was certain that there was no answer to that question that would.

"What about Thornton Scrunchy?" the Chief asked.

"Is he an architect?"

"I doubt it." The Chief stood and walked around his desk. "Come on, let's go look at the stiff."

I stood on still-unsteady legs and realized for the first time that my feet were hurting from the dress shoes that no longer perfectly fit.

The Chief led the way outside, then along the road two doors down to a one-story wooden house with a sign on the lawn that simply read, *Undertaking*. We walked in through the front door without knocking.

"Donald!" the Chief called out. "Don-ald!"

"Who is that yelling in here?" a tall, gray-headed man said as he came out of the back. "Chief?"

"Yeah, it's me."

Donald adjusted the straps of his overalls and regarded me suspiciously. "What's this all about?"

"Where's the body?" the Chief asked.

"Which body?"

"How many bodies do you have, Donald?"

"Just one."

"Well, that one."

"What about it?" Donald asked.

"I want to see him," the Chief said.

"Him, too?" Donald pointed to me with his nose.

"Him, too. Now, where is he?"

"I got him out in the garage." Donald turned and started away toward the back of the house.

"Garage?" I said.

"It's also my lab," the man said without looking back.

The Chief looked at me, seemed embarrassed. "Donald is our coroner. Sort of by default."

"I heard that," Donald said.

"I know you heard me, Donald. That's why I said it."

We entered the kitchen, passed through another back room with stacked magazines, *Boys' Life* and *Outdoor Gazette* and *National Geographic,* and through a door into what really was the garage. There was an old Plymouth on blocks on the far side and a stainless-steel table in the middle of the near side. Against the wall opposite the garage doors were three white chests that looked like deep freezers. Donald led us to the middle one.

"Here he is," Donald said, then pulled up the lid. He stood there, his arm extended, holding it open. He scratched his neck with his free hand.

I was standing well behind the Chief, and he turned to look at me. "Well, step on up here. I've already seen him. Just tell me if you know him."

I moved forward and leaned over. The man was young, black, with short-cropped hair. His eyes were closed. His lips were slightly parted. He was circumcised. He looked just like me. He looked exactly like me, a fact that was apparently lost on Donald and the Chief. I wanted to say, "That's me." The thought of saying it was strange feeling and scary. My chest was tight, and my ears were ringing. I was lying in the chest, and yet I wasn't. I said, "I don't know him." I was lying, I thought.

"Okay," the Chief said. "Close it up, Donald."

Donald let down the lid. "I heard somebody say that he came here to help them crazy nuns or whatever they are."

"What killed him?" I asked.

Donald cleared his throat. "Somebody smashed him on the back of the head with something harder than his skull."

"How do you know when he was killed?" I asked.

The Chief cocked his head and looked at me. "Because one minute he wasn't there, and the next minute he was, along with a lot of blood that wasn't nowhere except under him."

"Chief," I said, "I'd like to help you find the killer."

"That's a weird thing for you to say. What makes you think I'm looking for a killer?" he said.

"I just thought . . ."

"For all I know this boy beat himself in the back of the head with a bat. You want to find yourself a killer, go ahead." He looked at the ceiling and over at the disassembled Plymouth. "There ain't nothing here that makes a difference to nobody. Do what you want."

The face of the dead man haunted me. I stared at the closed lid of the deep freezer.

The Chief yawned. "Can we get out this way?" He pointed to the wide garage doors.

Donald hit a switch on the wall and one of the doors rolled up.

The sight of the late afternoon turning to dusk terrified me. There were people out there looking for me, wanting my fifty thousand dollars. I knew they would kill me for it and I wondered if in fact they already had. As we stepped out of the makeshift morgue I thought that if that body in the chest was Not Sidney Poitier, then I was not Not Sidney Poitier and that by all I knew of logic and double negatives, I was therefore Sidney Poitier. I was Sidney Poitier.

"When we get back to your office, may I use your phone? Collect call. After all, I never got my one. Don't prisoners usually get one call?"

"Yes, you *may*. One," he said. "One call. Collect."

Back in the dimly lit police station I placed a collect call to Podgy, who again reaffirmed his absolute refusal to come to any place called Smuteye. "What even does that mean?" he asked.

"I don't know. You don't have to come. Just call Ted and Professor Everett and tell them that I need them here."

Podgy said he would, and I hung up. I looked around at the station walls, at Horace in the corner watching me, at the dispatcher who might have been sleeping, at the calendar with a woman leaning over an Oldsmobile beside the passage to the cells, at the open door to the Chief's office. I wanted to ask if I could spend the night there, but I knew what that answer would be. Hell, they were probably tied in with the people who were after my money. I stepped over to the Chief's door.

"This might be a stupid question, but is there a motel in Smuteye?" I asked. I leaned against the jamb.

"No," he said, "there's no motel, but I do know where you can rent a room." He looked at his desk and nervously rearranged some papers. "I just now got off the phone. That was the state police over in Montgomery, and they told me that them boys up in Washington want this murder solved or they're gonna come down here and go through all of our drawers, the ones in my desk and the ones I'm wearing. They say this is a matter of civil rights. I say it's a matter of a boy being dead. I don't want no suits down here crawling up my ass. You think you can figure this out?"

"I'm not a cop."

"You're a smart guy. You don't think you can help the dumb crackers?" He smiled smugly at me. "Don't you want show up us peckerwoods?"

"I can find out who killed him." I didn't know why I said that, except for the fact that I somehow believed I would be investigating my own murder. I wanted to know who would kill me.

"You didn't think that man over there looked just like me?" I asked.

"You all look alike to me."

I felt stupid for having set that one up.

"Stay around and show up the poor white folks," he said.

"I think I will," I said. "I've asked some friends to come here. They'll help." Truth was I didn't know whether either of them would come, and I certainly didn't know whether they would help or whether they could help. But I wanted someone to know that someone knew where I was. I was, in effect, trying to cover my ass, my tremendously exposed and vulnerable ass. My black ass. "Where's this room that I can rent?"

"My house," the Chief said.

The Chief's house was a clapboard box set on cinder-block footings stuck far off the road in the center of a clearing of thin pines. The slow night drive there in his somewhat less foul-smelling police car was a bit nerve-racking. The idea of this white, rednecked, little southern town sheriff, or whatever he was, driving an unarmed, naïve, and solitary and stupid black man into the deep woods was unsettling at best, surreally terrifying at worst. The headlights panned across the yard and settled on the house. It was predictably dark, and it had the look of a man who lived alone.

"It ain't much, but it's paid for," he said.

"How much for the room?" I asked. "We never talked about that." I was afraid of what he might say. He knew that I had a thousand dollars on me. I wondered again if he knew about the rest of the money. Even if he wasn't involved with the people trying to get my money, perhaps Scrunchy had told him on the phone about my business in Montgomery.

"You know the kind of money you're carrying around is enough to get a boy killed," he said.

"I'll keep that in mind."

We walked into the front room. The Chief walked through the darkness to a standing lamp in the corner and switched it on. There was a saggy sofa, the original color of which was a mystery, and a matching stuffed chair. There was a rolltop desk under a window. There were no curtains on the windows. There were no rugs on the linoleum floor.

"You never told me how much the rent is."

"You don't have to pay me anything," he said. "Have a seat." He moved some magazines from the sofa, but I sat on the chair.

I sat.

"You want a drink?"

"I guess." I was uncomfortable. I was especially uncomfortable with the fact that he was all of a sudden acting cordially. "What are we drinking?"

"Rye whiskey," he said. He took a bottle from the desk and brought two glasses to the coffee table in front of me. He sat on the sofa, leaning forward. He poured the whiskey. "You like rye?"

"Never tried it," I said.

He laughed. "Drink it slow."

I sipped the drink. It burned my throat, but I didn't gag or cough, thus surprising myself, and so I think I let go a little smile.

"Good, ain't it?" he said.

On top of the desk was a dark lamp and a photograph. I stood and took the glass of whiskey with me. I was determined to nurse the three fingers he had poured for as long as possible. I walked over to the picture, looked at it without switching on the lamp. It was of a woman.

"Who's this?" I asked.

"My mama," the Chief said. "She's dead now."

"Did she live with you here?"

His eyes narrowed. "No, she did not live with me here. Does this look like the kind of house a decent lady would live in?"

I looked around at the bare windows, the dingy walls. "This house isn't so bad," I lied.

He knocked back the rest of the whiskey in his glass and automatically poured himself another. "How you doin'?" he asked. "That's enough whiskey for you, boy. Your judgment is already impaired." He laughed.

"Maybe so," I said. I sat back down.

"What do you do back there in Atlanta?"

"Nothing," I said, quite honestly.

"How do you make your money?"

"Inheritance."

"So, you're rich."

"You could say that."

"Well," the Chief said. "Around here, we're poor, dirt poor."

I nodded.

"You got a girlfriend?"

"Why do you ask?"

"Just curious."

His curiosity was strange and a bit annoying. I watched his lids get heavy. "I don't. Do you have a girlfriend?"

He laughed. I must have looked as if I were pitying him because he said, "No pity, now, boy. I don't need your pity. Nosiree, I do not need your pity." He poured himself another glass.

"Do you drink like this every night?" I asked.

"What if I do?"

I shrugged. "Expensive habit," I said, pretty much because I could think of nothing else.

He knocked back that glass and glared at me before closing his eyes, either because he could no longer stand to look at me or because he couldn't keep them open. I was trying to figure out where I was and why. I understood that I was in his house because he had more or less arranged it, but it was also clear that I was there because I was afraid to be anywhere else. I didn't know whether he was aware of my hidden money. He certainly knew I had a thousand dollars, which seemed to be a fortune to most of the residents of Smuteye, though he seemed unimpressed enough. Certainly this man didn't believe that I could help him solve a crime. However, I in part had chosen to remain because I needed to solve the murder; I believed somehow that the body I had seen in the freezer was my own. I sat there through the night as the dust and mustiness bothered my nose, the policeman's snoring filled the room, the sick light from the lamp at once too harsh and too dim.

The morning came with my stupid ass still sitting in that same lumpy chair. Watching. Watching the red, puffy, snoring face of the Chief. Watching the rain. As soon as there was light, there was rain—a hard-driving rain with wind that bent the pines severely. While he continued to sleep I got up and walked into the kitchen. To my surprise, it was not the sty I expected. It was in fact spotless. The sink was extremely white and the short curtains above it were crisp, bright yellow, and pulled aside evenly. One cup and one saucer were left on the drying rack. I actually turned to look at the doorway to the living room to be sure I was still in the same house. It was so strangely clean that I felt uncomfortable and so returned to my chair.

"Storm," the Chief said, waking, rubbing his eyes. He sat up and poured himself another drink. "You sleep?"

I shook my head. "What now?"

"You're the one that wants to find a killer."

"What do you know about me?" I asked. "I mean what did the bank man tell you about my business with him?"

"He just told me he remembered seeing you."

I wanted to believe him. "He didn't tell you what my business was?"

The Chief just looked at me.

"Do you think that dead man looks like me? And don't give me that shit about how we all look alike."

"A little."

"A lot."

"Okay," he said. "A lot. What's your point?"

"I was in Montgomery picking up fifty thousand dollars," I told him and then waited for a reaction to show on his face. None appeared. This I found odd. "That doesn't surprise you?"

He drank from his glass. "What do you want me to say, Sidney? You want me to say, 'Wow, that's a lot of money'? What do you expect?"

"I don't know what I expect."

For whatever unfathomable and idiotic reason I decided to level with him further. "I became afraid that I was followed from the bank, that somebody was going to steal my money. And then when I met that Thornton Scrunchy, you know with the same last name as the guy from the bank, I got really scared."

Still, he listened without showing any reaction.

"Why so much cash?"

"It was for the sisters. It's for their church. They seemed to think god sent me down here to build their blasted temple. I don't know how to build anything, so I had some money wired to the bank in Montgomery. The money was for them. I would have given it to them, but that Scrunchy was there."

"So, you're one of them good Samaritans."

I laughed. "An idiot."

"Where's the money now?"

"I hid it."

"Good move."

"Is this where you point a pistol at my head and make me take you to it?" I asked, half smiling.

He swallowed the last of what was in his glass. "No, this is where I close my eyes and sleep for another five or ten minutes. You think about this killer you want to catch. Maybe I'll dream about your kind of money. Fifty thousand good ol' Uncle Samuel Greenbacks. Man oh man." He laughed softly as he seemed to drift off.

If I wasn't digging myself deeper, I was certainly lengthening the trench. The rain was not letting up, but was now smashing into the windows. I couldn't see the trees clearly anymore.

What I did see clearly was the murder of the doppelganger of Not Sidney Poitier. He was struck on the back of the head by a redneck named Thornton Scrunchy who was subsequently disappointed to find no cash in the dead man's pockets. Probably every KKK-connected miscreant in a five-county swath of Alabama was in on the murder and the search for the money. Whether the Chief was, I obviously didn't know. But as he slept there I resolved to attempt to Fesmerize him upon his waking. I thought I might have a better chance and an easier job if I awoke him before he was ready. I perched myself on the edge of my seat and leaned into my stare — my eyebrow arched, my head tilted slightly, and I cleared my throat, again, louder, again. The man stirred, slowly opened his eyes, grew immediately alarmed by my posture, then fell into what I recognized as a successful Fesmerian submersion. He sat there even more like a lump and stared into the space that was me.

"Can you hear me, Chief?" I asked.

"Yes."

"Tell me your full name."

"My name is Francis Rene Funk."

"Really?" I leaned closer to him. "When did you learn about the fifty thousand dollars?"

"When you told me," he said.

"Do you know who killed the man in the chest?"

"No."

"Do you suspect anyone?"

"Yes," he said.

"Whom do you suspect?"

"Thornton Scrunchy."

"Why?"

"Because of what you said. He thought the black boy looked like you. He does look like you."

"Do you want to hurt me?"

"No," he said.

"Will you hurt me?" I asked.

"I don't know."

"Do you believe my life is in danger?"

"Yes."

"Look into my eyes," I told him, and when he did, I said, 'When I say 'Chief, I need your help,' you will help me. Do you understand?"

"Yes."

"You will defend me, protect me if I need you, if anyone is trying to hurt me. Do you understand?"

"Yes."

I told him to go back to sleep and wake up in ten minutes. I sat there just a little less afraid than I had been, convinced at least of the fact the man with me meant me no harm. I was certainly no less confused. I felt terribly guilty for the man who looked enough like me to have been killed. I didn't know what to do about the money. I had been stupid about it. I should have taken Sister Irenaeus to the bank and simply had her open an account, but it was too late to change any of that. I thought of the money hidden in the satchel and wondered how it was faring in the rain and wind. For all I knew one-hundred-dollar bills were floating all over southern Alabama.

The rain was letting up when Chief Francis Rene Funk awoke, but there was no sign or promise of a blue sky to come. There was only gray, dark clouds, wind, and mud. We got back into the Chief's car and slipped and slid our way back to the highway. We drove to the diner, and I saw my car in the parking lot, at least what was left of it. It had been stripped and left open and bleeding in the pouring rain. The only consolation to what I saw as the loss of a friend was the fact that the thugs had not found what they were looking for.

"What now, city boy?" the Chief asked.

I shook my head, shrugged.

"Well, let's eat something." He parked beside my Skylark. "Need to eat something."

"Tell me, Chief, what is a Smuteye?"

"You never had corn smut? Come on, boy."

In the diner, Diana was surprised and pleased to see me. "Sidney," she said. "They didn't kill you?"

"That's a matter of opinion," I said.

She laughed.

"Give this boy some corn smut," the Chief said.

"You sure you're ready for this?" Diana asked.

"No. What is it?"

"Corn cancer is what it is," said the man in the tractor cap who was sitting right where he had been seated when I was arrested.

"It's a fungus," she said. "Tastes real good. We eat it with eggs. The Mexicans called it *Huitlacoche*."

"What Mexicans?" I asked.

"The two that come through here about three years ago. They said it means raven shit."

I looked at the Chief's face and recalled his charge to not let any harm come to me. I nodded. "Okay, let me have some."

Diana scrambled some eggs in a pan, divided them onto two plates, slapped some toast beside the servings, and the opened a plain jar from which she scraped black matter. She slid the plates in front of us.

"Have at," the Chief said. "The Mexicans said it's good for you-know." He glanced down at his crotch.

"What happened to these Mexicans?" I asked.

The Chief smirked. "Well, we chased them into the swamp, and one of them never come out. We caught the other one, what was left of him, and sent him to the county jail farm."

"What did they do?" I asked.

"I don't rightly recall."

I finally took a bite of the corn smut. I didn't gag like I thought I might. It was a little like mushrooms. I at once sort of liked it and wanted to spit it out across the counter.

"What do you think?" Diana asked.

I was saved from having to answer by the opening of the screen door. A familiar voice split the room.

"Anybody here seen a fellow who looks just like Sidney Poitier?" It was Ted.

"Ted," I said.

"Nu'ott?"

"It's me," I said.

"If you say so. Podgy told me you needed some help. What are you eating?"

"It's called corn smut," I said.

"And you're eating it? Is it good?"

I shrugged.

Ted looked at Diana. "Hey," he said.

"Hey," said Diana.

"Fix me up a plate of that," Ted said.

"You can have mine," I said.

Ted sat beside me, and I pushed my plate in front of him. "Ted Turner," I said, "this is the chief of police."

"How you doing?" Ted said, a mouth full of eggs and corn smut. "This ain't terrible." He pointed his fork at Diana. "But I wouldn't order it a second time. No offense."

"None taken," she said.

"And this is Diana," I said.

"You ever notice how some people spell your name with two n's and some with one? How do you spell it?"

"One," Diana said.

"Now, see, that makes sense to me. Why would you need two of them doing the same duty? What is this shit called again?"

"Corn smut," I said.

"I don't doubt it. Tell me, Nu'ott, why am I here?"

"Someone is trying to kill me," I said.

He looked at the plate in front of him.

"Not with that."

"Don't be so sure."

I wanted to suggest to him further that perhaps I had already been killed, but that would have sounded as crazy to him as it did to me. "I did something stupid. I needed fifty thousand dollars to help these religious women build a church, and I got it in cash, and now somebody wants to kill me for it."

Diana and the tractor-cap man were hearing about the money for the first time, and their mouths dropped open. The story I had just tried to tell in shorthand would have come across as nutty and surreal to anyone but Ted.

"Did you get your money in twenties or hundreds?" Ted asked.
"Hundreds."

"That's where you went wrong. People go crazy for hundred-dollar bills. You can give a caddy seven twenties and he'll forget you in a week, but give him a hundred, and he'll remember you forever." He nodded to the Chief. "And that's why I don't play golf."

"Who are you?" the Chief asked.

"My name's Ted Turner. What's yours?"

"Chief."

"Interesting." He ate another bit of corn smut. "You know, Diana-with-one-n, this isn't half bad. It's more like three-quarters bad."

"Glad you like it," Diana said.

Just then Horace burst into the trailer. "I got him, Chief! This time I got me the right one! No question about it!"

"Got who?" the Chief asked.

"The killer. Caught him snooping around the outside of the hardware store. He's a nigger, so I arrested him."

"Well, let's go see what the hell you're talking about." The Chief slid off his stool and walked out. Horace, Ted, and I followed.

"What exactly is going on here?" Ted asked me as we sat in the backseat of the Chief's car.

"I'm not sure," I said.

At the police station, we filed in and heard laughter coming from the cells. The big-haired dispatcher said, "Been like that since you put him back there, Horace."

The Chief walked toward the back, and I followed. And there was Professor Everett, doing push-ups and counting loudly. "Sixty-three." He paused at the top and laughed. "Sixty-four."

Billy, my former cellmate, was counting with him, laughing as well.

"What the hell is going on here?!" the Chief shouted.

"Push-ups," Everett said.

My first thought was that he could not possibly have done sixty-four push-ups. My second thought was an affirmation of my previous suspicion that Horace's murder suspect was Everett.

Everett sat on the floor, his back against the wall. "Okay, Billy Bob Jack, whatever-the-fuck your name is. Beat that." He looked up at me and smiled. "I've been working out."

"I guess so."

"How are you, Mr. Poitier?" Everett asked.

"You realize you're in here for murder," I said.

"My friend Billy told me as much. Who did I kill?"

"Me," I said.

He looked me up and down. "I didn't do a very good job."

"Who is this guy?" the Chief asked me.

"He's one of my professors. I called and asked him to come down here."

The Chief moaned. "Horace, would you please let this man out of the cell? And don't speak to me for the rest of the day."

"Yes, sir," Horace said and unlocked the door.

Everett stretched as he exited the cell. "Billy, it was good doing time with you. Look me up when you get out." He looked at me. "Now, tell me, what the hell am I doing here?"

I didn't answer his question, instead I introduced him to Ted. "Percival Everett, Ted Turner. Ted, this is my professor."

"Was," Everett said. He looked at my face. "You look a lot older."

"He's right," Ted said.

Everett shook Ted's hand. "Ted."

"Prof."

"Well, ain't this just sweet and friendly," the Chief said. "This is a damn jail. Everybody out of here."

Everett reached through the bars and shook hands with Billy. "Take care of yourself, you pathetic peckerwood motherfucker."

"You, too, you darkie sumbitch."

Everett smiled at me. "It's a special thing when you do time with a fellow." He led the way back into the main room of the station. "So, tell me how I killed you, and why it didn't stick," he said.

I ignored Everett's question and told him what I'd told Ted, that someone wanted to kill me. I then told him why.

"That was stupid," he said. "That's one of the stupidest things I've ever heard." He looked over at Ted. "I hate colorization." He then turned to the Chief. "I'm not speaking metaphorically."

"I have mixed feelings about it myself," Ted said. "Don't you just hate when you're watching a movie, and you can't remember if it's the first version or a remake. You know, like *Heaven Can Wait*."

"No, I kind of like that feeling." Everett turned and looked me up and down. "What's with the monkey suit?"

Ted looked at his thumb. "What do you call it when you get that painful bit of nail on the side of your cuticle and you can't help but push up and make it hurt more and you never have a clipper with you?"

"I never knew what that was exactly. Is that what I'm supposed to call a hangnail?" Everett asked.

"I guess that's what you call it," Ted said.

"You're right, though. It is really annoying," Everett said. "I always get them right before I'm about to have sex for some reason."

"Would you two shut up?" I said.

The Chief and Horace looked on as if they had been invaded by Russian-speaking madmen. The big-haired dispatcher dozed in her chair. The rain had started up outside again, and the wind howled.

"I say we go get your money and put it in the bank," Ted said.

"I agree," Everett said. "That doesn't mean it's the right or smartest thing to do, but I agree with it."

It was the thing to do. And as long as I kept the Chief with me, I figured I was relatively safe. Even though the rain was falling more heavily than ever, I felt an urgency about getting the money. I looked out the window and at the black sky.

"Listen, I want everybody out of this goddamn station right now," the Chief barked.

The dispatcher sat up and said, "Weather Service just announced a tornado watch for all of Bullock County."

Horace whistled. "It does look bad out there."

"What's the difference between a tornado watch and a tornado warning?" Ted asked. "I mean, which one is worse?"

"I think a warning means somebody's seen one," Everett said.

"But how can you watch something that's not there?" Ted asked.

Everett scratched his head.

Ted looked at Everett's face. "Percival Everett. Didn't you write a book called *Erasure*?"

Everett nodded.

"I didn't like it," Ted said.

"Nor I," Everett said. "I didn't like writing it, and I didn't like it when I was done with it."

"Well, actually, I loved the novel in the novel. I thought that story was real gripping. You know, true to life."

"I've heard that."

It grew darker outside. The wind screamed. The dispatcher calmly crawled under her desk. The front door blew open, hit the wall, and then slammed shut. Horace was shaking.

"Wow," Everett said. "I've always wanted to see a tornado, if in fact this is one. Could be just a bad storm."

"I read that tornado is a messed-up form of some Spanish word, *tronada* or something like that."

Everett scratched his head. "Could be from the Latin *tonare,* to thunder. Anyway, I like the word *twister* better."

"Maybe you two should step outside there and get a close-up look," the Chief said.

"Maybe I will," Everett said. He smiled at the Chief. "Tell me, constable, just what is a Smuteye?"

"It's a dish," I said.

"I tried it," Ted said. "Tastes like shit."

Everett looked at the Chief and around the station. "I can well imagine."

The whole building rattled.

"Well, we can't go out in this mess," the Chief said. "The best we can do is hunker down in here. And the best place for that is back in the cells." He leaned over the dispatcher's desk. "You're gonna have to come on back, Lucy."

So we did. Horace unlocked the cell doors and we all joined Billy sitting on bunks and against the walls.

Everett stared at the disgusting, seatless toilet. "I grew to hate that during my incarceration," he said.

The roof shook, and we all looked up. Dust fell from the ceiling into our eyes. The wind roared like an engine.

"It's a bad one," Horace said.

"Thanks for the news," the Chief said.

I pictured the satchel of money swirling up into the funnel cloud, opening and scattering the bills across six counties and into Georgia. I felt nothing for the money; it was only fifty thousand, a drop in my so-called bucket. However, I felt I needed it in order to make a show of depositing it into the bank—a move designed to protect myself from the would-be robbers. And I wanted the sisters to have it, though I was unsure why that was important to me, if in fact it was and not some mere and strange act of perversion on my part.

Ted was marveling at the storm and saying *wow* over and over. "I read that twisters in the northern hemisphere rotate counterclockwise, I think, opposite from the ones in the southern hemisphere. Hey, you ever try on trousers and they're too short in the rise and for some reason you buy them anyway?"

"That happens to me a lot," Everett said. "I don't know why. Mr. Poitier was one of my favorite students. That is until he cowardly dropped out of school. I think it's because no girls would sleep with him."

The roof made a loud cracking noise, and we let out a collective gasp, but the structure stayed together. The dispatcher prayed loudly. Billy comforted her, called her "Mama."

Horace said, "Think we're going to die, Chief?"

"We'd never be so lucky," the Chief said. "If I could only get that fucking lucky."

Then the wind stopped. Rain leaked in through the damaged roof, but the blowing stopped. All was silent. "I guess that's it," the Chief said, disgust in his voice. He walked away back into the station room.

I followed him. "Chief, I think we ought to go get that money now the weather has broken."

"Oh, you do," he said. "That's just like one of you selfish muckety-mucks from the city. I've got to go out there and check on the folks. I might have to rescue some poor peckerwoods from the tops of trees or some such. And all you can think about is your money."

"Actually, it's the sisters' money," I said.

"You and your friends go and find your damn money. I got pressing business to attend to."

"But I'm afraid I'll be in danger," I said, slowly.

He looked blankly at me, then said, "Horace, drive around and see what's what while I help this boy find his money. And do it right now and don't go visiting that Sarah Purdy that you think I don't know you visit every day."

"Yes, sir, Chief."

The road outside was strewn with fallen limbs and whatever garbage there was in the town of Smuteye, but it didn't appear that any of the buildings had been ripped from their foundations. Ted and Everett sat in the back of the car while I sat in the front and reminded the Chief how to get to the sisters' place. We turned off the road and bounced over a few limbs. Then I saw her. Actually, I first saw the white head of Thornton Scrunchy, then I saw Sister Irenaeus. I told the Chief to stop, and we got out. Sister Irenaeus and the man were shoving bills back into what I recognized as my satchel. When they saw us, they ran through the woods toward a pickup parked at the side of the road. Sister Irenaeus looked back when she reached the passenger-side door. She looked wild eyed, nothing like the woman I had met before. She turned, got into the cab, and slammed the door. Thornton Scrunchy punched the accelerator and sprayed the bushes behind him with mud and gravel. The truck sped away into the wet, windy, dismal gray of Bullock County.

I walked over to what had been the money's hiding spot. Bills were still all over the place—in the crooks of tree branches, in puddles, on the muddy ground. They hadn't gotten nearly all of them. Everett started collecting the money he could reach and stuffed it in his pockets.

"We have to catch him," I said, realizing suddenly just what was happening. "He's the one who killed me."

The Chief, Ted, and Everett studied me, quizzically.

"We have to stop him," I said, again. My heart was pounding. "He killed that man because he thought he was me. Someone is dead because of me. Because of my stupidity."

We hurried back to the car. The Chief slammed his foot on the gas as we hit the highway again. The weather began to turn bad once more. We were driving into another storm. Sheets of rain washed along the road and then over us. The rain fell so hard that the wipers did little to help our vision through the windshield. The rain stopped, all of a sudden.

In front of us was the overturned and mangled blue Ford pickup of Thornton Scrunchy. Engine parts littered the road. As did Sister Irenaeus and Scrunchy and Scrunchy's hair. The utility pole into which it had crashed was broken and lay on the ground beside it; the wires were sizzling and popping on the wet road.

Ted whistled as we stood there staring from a safe distance. "Hell of a thing," he said.

"Do you think they're dead?" Everett asked.

"Dead enough," the Chief said. He was at the open door of his car and on his radio. "Lucy, call Donald and have him come over to Two Forks Road and the highway with his wagon. And call the county and tell we need a cleanup, some power lines down."

"What if they're alive?" I asked. The electrical line bounced and danced across the asphalt.

Ted turned to Everett. "Does rock beat paper or does paper beat rock?"

"Paper beats rock, but I have no idea why," Everett said. "A rock should go right through paper, don't you think? I mean, I love paper as much as, or more than, the next guy. My guess is that it's the function of some kind of privileged intradialogical and embedded enunciator."

"What are you talking about?" Ted asked.

"Paper beats rock. What beats paper?"

"Scissors."

"Ah, yeah."

"Your friends are nuts," the Chief said to me.

I had to agree. And so I did. I didn't know why I'd asked them to come. But somehow things had worked out for me. The same could not be said for Sister Irenaeus. Neither could it be said for the unfortunate young man in the freezer who may or may not have been me.

The sun burst through the dingy steel gray sky and made everything bright. For whatever reason the power line appeared to discharge and then after a few last pops lay there quietly, unmoving. The Chief and I stepped forward toward the bodies. Except for the twisted metal and carnage on the road, the sun had made it a beautiful day. It was pretty clear once we were close that both Sister Irenaeus and Scrunchy were quite dead. All four eyes were wide open and staring into what I believed the sisters would have called the afterlife — into what my mother would have called nothing.

The Chief pointed to the satchel. It had been tossed clear of the truck and was lying in the tall brown grass at the side of the highway. "There it is. Take it. It's your money."

"It's not evidence?" I said.

He gave me a *get-real* look.

I picked up the bag. "I'll give this to the sisters." I walked back over to Everett and Ted.

Everett handed me the money he'd collected in the woods. "What do I need with money? I'll just gamble it away."

"You have a gambling problem?" I asked.

"Not yet." He looked at my face. "What now?"

"Why don't you just fly to Los Angeles?" Ted said.

CHAPTER 7

I flew to LAX. Podgy told me he'd arranged a car for me. For a while at least I would live the way my money allowed. I called it a kind of vacation after Alabama. At the bottom of the escalator at baggage claim I saw several black-suited drivers holding signs with names. There was one with a placard that read *Sidney Poitier.* I stood in front of him.

He said with a British accent, "Are you not Sidney Poitier?"

"I am," I said.

"I'm Gilbert. Do you have any luggage, Mr. Poitier?"

"This is it, Gilbert," I said.

He took my small bag from me, and I followed him out and across the lanes of traffic to the dusty parking garage.

I sat in the back of the black sedan as he paid the Somali attendant and might have flirted with her, I couldn't tell. I looked out at Los Angeles as he curved around onto Sepulveda. He took me on a slow drive to the Beverly Hills Hotel. Stale glitz and money conspired to make me feel comfortable. Everyone there knew me — the men outside the door, the men inside the door. Mr. Poitier this and Mr. Poitier that, welcome back, long time no see. The driver left me at the desk, told me that he would be back to collect me at fifteen past seven. I did not tip him, and this seemed to make him happy. I turned to face the desk clerk.

"Mr. Poitier, so good to see you," the young woman said.

"It's good to see you, too."

She was pleased that I had perhaps remembered her.

"May I say that you're looking younger?"

"You may," I said. "And thank you."

I accepted my key, with a graze of her soft hand, and was led up to my suite by a quiet little man. I showered for a long time, put on a robe, and ordered a sandwich from room service. I then sat on the sofa and watched a man who looked for the world like me in a movie called *For the Love of Ivy*.

At six thirty, a valet delivered black dress pants, a white shirt, and a dinner jacket to my room. At seven, I was dressed. I walked through the lobby, and a young woman came up to me and asked for my autograph. She said, "I just love you, Mr. Poitier." I didn't know why. I asked her name. She said it was Evelyn.

I wrote: *For Evelyn, All the best, Not Sidney Poitier.*

She was puzzled as she read. "You're not Sidney Poitier?"

"I am."

Gilbert was entering the lobby as I approached the door. He seemed upset that I was there before him.

"I'm so sorry, Mr. Poitier."

"That's okay, Gilbert."

"We'll be there in no time."

"Very well, Gilbert."

"Good to be back?" Gilbert asked.

"I suppose."

"Big night," the driver said.

"If you say so, Gilbert." I noticed that he was taking me toward the middle of the city, toward my old neighborhood of West Adams. "Gilbert, could you turn here please?"

"Certainly, sir."

"And a left here," I said. I was feeling my way through a place that had changed and that I didn't remember all that well.

"Yes, sir. This is a rather, shall I say, rough neighborhood."

"It's okay, Gilbert."

"May I ask what we're looking for, sir?"

"We're looking for my home," I said.

Gilbert said nothing.

We were a source of interest to the people on the street. My window was down, and everyone could see my face. Some women seemed to recognize me. They didn't wave, they pointed.

We wended through the streets.

And there was the house I'd lived in with my mother. Other children played in the yard now. A fat man rocked on the porch. It was less profound for me than I had imagined. I wanted to hear my mother's voice, but it never came. I stared at the same front door through which I had passed so many times. I could smell my mother's cookies, cookies that were always *just okay,* she would say, and she was correct. I could see the flow of her open house-coat as she crossed the yard. But I couldn't hear her voice.

"Drive on, Gilbert," I said.

Gilbert did, and he took me to the Shrine Auditorium. Hundreds of people cheered and applauded as I stepped out onto the red carpet. Cameras flashed and flashed and flashed. People called my name. A woman with dyed blond hair, too skinny for her own good, and who looked just like the woman walking several yards behind her, came to me and said, "This way."

I followed her to a room with champagne and caviar and well-dressed people who welcomed me with raised glasses. I drank wine and ate cheese. I was hugged by Elizabeth Taylor and kissed on the cheek by Harry Belafonte.

"I love your dress," I said to Liz.

She twirled. "Thank you, Sidney."

Harry handed me a glass of champagne. "Big night," he said.

"The world is my oyster," I said.

And then I didn't understand a word that was said to me. But of course I was there. Was I Not Sidney Poitier or was I not Sidney Poitier? The emaciated blond or one like her came, took me by the arm, and showed me to my seat in the second row, near the left aisle.

After award after award in categories I didn't know and didn't care to know, I found myself squirming in my seat. The emcee made a joke about Jack Nicholson and everyone laughed, mouths open, heads tossed back. He then became solemn, almost sedate. He looked at me. "And now," he said, "to present the next, special award, Harry Belafonte and Elizabeth Taylor."

"A tribute tonight to an icon of American character," said Liz Taylor.

"To a man that sets the standard," said Harry. "This special award for Most Dignified Figure in American Culture."

"Goes to none other than Sidney Poitier," Liz said.

Applause erupted. I was pushed to standing by the people beside and behind me. I walked down the aisle and then up the stairs to the podium. I was handed an award—a statue of a standing man, gold in color, his arms bent and his hands disappearing in front of him.

I faced the microphone. "Thank you," I said. "I came back to this place to find something, to connect with something lost, to reunite if not with my whole self, then with a piece of it. What I've discovered is that this thing is not here. In fact, it is nowhere. I have learned that my name is not my name. It seems you all know me and nothing could be further from the truth and yet you know me better than I know myself, perhaps better than I can know myself. My mother is buried not far from this auditorium, and there are no words on her headstone. As I glance out now, as I feel the weight of this trophy in my hands, as I stand like a specimen before these strangely unstrange faces, I know finally what should be written on that stone. It should say what mine will say:

I AM NOT MYSELF TODAY."

PERCIVAL EVERETT is Distinguished Professor of English at the University of Southern California and the author of seventeen novels, including *The Water Cure, Wounded,* and *Erasure.*

I Am Not Sidney Poitier has been typeset in Dante, a font created by Giovanni Mardersteig and Charles Malin in the mid-1950s. Book design by Wendy Holdman. Composition by BookMobile Design and Publishing Services, Minneapolis, Minnesota. Manufactured by Versa Press on acid-free paper.